THE IMPROBABLE EVENTS OF
A HOUSE DIVIDED

THE ACCURSED INHERITANCE OF HENRIETTA ACHILLES
AND
A LIGHT IN THE DARKNESS, A LOCK IN THE DOOR

After years as an orphan, Henrietta Achilles has learned she's the last living relative of deceased wizard Ornun Zol—and she has inherited her uncle's estate. When she enters Zol's towering manor, she discovers a war among squatters: bandits searching for treasure, soldiers out to capture them, and tiny monsters swearing revenge after their banishment from the kitchen.

Stranger still, a massive cat is stalking Henrietta. Once it corners her, their clash creates a flood throughout the manor. The deluge demands an uneasy alliance. Henrietta and the other occupants unite to end the flood, forcing bandit leader Nate Flemming and his enemy Captain Booner to face their shared past.

When a blast of water separates Henrietta from her new allies, she makes another fateful discovery: a candle in the shape of a boy. A creation of Ornun Zol, this simulacrum soon envies her status as wizard's heir. They navigate the house together until the cat once again confronts Henrietta. She learns it's a product of the house's magic—and an artifact of her war-torn past.

Henrietta embraces the cat, soothing its rage but making an enemy of the simulacrum. After the soldiers and bandits come to Henrietta's rescue, they stop the flooding and defeat the candle creature. But victory comes at a cost: a final wave consumes the cat, and Flemming falls from a bridge after an unlikely act of heroism. Meanwhile, somewhere beyond the house's walls, strange forces begin to stir . . .

Big thanks to Parvin Jahanshad and Margarite Heimbuch
for their assistance! Ongoing thanks to Eve Jay and
Annelie Wagner for their help and support.

Translation by Haiko Hörnig
Script by Haiko Hörnig
Art by Marius Pawlitza

First American edition published in 2021 by Graphic Universe™

Graphic Universe™
An imprint of Lerner Publishing Group, Inc.
241 First Avenue North
Minneapolis, MN 55401 USA

For reading levels and more information, look up this title at
www.lernerbooks.com.

Main body text set in CC Dave Gibbons Lower.
Typeface provided by Comicraft.

Library of Congress Cataloging-in-Publication Data

Names: Hörnig, Haiko, 1984- author. | Pawlitza, Marius, 1984- illustrator.
Title: The winter of walking stone : Haiko Hörnig, Marius Pawlitza.
Description: First American edition. | Minneapolis, MN : Graphic Universe, 2021. | Series: A house
    divided ; Book 3 | Audience: Ages 12–18 | Audience: Grades 7–9 | Summary: "After saving her house
    and her friends from a magical flood, Henrietta Achilles settles in for the winter. But as her allies
    depart the manor, a strange army of walking statues begins heading her way . . . "— Provided by
    publisher.
Identifiers: LCCN 2020028579 (print) | LCCN 2020028580 (ebook) | ISBN 9781541572454 (library binding)
    | ISBN 9781728420141 (paperback) | ISBN 9781728417448 (ebook)
Subjects: LCSH: Graphic novels. | CYAC: Graphic novels. | Magic—Fiction.
Classification: LCC PZ7.7.H665 Wi 2021 (print) | LCC PZ7.7.H665 (ebook) | DDC 741.5/973—dc23

LC record available at https://lccn.loc.gov/2020028579
LC ebook record available at https://lccn.loc.gov/2020028580

Manufactured in the United States of America
1-46522-47551-9/24/2020

THE WINTER OF WALKING STONE

HAIKO HÖRNIG • MARIUS PAWLITZA

GRAPHIC UNIVERSE™ • MINNEAPOLIS

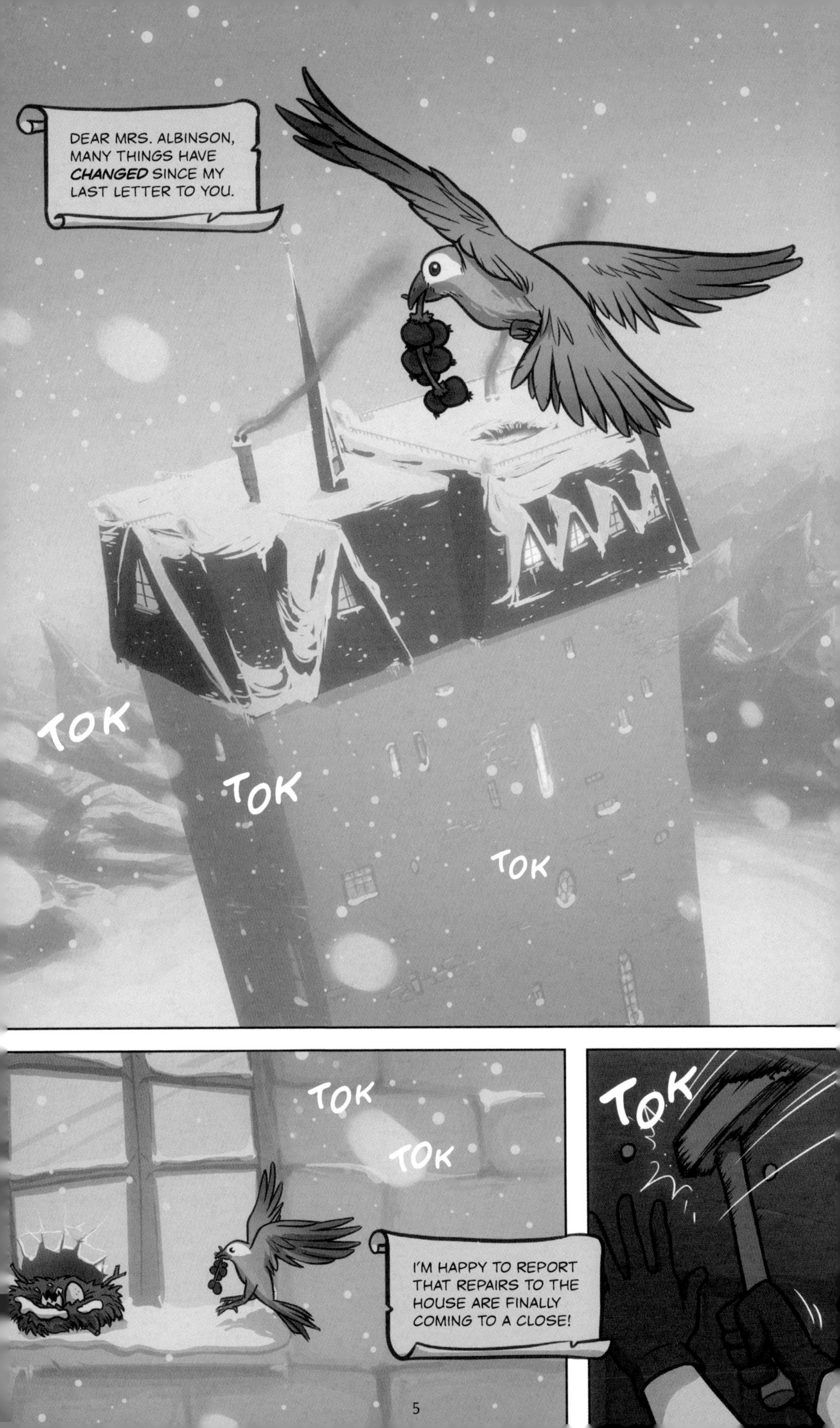
DEAR MRS. ALBINSON, MANY THINGS HAVE ***CHANGED*** SINCE MY LAST LETTER TO YOU.
TOK
TOK
TOK
TOK
TOK
I'M HAPPY TO REPORT THAT REPAIRS TO THE HOUSE ARE FINALLY COMING TO A CLOSE!
TOK

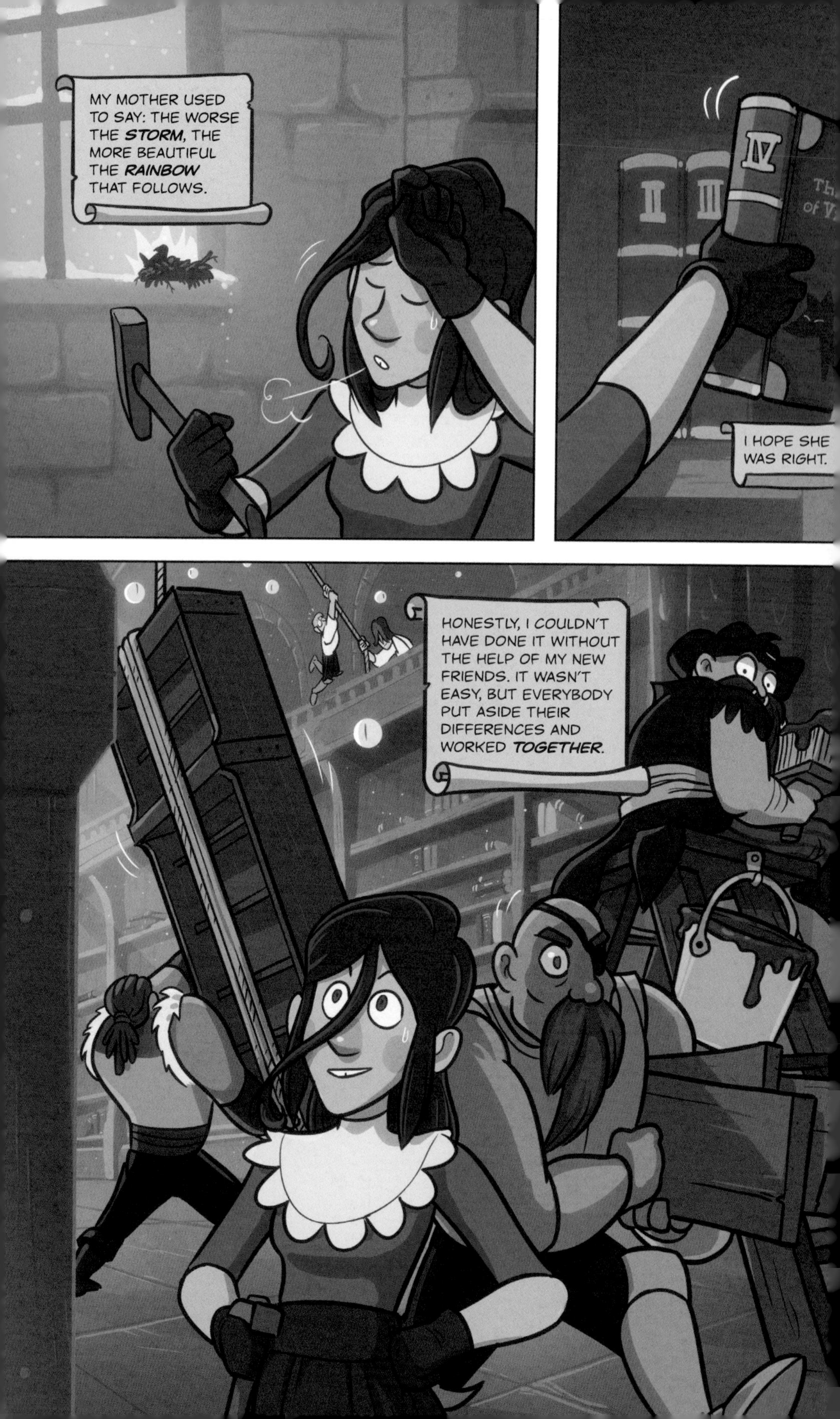
MY MOTHER USED TO SAY: THE WORSE THE STORM, THE MORE BEAUTIFUL THE RAINBOW THAT FOLLOWS.
IV
II
III
I HOPE SHE WAS RIGHT.
HONESTLY, I COULDN'T HAVE DONE IT WITHOUT THE HELP OF MY NEW FRIENDS. IT WASN'T EASY, BUT EVERYBODY PUT ASIDE THEIR DIFFERENCES AND WORKED TOGETHER.

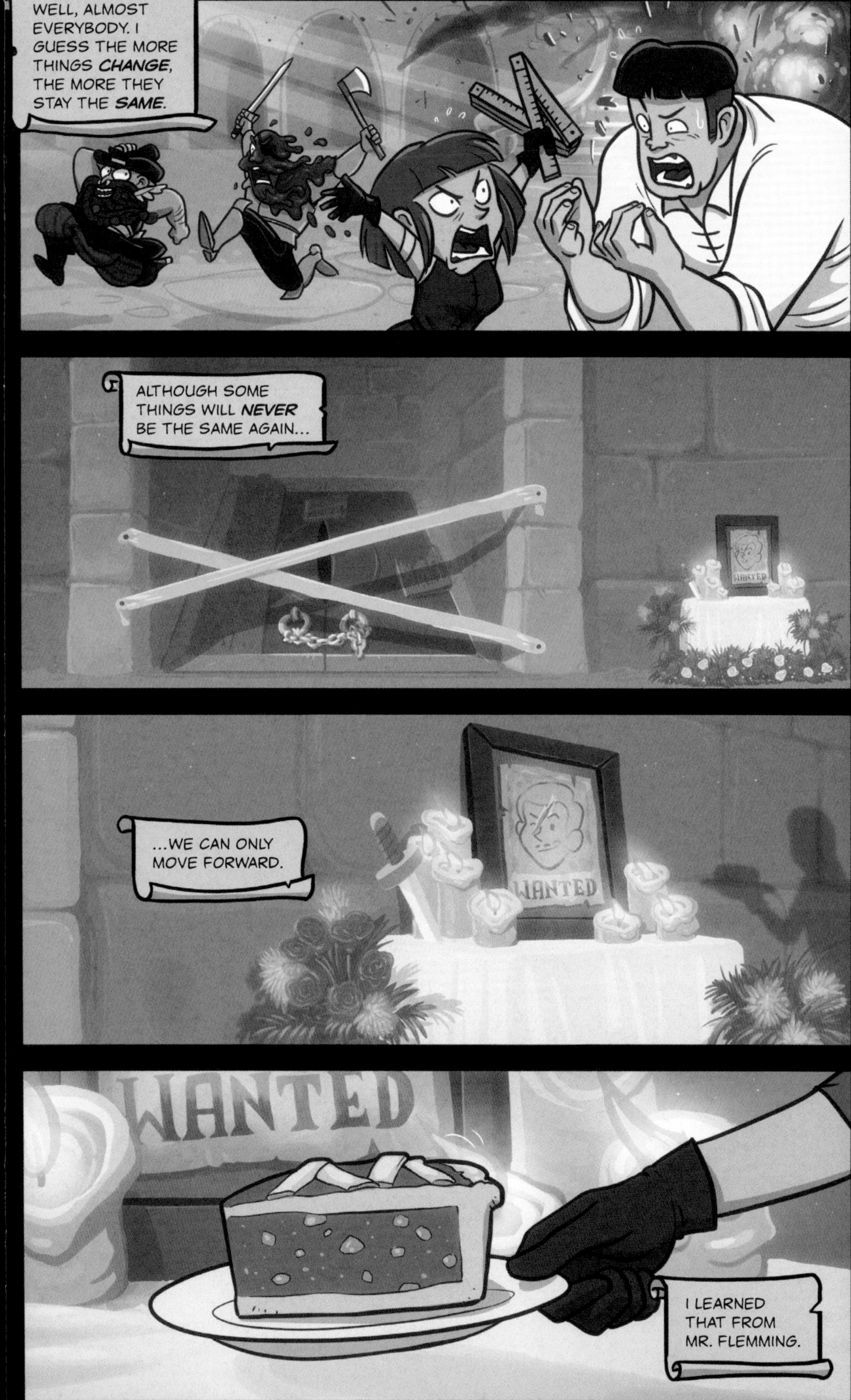
WELL, ALMOST EVERYBODY. I GUESS THE MORE THINGS *CHANGE*, THE MORE THEY STAY THE *SAME*.
ALTHOUGH SOME THINGS WILL *NEVER* BE THE SAME AGAIN...
WANTED
...WE CAN ONLY MOVE FORWARD.
WANTED
WANTED
I LEARNED THAT FROM MR. FLEMMING.

SO *FORWARD* I GO...

CHOO
CHOO
CHOO
CHOO
CHOO
CHOO

5

UPPER GARDENS

TSHHHHHY

...BUT THE *CLOSER* I TRY TO GET TO THE MYSTERIES OF ORNUN ZOL...

CHOO
CHOO
CHOO

101 IDEAS FOR ENERGY SHIELDS

TRANSMUTATION FOR TEENS

MONSTERS: A MANUAL

SELEKTIVE ERINNERUNG

...THE MORE THEY SEEM TO *EVADE* ME.

MENDING AND REPAIRS VOL. I

PLUMBING MADE FUN

STILL, THE MANY CHORES KEEP ME QUITE BUSY.

SCRUB

SOMETIMES IT FEELS LIKE THERE'S MORE THAN A LIFETIME OF WORK WAITING FOR ME.

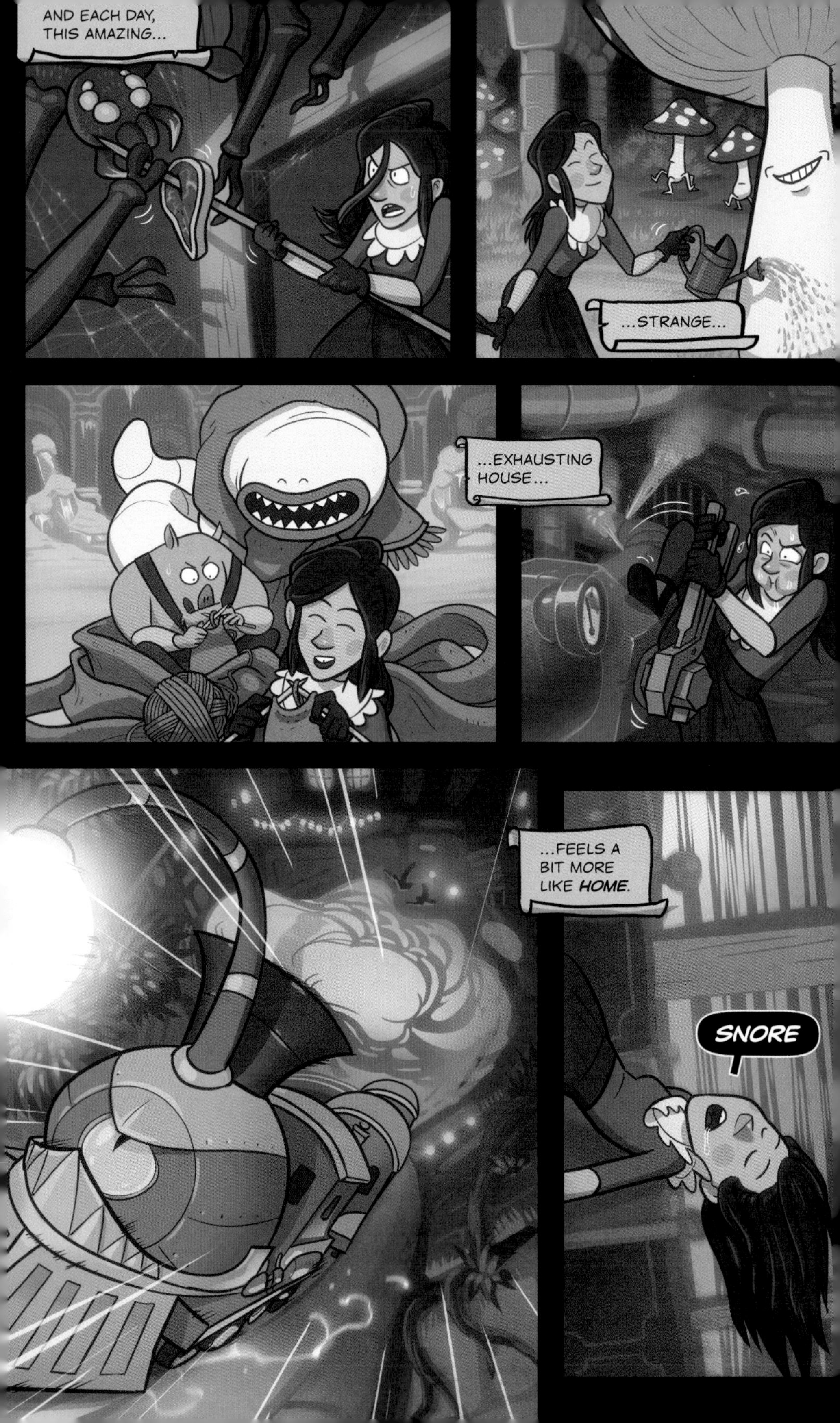

AND EACH DAY, THIS AMAZING...
...STRANGE...
...EXHAUSTING HOUSE...
...FEELS A BIT MORE LIKE HOME.
SNORE

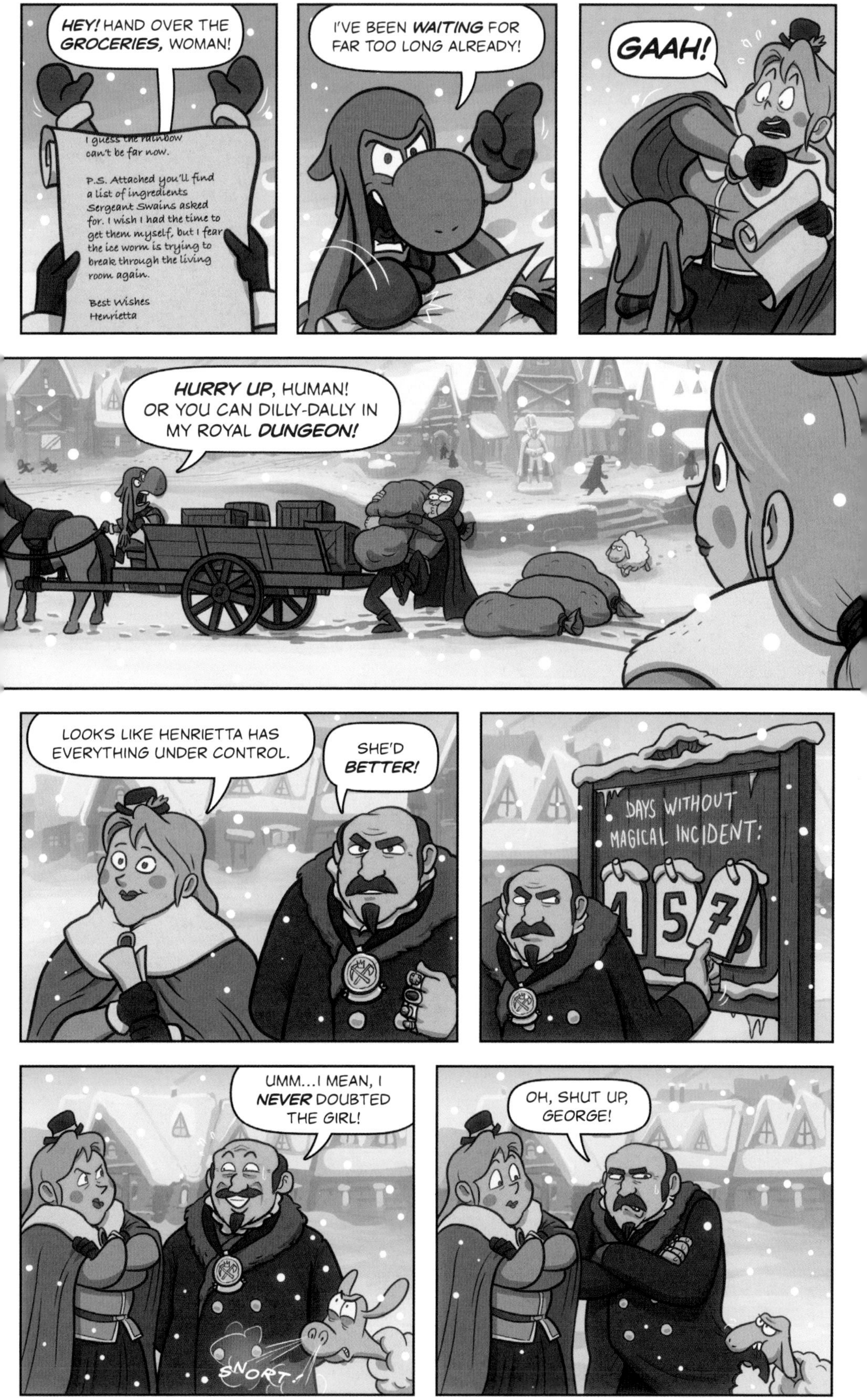
HEY! HAND OVER THE GROCERIES, WOMAN!
I guess the rainbow can't be far now.
P.S. Attached you'll find a list of ingredients Sergeant Swains asked for. I wish I had the time to get them myself, but I fear the ice worm is trying to break through the living room again.
Best Wishes
Henrietta
I'VE BEEN WAITING FOR FAR TOO LONG ALREADY!
GAAH!
HURRY UP, HUMAN! OR YOU CAN DILLY-DALLY IN MY ROYAL DUNGEON!
LOOKS LIKE HENRIETTA HAS EVERYTHING UNDER CONTROL.
SHE'D BETTER!
DAYS WITHOUT MAGICAL INCIDENT:
157
UMM...I MEAN, I NEVER DOUBTED THE GIRL!
SNORT!
OH, SHUT UP, GEORGE!

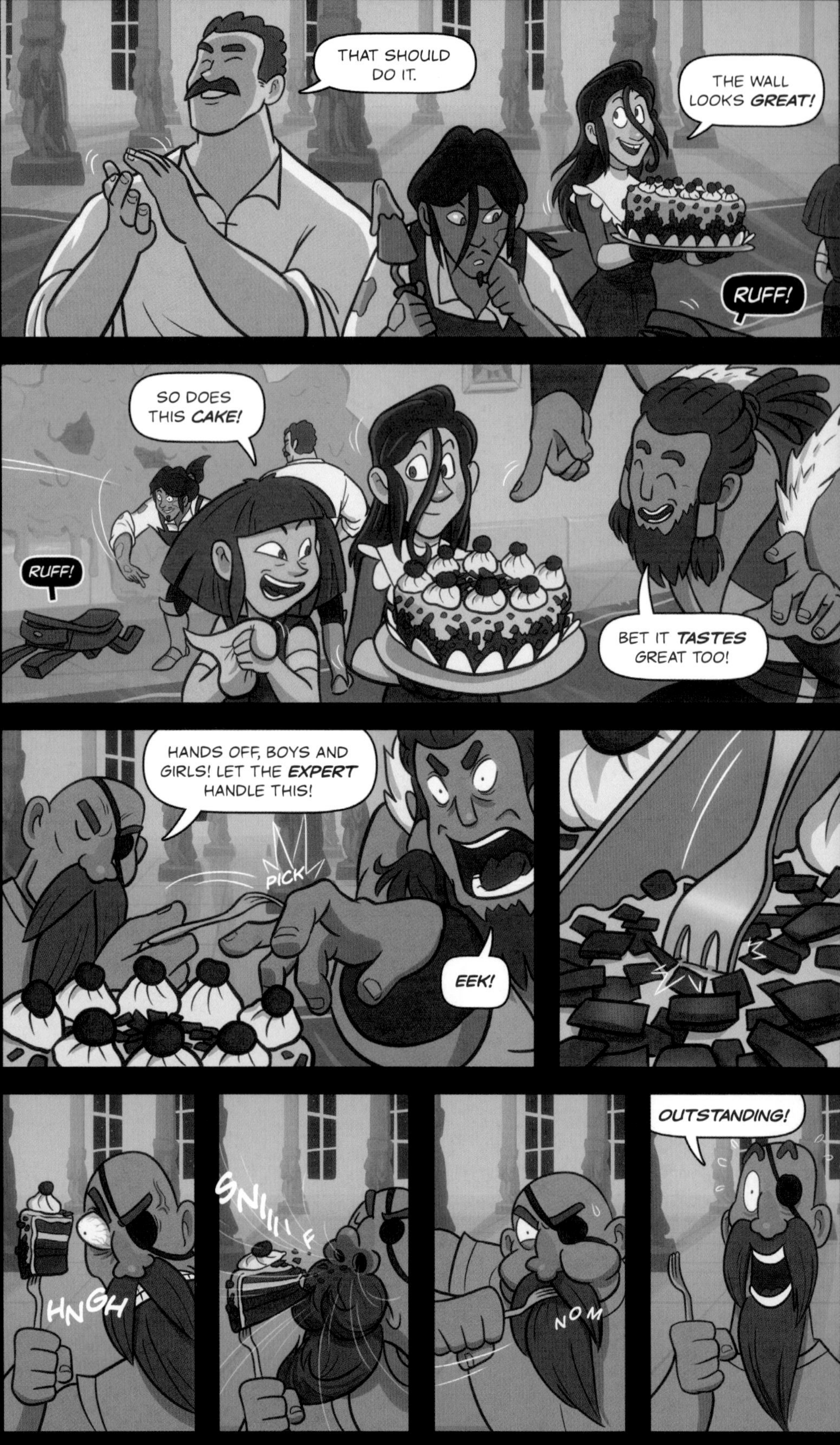
THAT SHOULD DO IT.
THE WALL LOOKS **GREAT!**
RUFF!
SO DOES THIS **CAKE!**
RUFF!
BET IT **TASTES** GREAT TOO!
HANDS OFF, BOYS AND GIRLS! LET THE **EXPERT** HANDLE THIS!
PICK
EEK!
HNGH
SNIIIIF
NOM
OUTSTANDING!

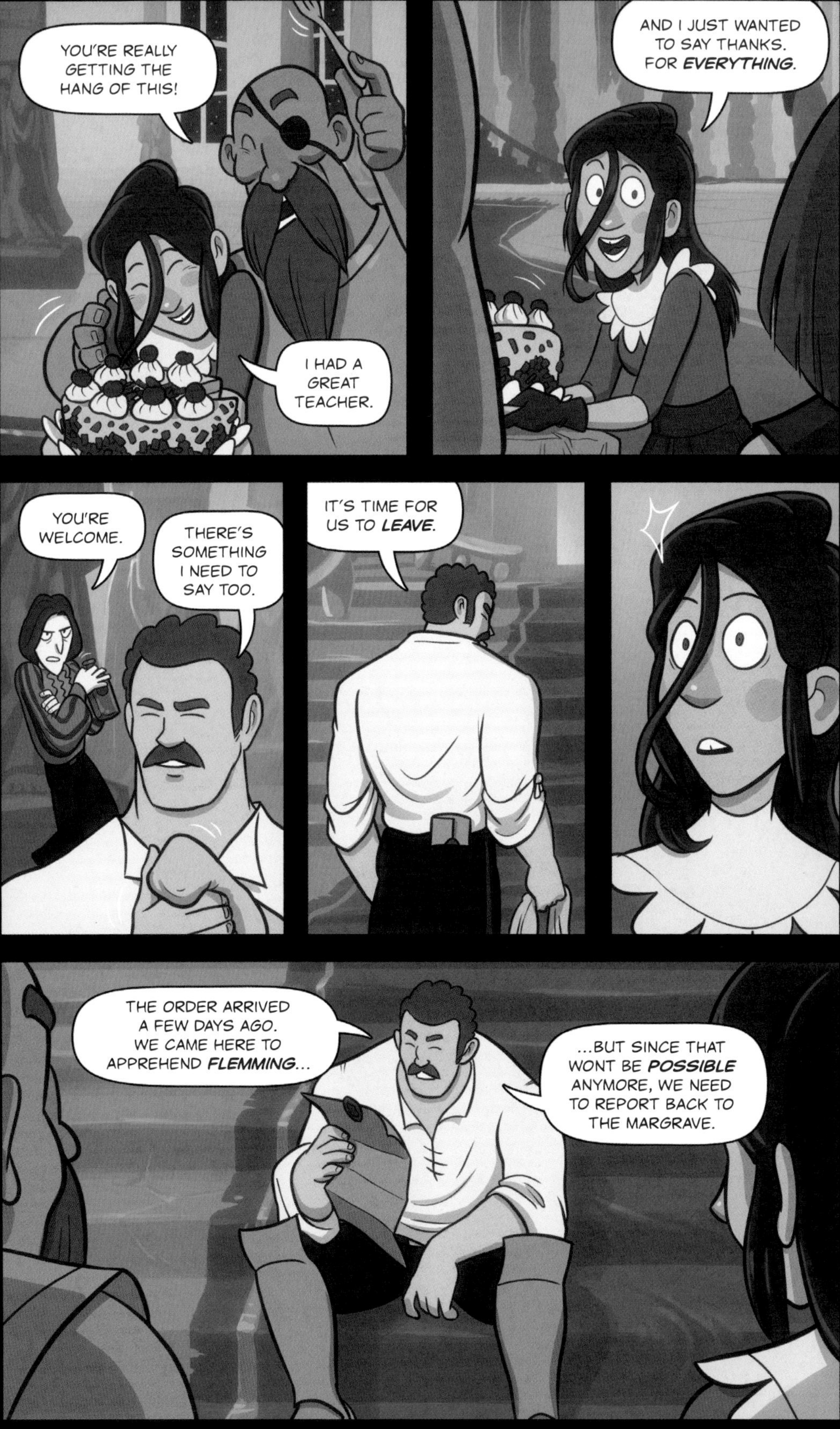
YOU'RE REALLY GETTING THE HANG OF THIS!
I HAD A GREAT TEACHER.
AND I JUST WANTED TO SAY THANKS. FOR *EVERYTHING*.
YOU'RE WELCOME.
THERE'S SOMETHING I NEED TO SAY TOO.
IT'S TIME FOR US TO *LEAVE*.
THE ORDER ARRIVED A FEW DAYS AGO. WE CAME HERE TO APPREHEND *FLEMMING*...
...BUT SINCE THAT WONT BE *POSSIBLE* ANYMORE, WE NEED TO REPORT BACK TO THE MARGRAVE.

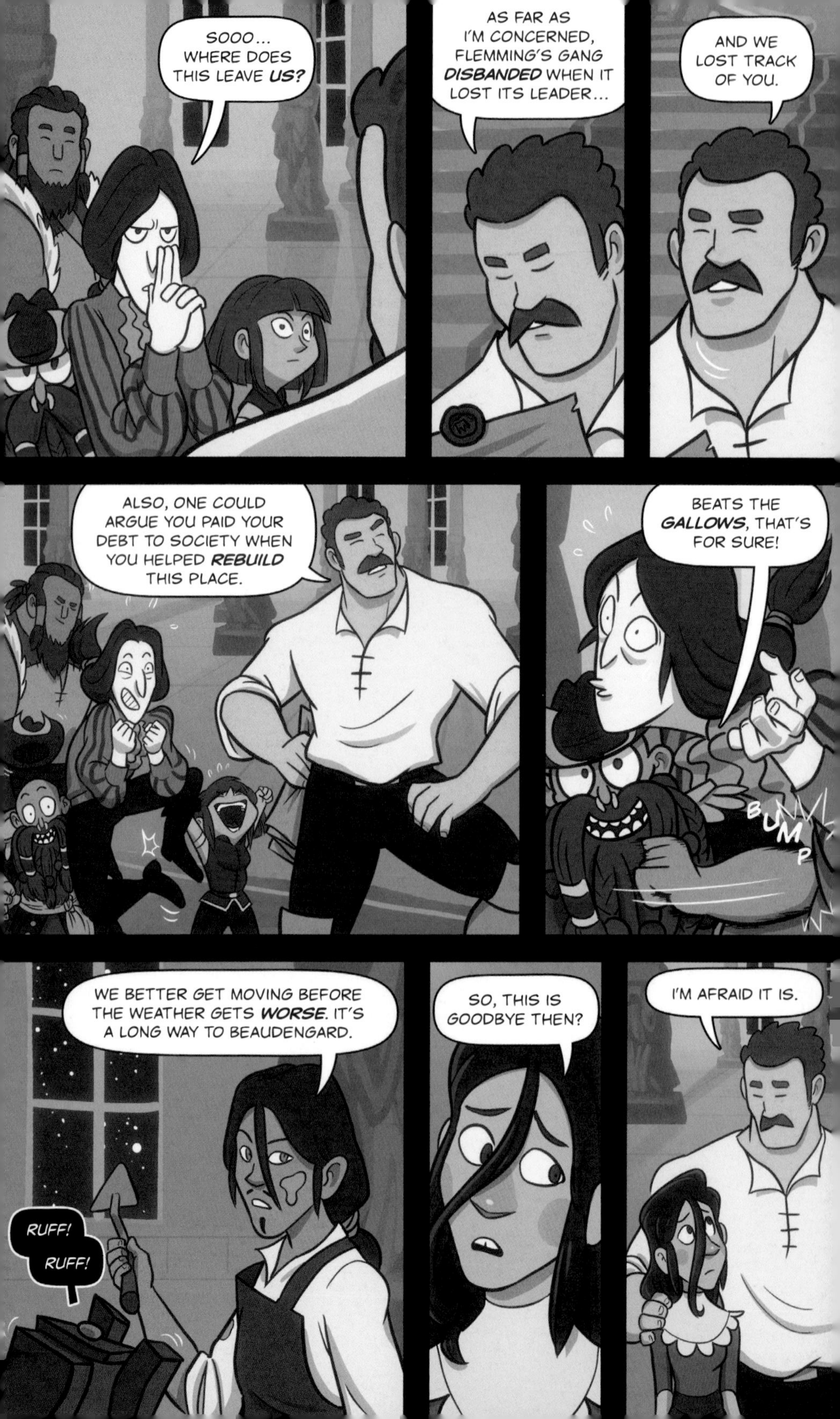
SOOO... WHERE DOES THIS LEAVE *US?*
AS FAR AS I'M CONCERNED, FLEMMING'S GANG *DISBANDED* WHEN IT LOST ITS LEADER...
AND WE LOST TRACK OF YOU.
ALSO, ONE COULD ARGUE YOU PAID YOUR DEBT TO SOCIETY WHEN YOU HELPED *REBUILD* THIS PLACE.
BEATS THE *GALLOWS*, THAT'S FOR SURE!
BUMP
WE BETTER GET MOVING BEFORE THE WEATHER GETS *WORSE*. IT'S A LONG WAY TO BEAUDENGARD.
RUFF!
RUFF!
SO, THIS IS GOODBYE THEN?
I'M AFRAID IT IS.

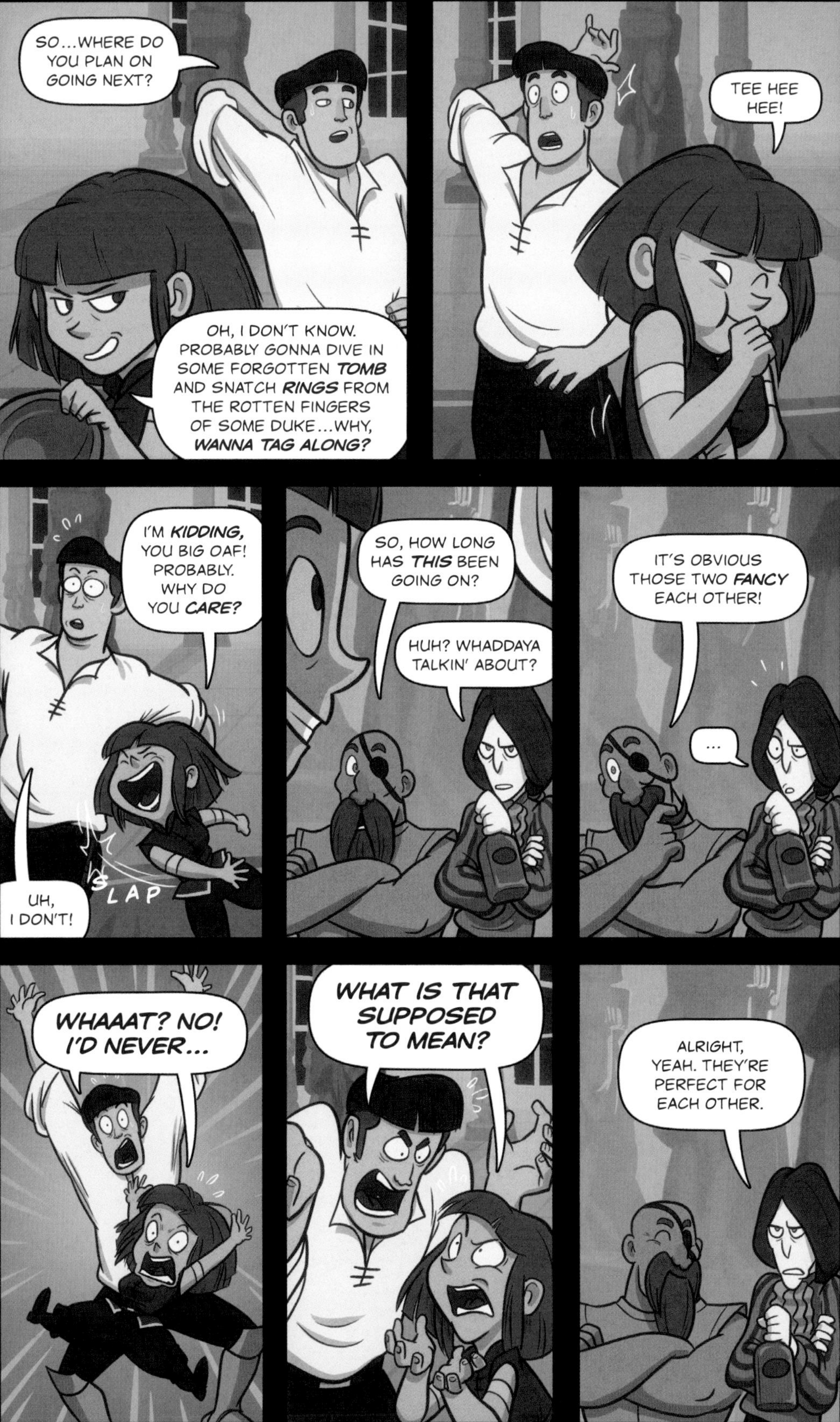
SO...WHERE DO YOU PLAN ON GOING NEXT?
OH, I DON'T KNOW. PROBABLY GONNA DIVE IN SOME FORGOTTEN **TOMB** AND SNATCH **RINGS** FROM THE ROTTEN FINGERS OF SOME DUKE...WHY, **WANNA TAG ALONG?**
TEE HEE HEE!
I'M **KIDDING,** YOU BIG OAF! PROBABLY. WHY DO YOU **CARE?**
SLAP
UH, I DON'T!
SO, HOW LONG HAS **THIS** BEEN GOING ON?
HUH? WHADDAYA TALKIN' ABOUT?
IT'S OBVIOUS THOSE TWO **FANCY** EACH OTHER!
...
WHAAAT? NO! I'D NEVER...
WHAT IS THAT SUPPOSED TO MEAN?
ALRIGHT, YEAH. THEY'RE PERFECT FOR EACH OTHER.

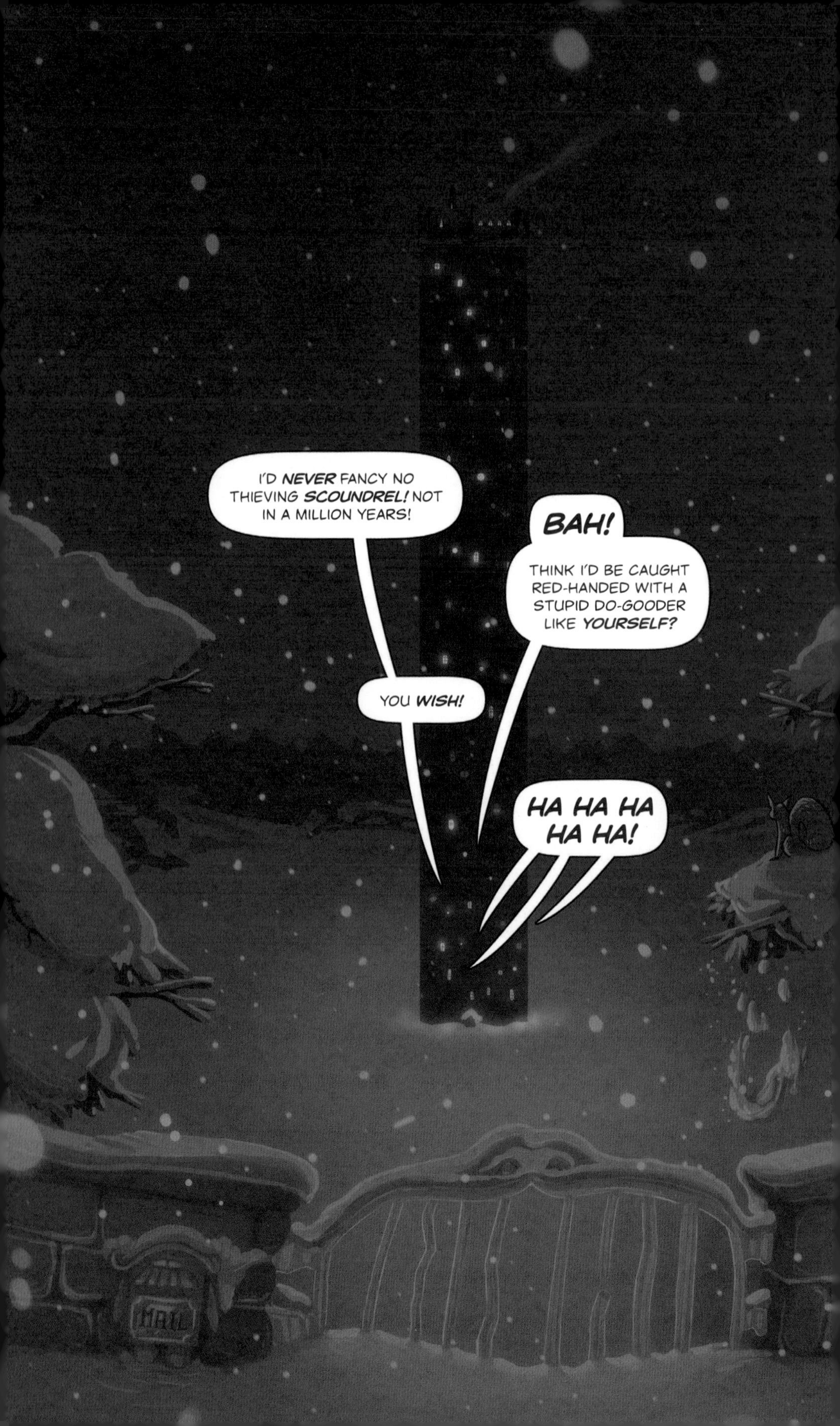
I'D NEVER FANCY NO THIEVING SCOUNDREL! NOT IN A MILLION YEARS!
YOU WISH!
BAH!
THINK I'D BE CAUGHT RED-HANDED WITH A STUPID DO-GOODER LIKE YOURSELF?
HA HA HA HA HA!
MAIL

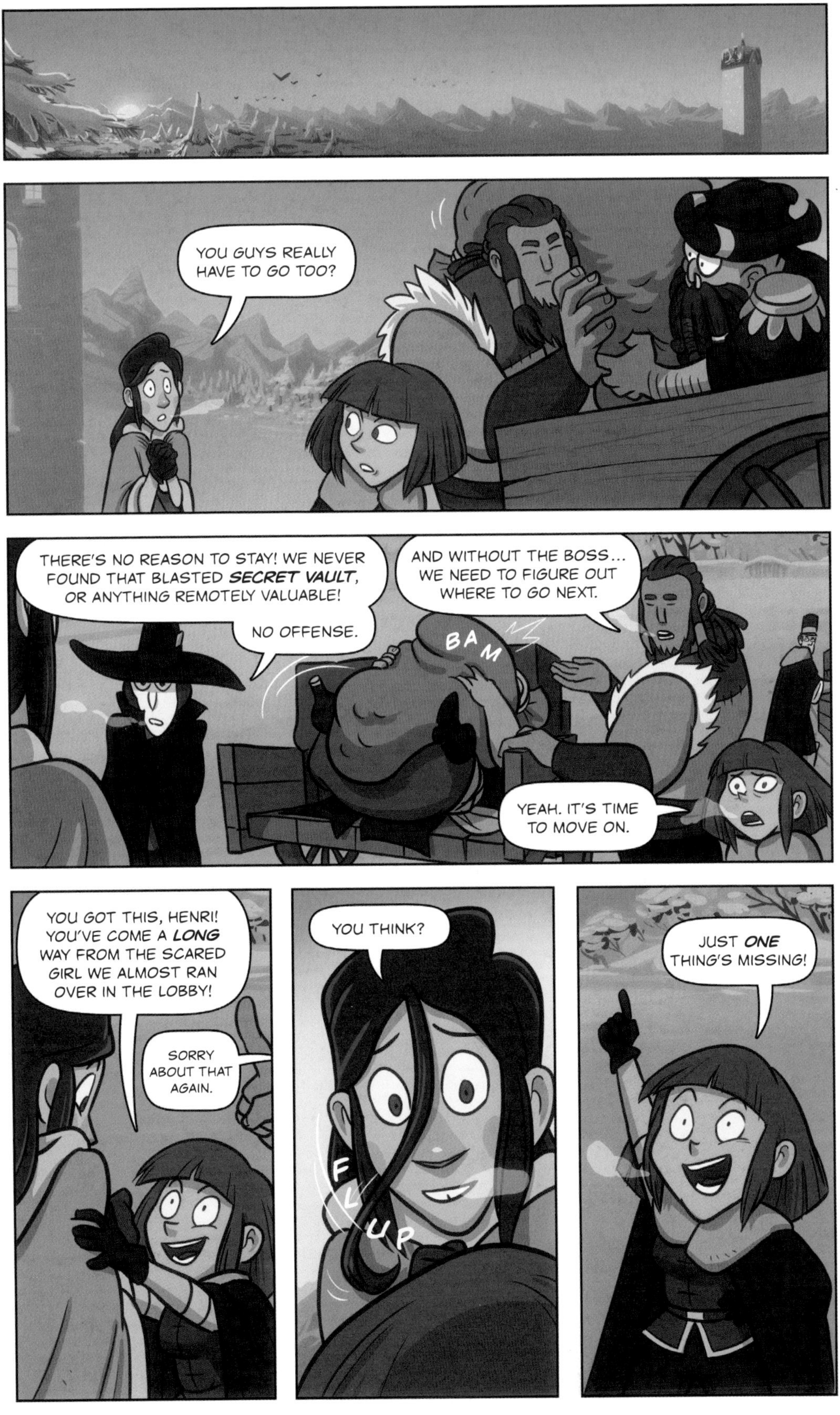
YOU GUYS REALLY HAVE TO GO TOO?
THERE'S NO REASON TO STAY! WE NEVER FOUND THAT BLASTED ***SECRET VAULT***, OR ANYTHING REMOTELY VALUABLE!
NO OFFENSE.
AND WITHOUT THE BOSS... WE NEED TO FIGURE OUT WHERE TO GO NEXT.
BAM
YEAH. IT'S TIME TO MOVE ON.
YOU GOT THIS, HENRI! YOU'VE COME A ***LONG*** WAY FROM THE SCARED GIRL WE ALMOST RAN OVER IN THE LOBBY!
SORRY ABOUT THAT AGAIN.
YOU THINK?
FLUP
JUST ***ONE*** THING'S MISSING!

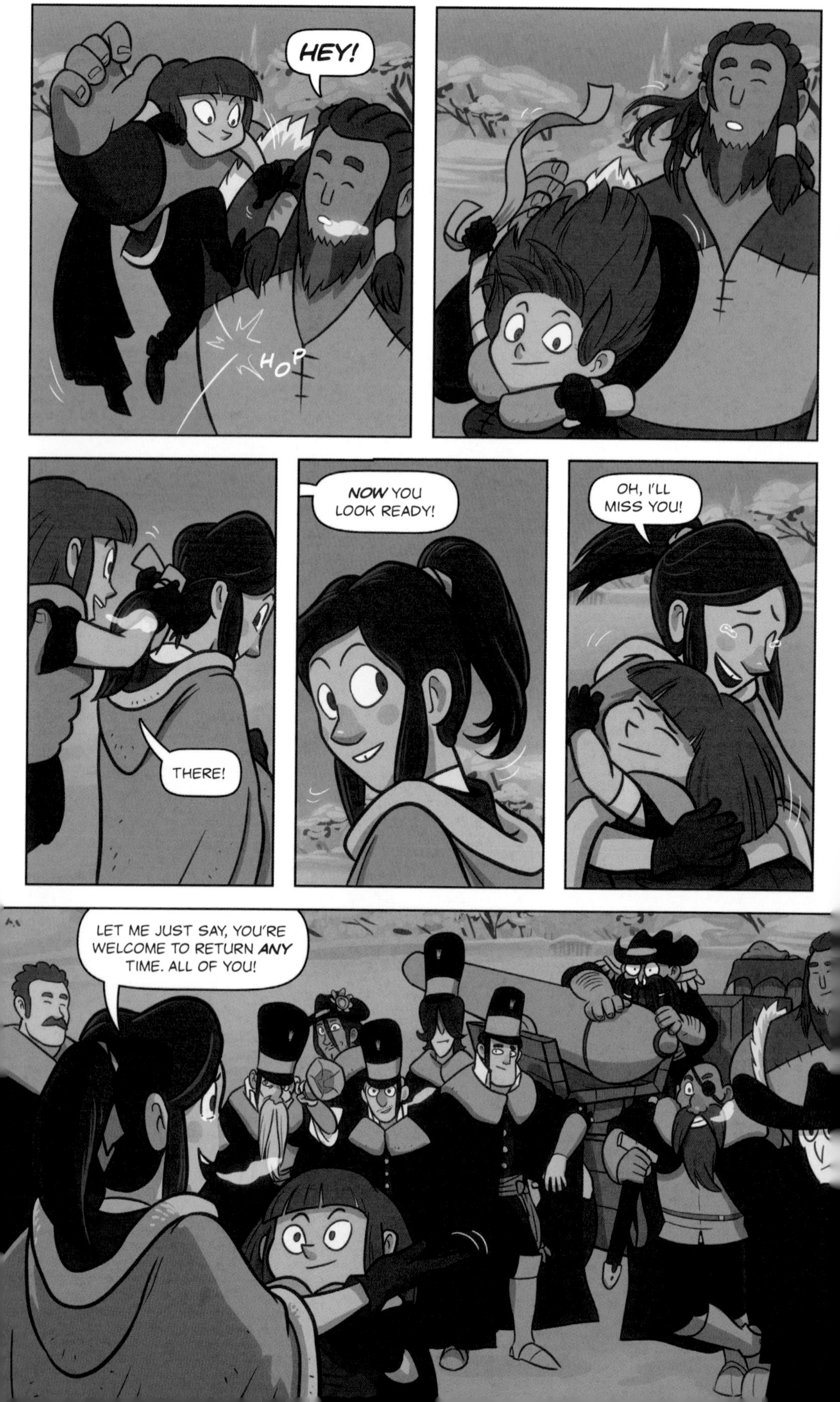
HEY!
HOP
NOW YOU LOOK READY!
THERE!
OH, I'LL MISS YOU!
LET ME JUST SAY, YOU'RE WELCOME TO RETURN *ANY* TIME. ALL OF YOU!

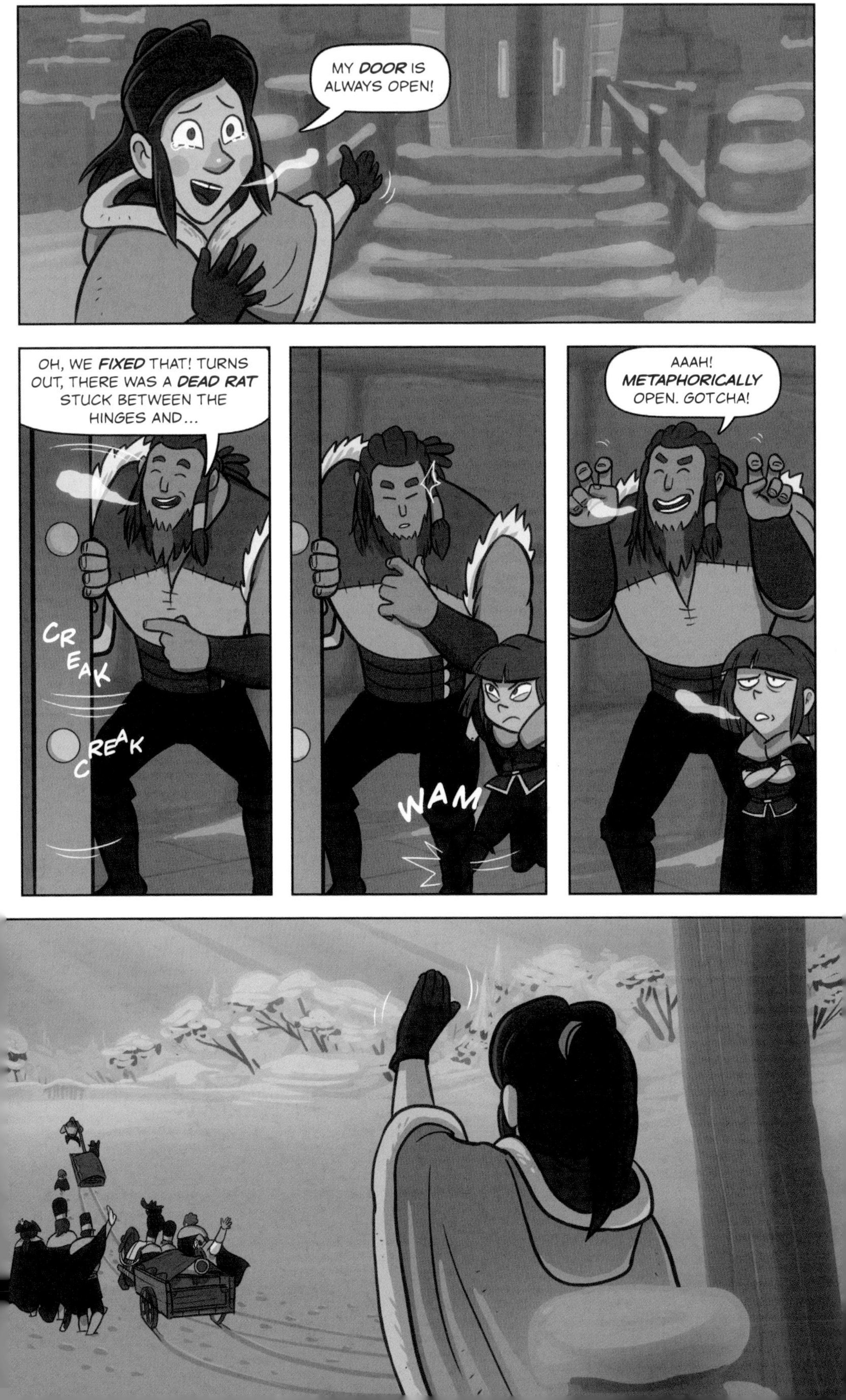
MY DOOR IS ALWAYS OPEN!
OH, WE FIXED THAT! TURNS OUT, THERE WAS A DEAD RAT STUCK BETWEEN THE HINGES AND...
CREAK
CREAK
WAM
AAAH! METAPHORICALLY OPEN. GOTCHA!

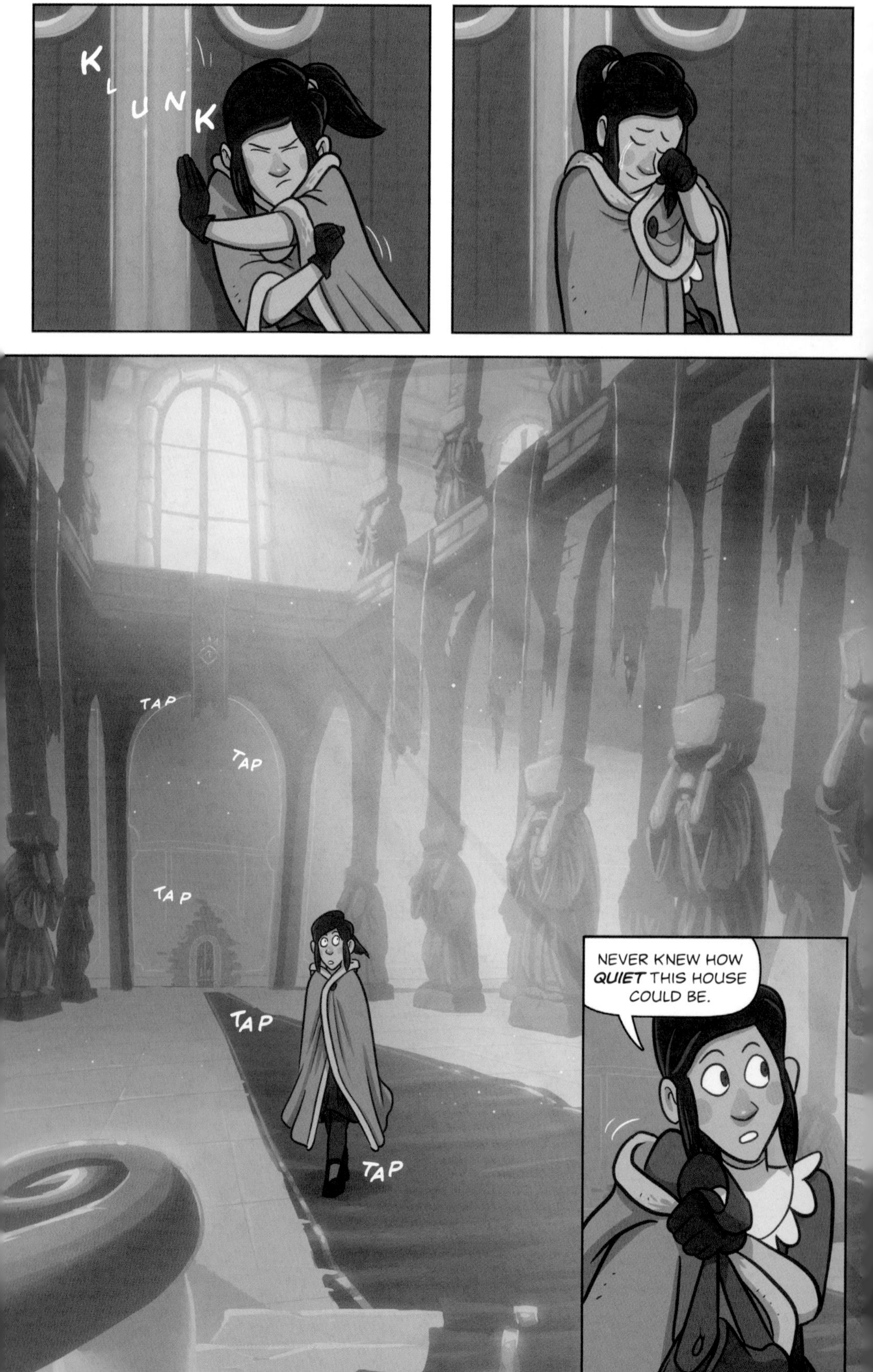
KLUNK
TAP
TAP
TAP
TAP
TAP
NEVER KNEW HOW *QUIET* THIS HOUSE COULD BE.

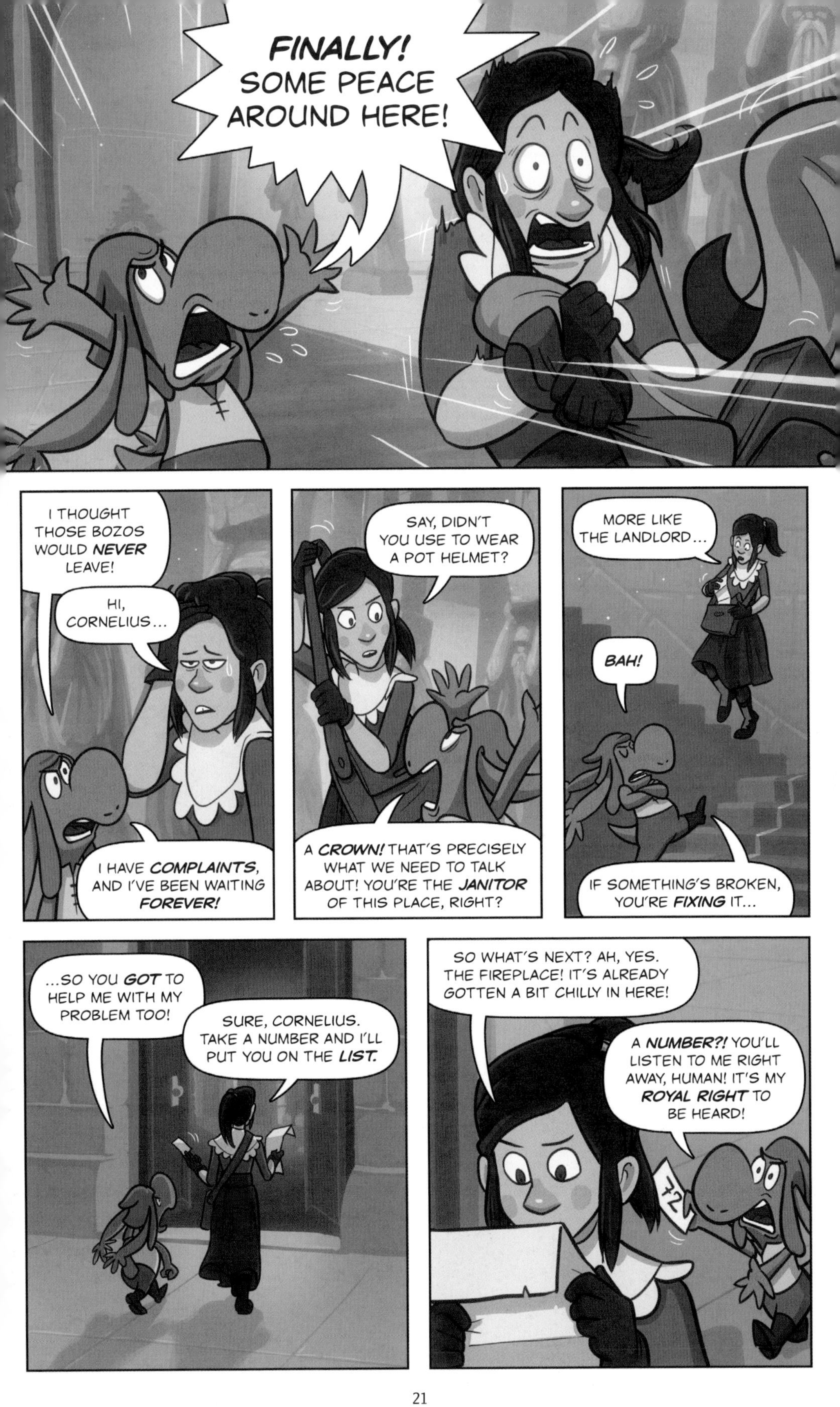
FINALLY! SOME PEACE AROUND HERE!
I THOUGHT THOSE BOZOS WOULD NEVER LEAVE!
HI, CORNELIUS...
I HAVE COMPLAINTS, AND I'VE BEEN WAITING FOREVER!
SAY, DIDN'T YOU USE TO WEAR A POT HELMET?
A CROWN! THAT'S PRECISELY WHAT WE NEED TO TALK ABOUT! YOU'RE THE JANITOR OF THIS PLACE, RIGHT?
MORE LIKE THE LANDLORD...
BAH!
IF SOMETHING'S BROKEN, YOU'RE FIXING IT...
...SO YOU GOT TO HELP ME WITH MY PROBLEM TOO!
SURE, CORNELIUS. TAKE A NUMBER AND I'LL PUT YOU ON THE LIST.
SO WHAT'S NEXT? AH, YES. THE FIREPLACE! IT'S ALREADY GOTTEN A BIT CHILLY IN HERE!
A NUMBER?! YOU'LL LISTEN TO ME RIGHT AWAY, HUMAN! IT'S MY ROYAL RIGHT TO BE HEARD!
72

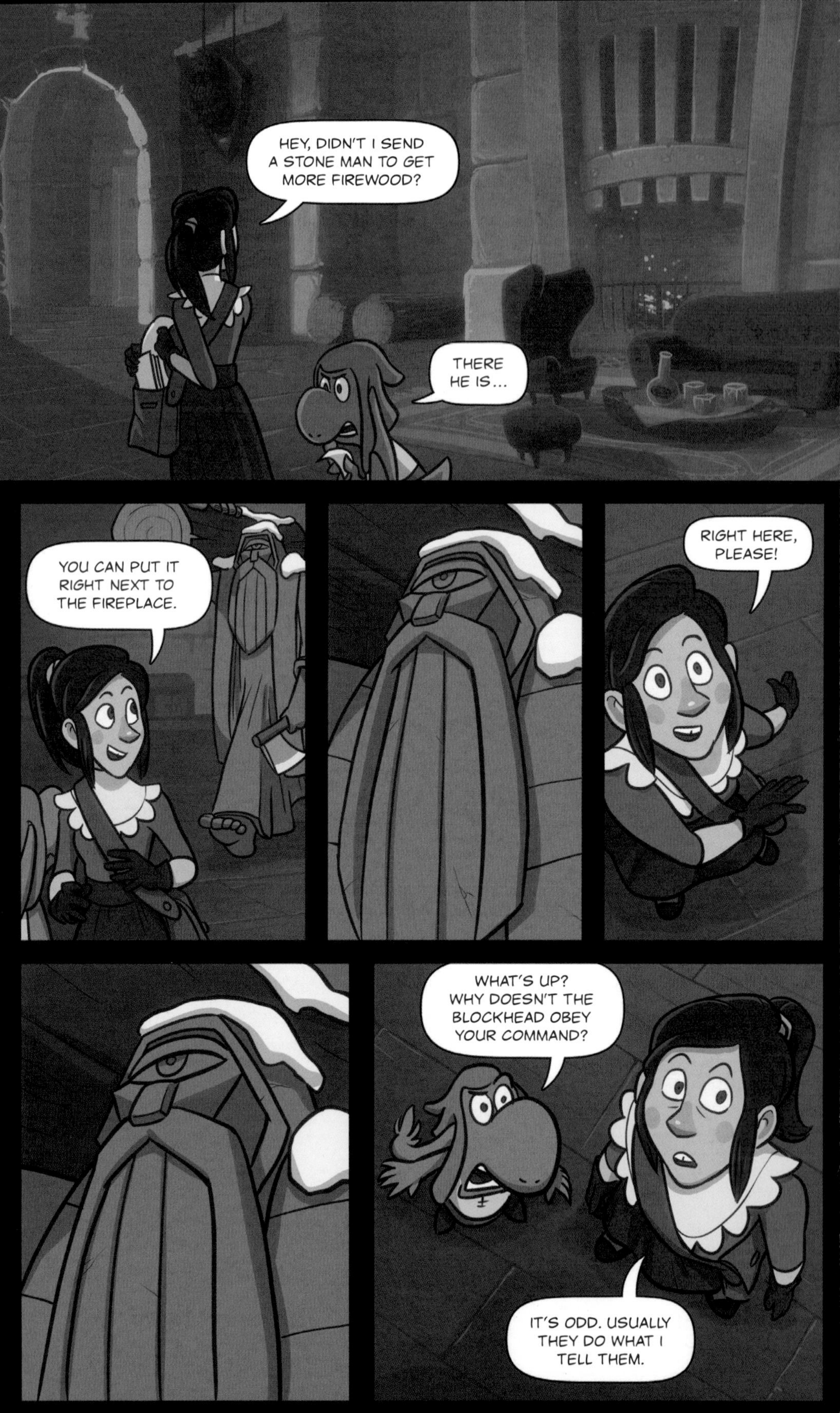
HEY, DIDN'T I SEND A STONE MAN TO GET MORE FIREWOOD?
THERE HE IS...
YOU CAN PUT IT RIGHT NEXT TO THE FIREPLACE.
RIGHT HERE, PLEASE!
WHAT'S UP? WHY DOESN'T THE BLOCKHEAD OBEY YOUR COMMAND?
IT'S ODD. USUALLY THEY DO WHAT I TELL THEM.

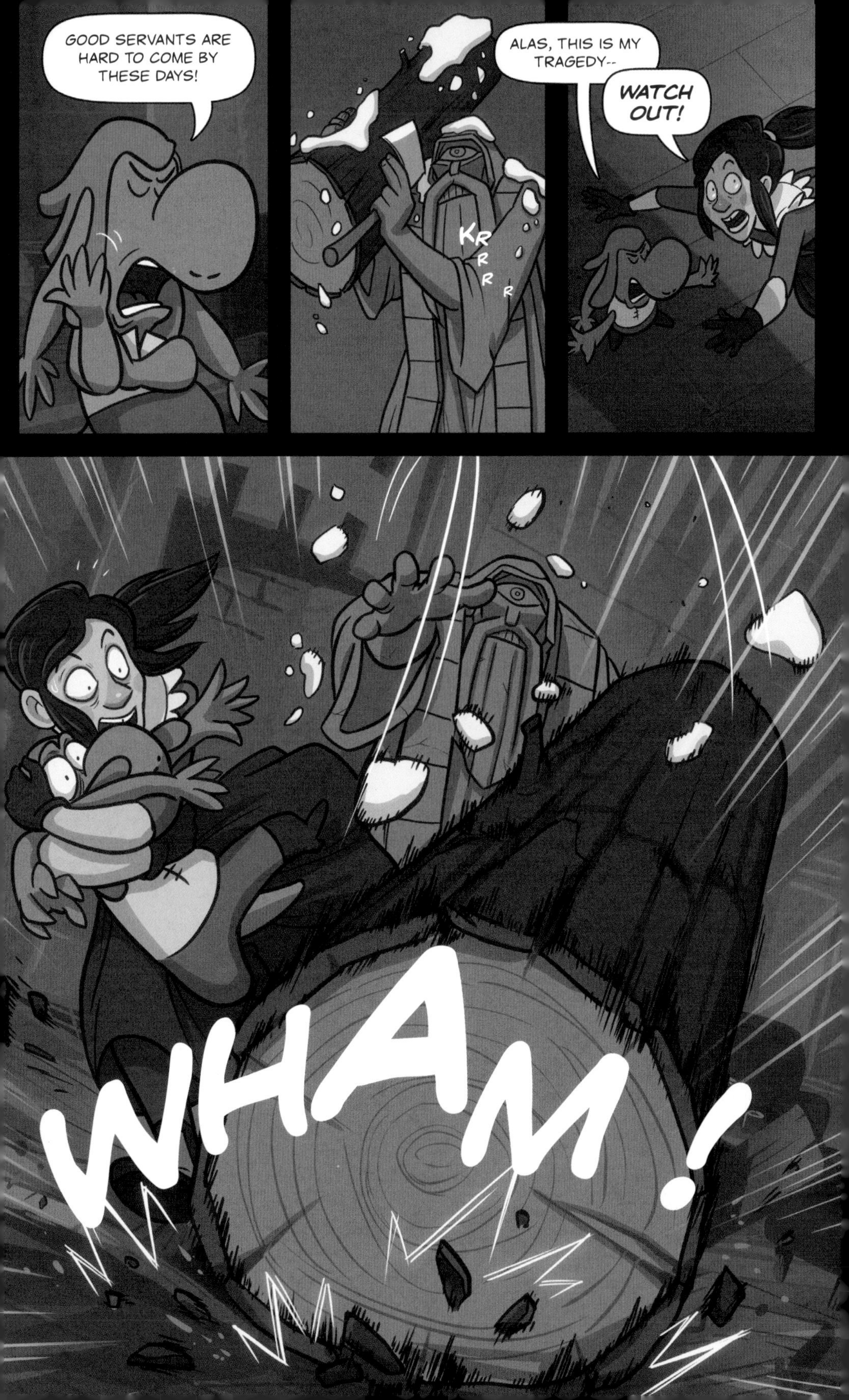
GOOD SERVANTS ARE HARD TO COME BY THESE DAYS!
ALAS, THIS IS MY TRAGEDY--
KRRRR
WATCH OUT!
WHAM!

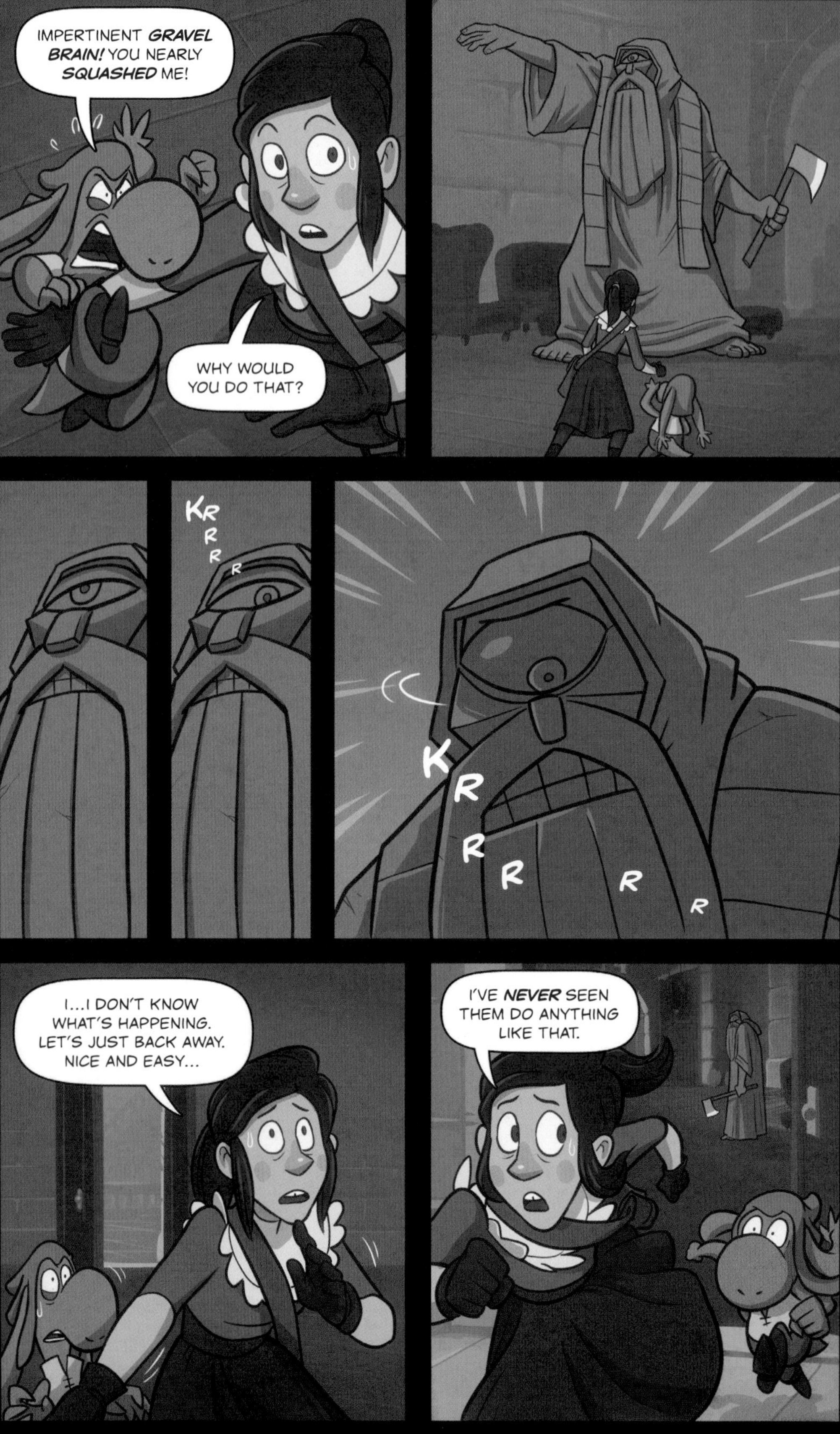
IMPERTINENT GRAVEL BRAIN! YOU NEARLY SQUASHED ME!
WHY WOULD YOU DO THAT?
KRRRR
KRRRRR
I...I DON'T KNOW WHAT'S HAPPENING. LET'S JUST BACK AWAY. NICE AND EASY...
I'VE NEVER SEEN THEM DO ANYTHING LIKE THAT.

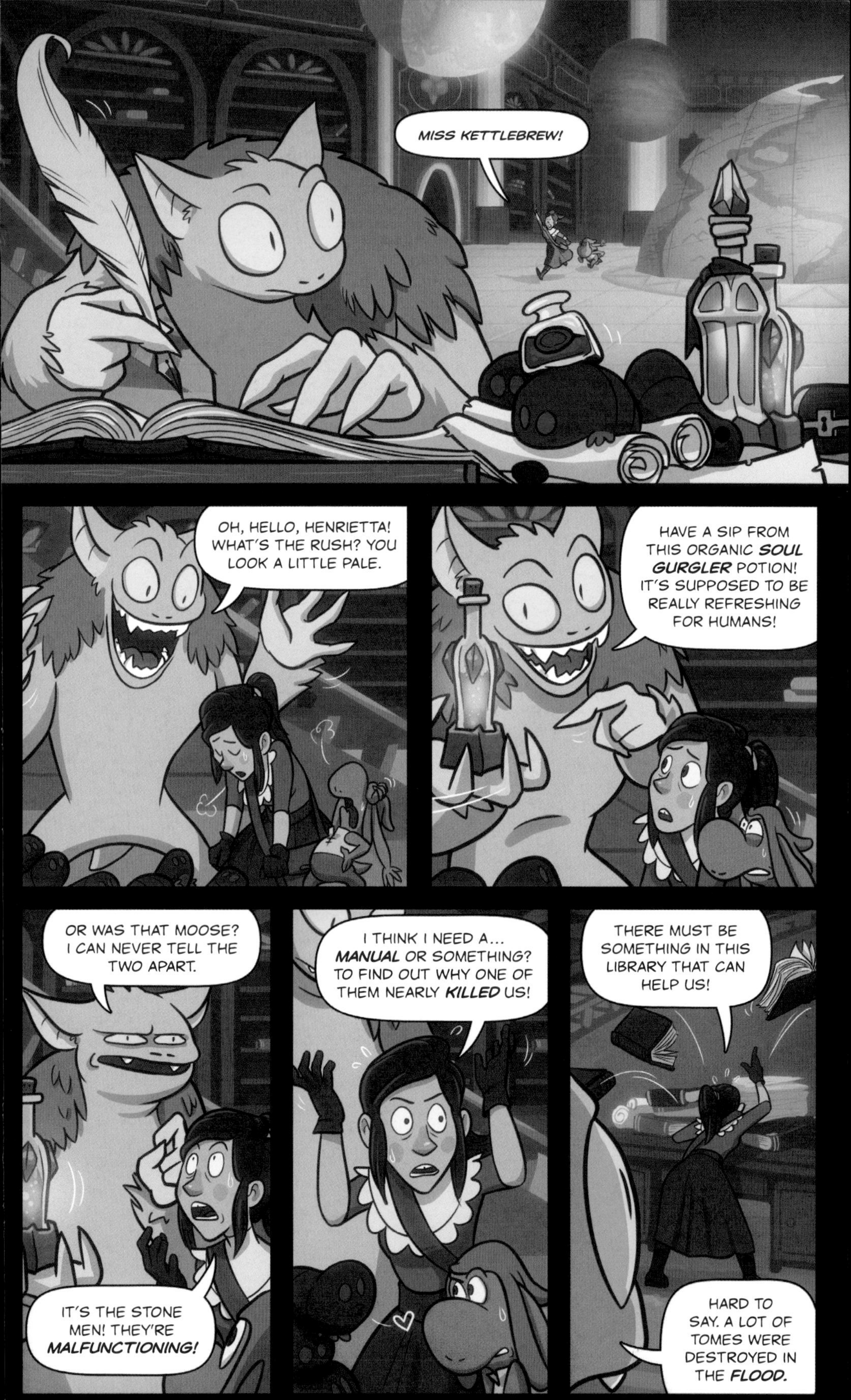

MISS KETTLEBREW!
OH, HELLO, HENRIETTA! WHAT'S THE RUSH? YOU LOOK A LITTLE PALE.
HAVE A SIP FROM THIS ORGANIC SOUL GURGLER POTION! IT'S SUPPOSED TO BE REALLY REFRESHING FOR HUMANS!
OR WAS THAT MOOSE? I CAN NEVER TELL THE TWO APART.
IT'S THE STONE MEN! THEY'RE MALFUNCTIONING!
I THINK I NEED A... MANUAL OR SOMETHING? TO FIND OUT WHY ONE OF THEM NEARLY KILLED US!
THERE MUST BE SOMETHING IN THIS LIBRARY THAT CAN HELP US!
HARD TO SAY. A LOT OF TOMES WERE DESTROYED IN THE FLOOD.

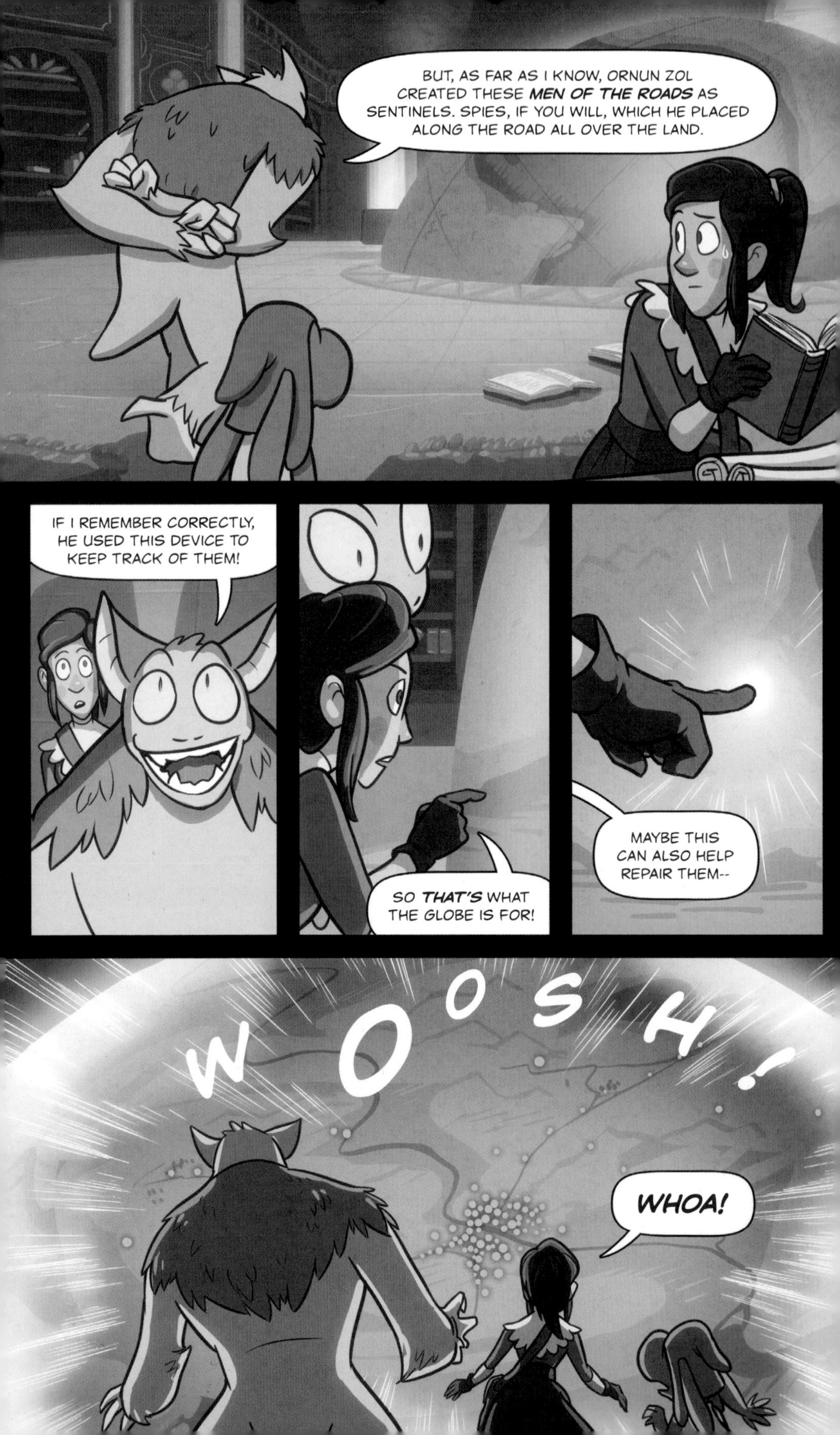
BUT, AS FAR AS I KNOW, ORNUN ZOL CREATED THESE ***MEN OF THE ROADS*** AS SENTINELS. SPIES, IF YOU WILL, WHICH HE PLACED ALONG THE ROAD ALL OVER THE LAND.
IF I REMEMBER CORRECTLY, HE USED THIS DEVICE TO KEEP TRACK OF THEM!
SO ***THAT'S*** WHAT THE GLOBE IS FOR!
MAYBE THIS CAN ALSO HELP REPAIR THEM--
WOOSH!
WHOA!

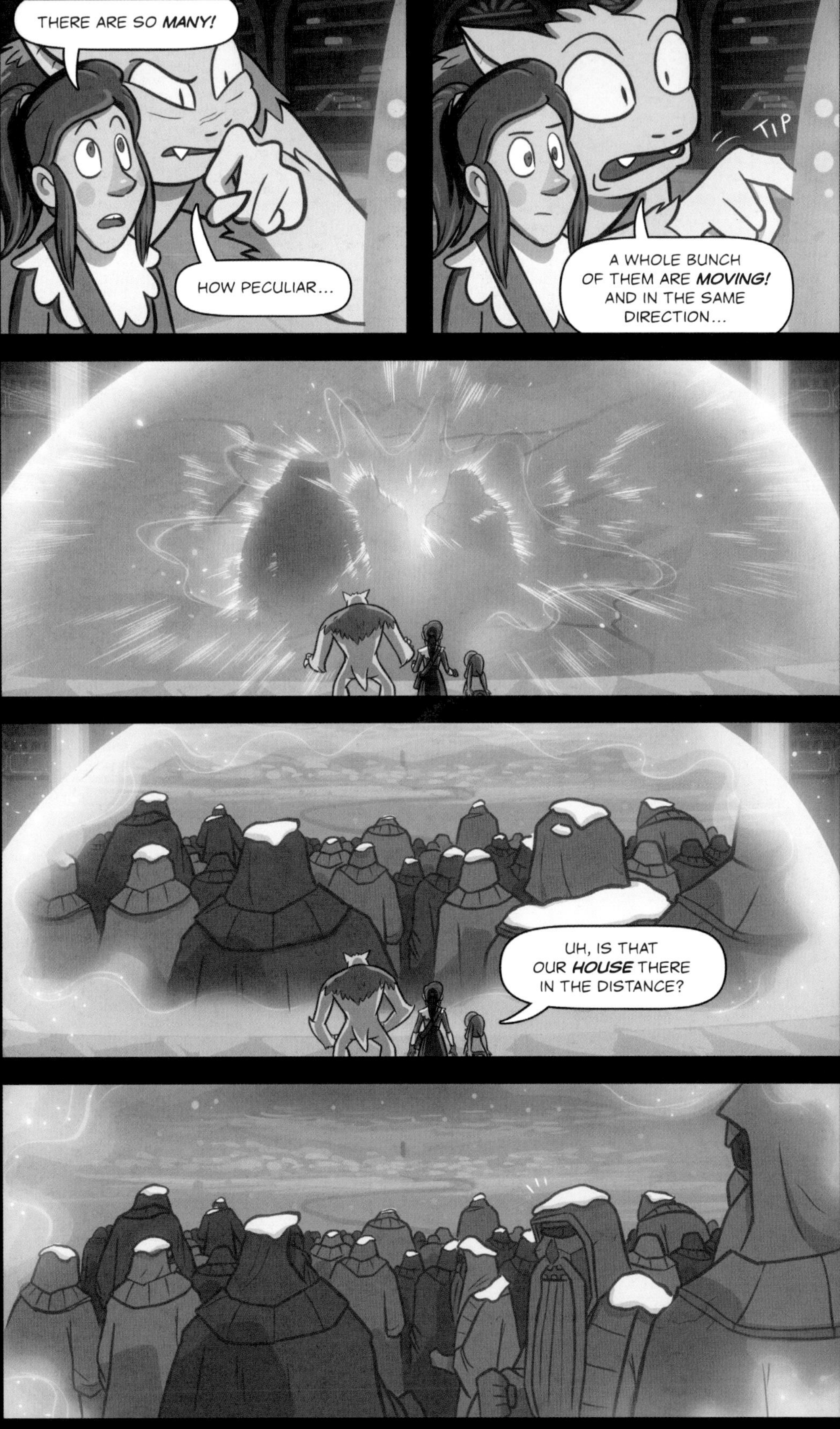
THERE ARE SO **MANY!**
HOW PECULIAR...
TIP
A WHOLE BUNCH OF THEM ARE **MOVING!** AND IN THE SAME DIRECTION...
UH, IS THAT OUR **HOUSE** THERE IN THE DISTANCE?

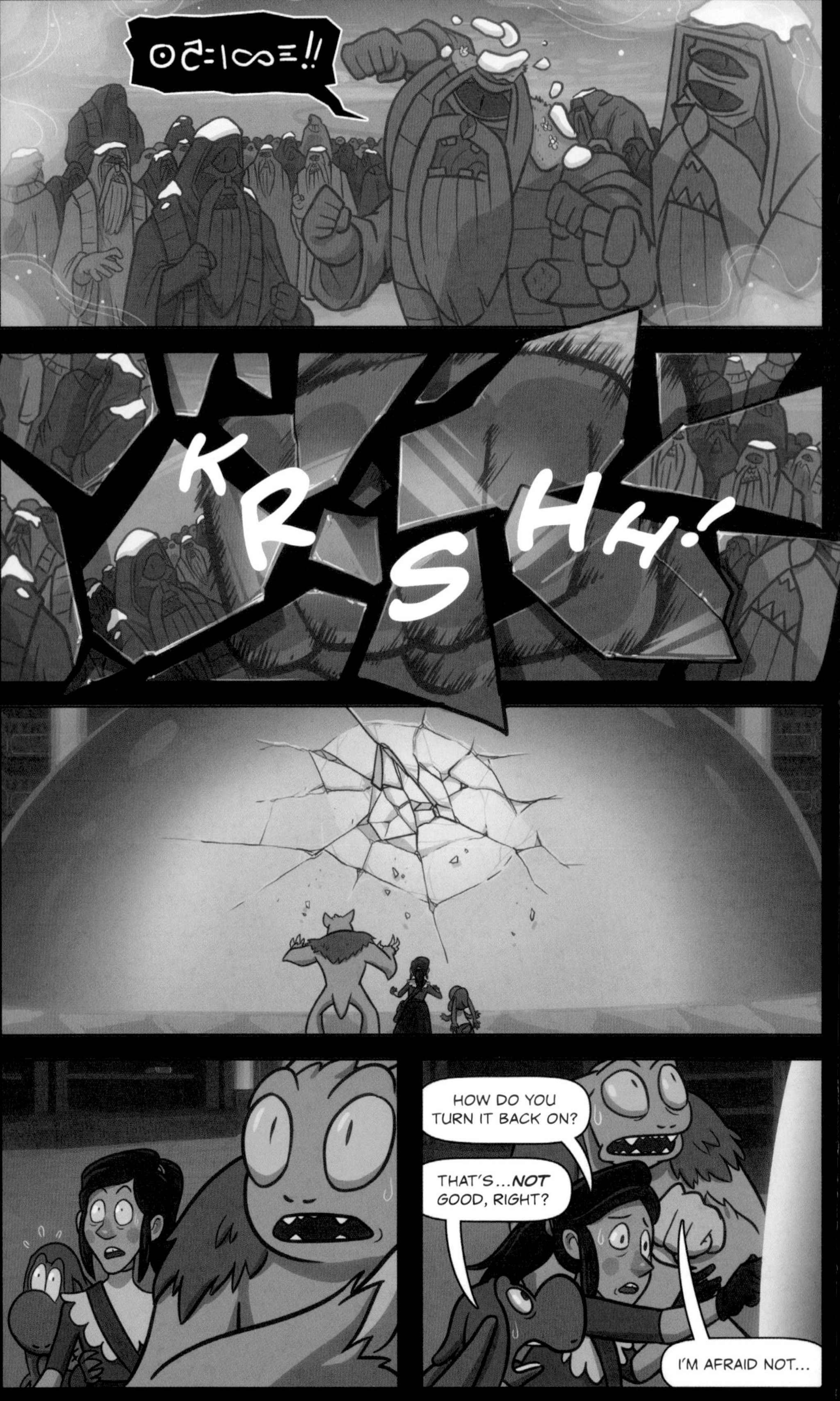
KRSHH!
HOW DO YOU TURN IT BACK ON?
THAT'S...*NOT* GOOD, RIGHT?
I'M AFRAID NOT...

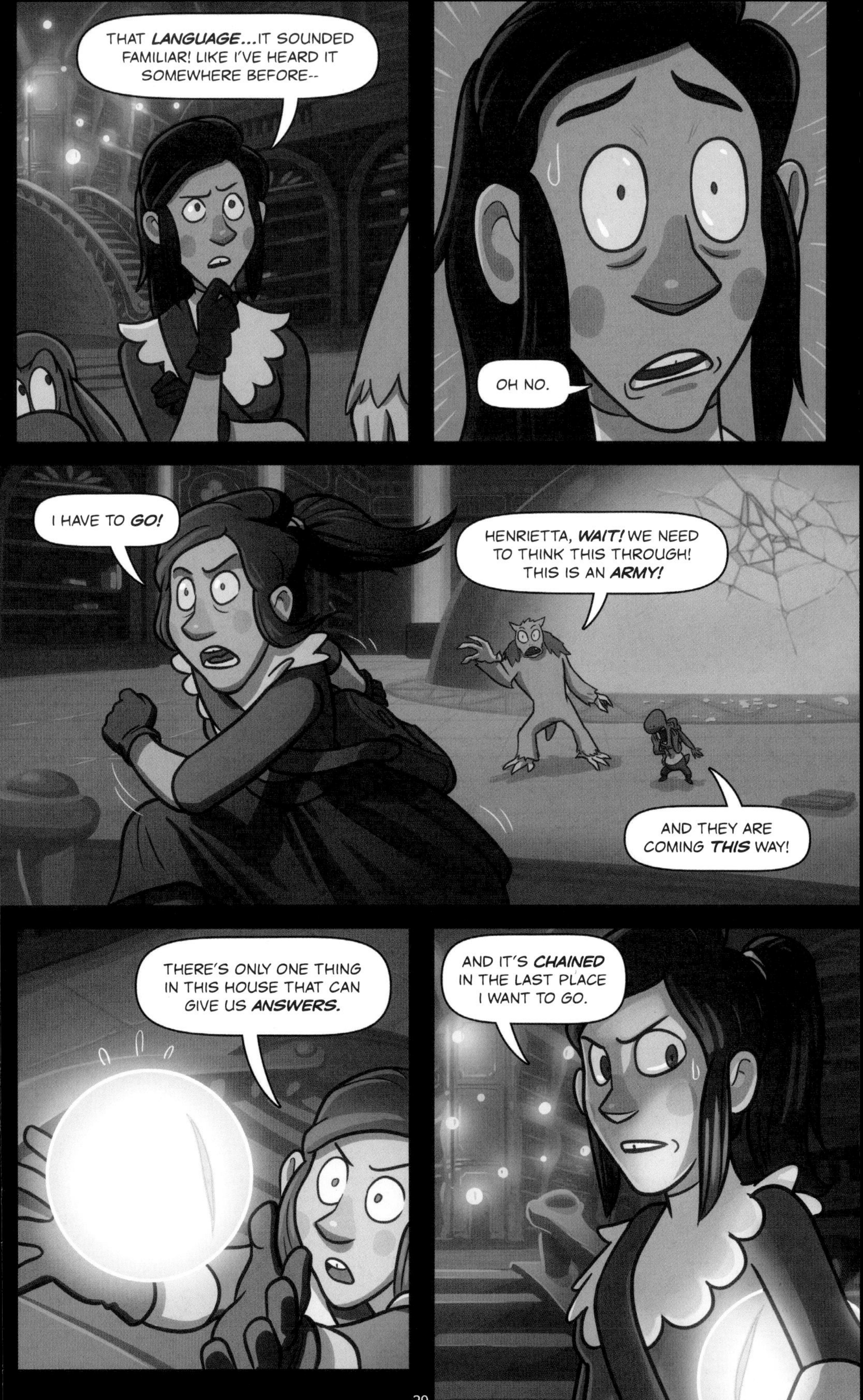
THAT LANGUAGE...IT SOUNDED FAMILIAR! LIKE I'VE HEARD IT SOMEWHERE BEFORE--
OH NO.
I HAVE TO GO!
HENRIETTA, WAIT! WE NEED TO THINK THIS THROUGH! THIS IS AN ARMY!
AND THEY ARE COMING THIS WAY!
THERE'S ONLY ONE THING IN THIS HOUSE THAT CAN GIVE US ANSWERS.
AND IT'S CHAINED IN THE LAST PLACE I WANT TO GO.

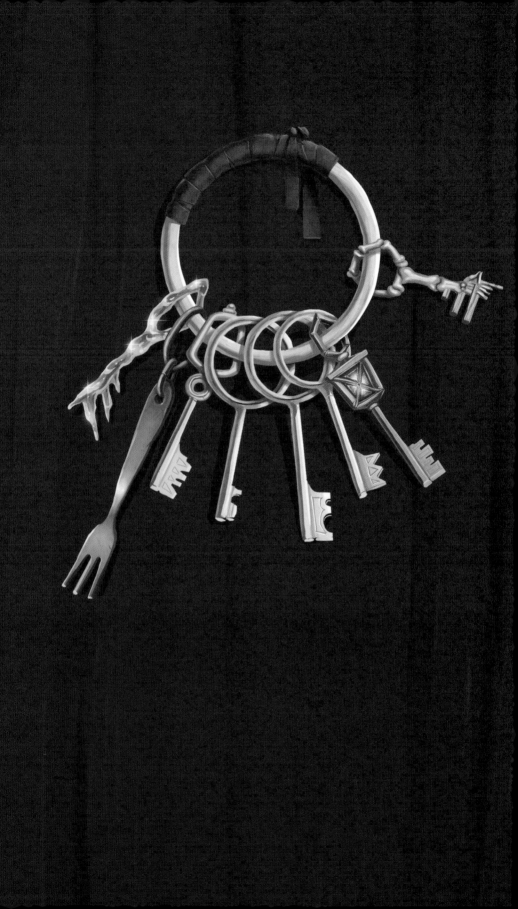

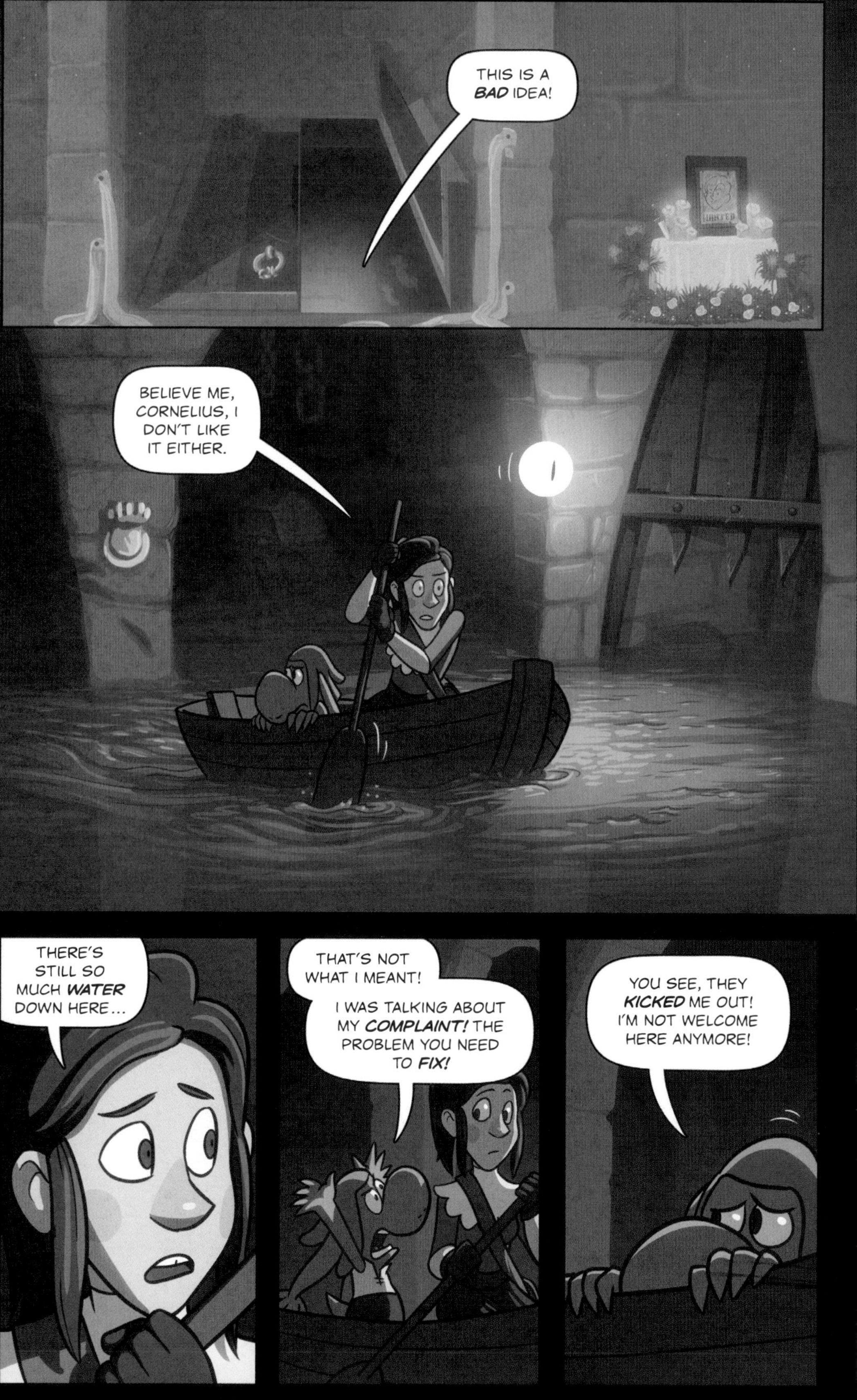
THIS IS A BAD IDEA!
BELIEVE ME, CORNELIUS, I DON'T LIKE IT EITHER.
THERE'S STILL SO MUCH WATER DOWN HERE...
THAT'S NOT WHAT I MEANT!
I WAS TALKING ABOUT MY COMPLAINT! THE PROBLEM YOU NEED TO FIX!
YOU SEE, THEY KICKED ME OUT! I'M NOT WELCOME HERE ANYMORE!

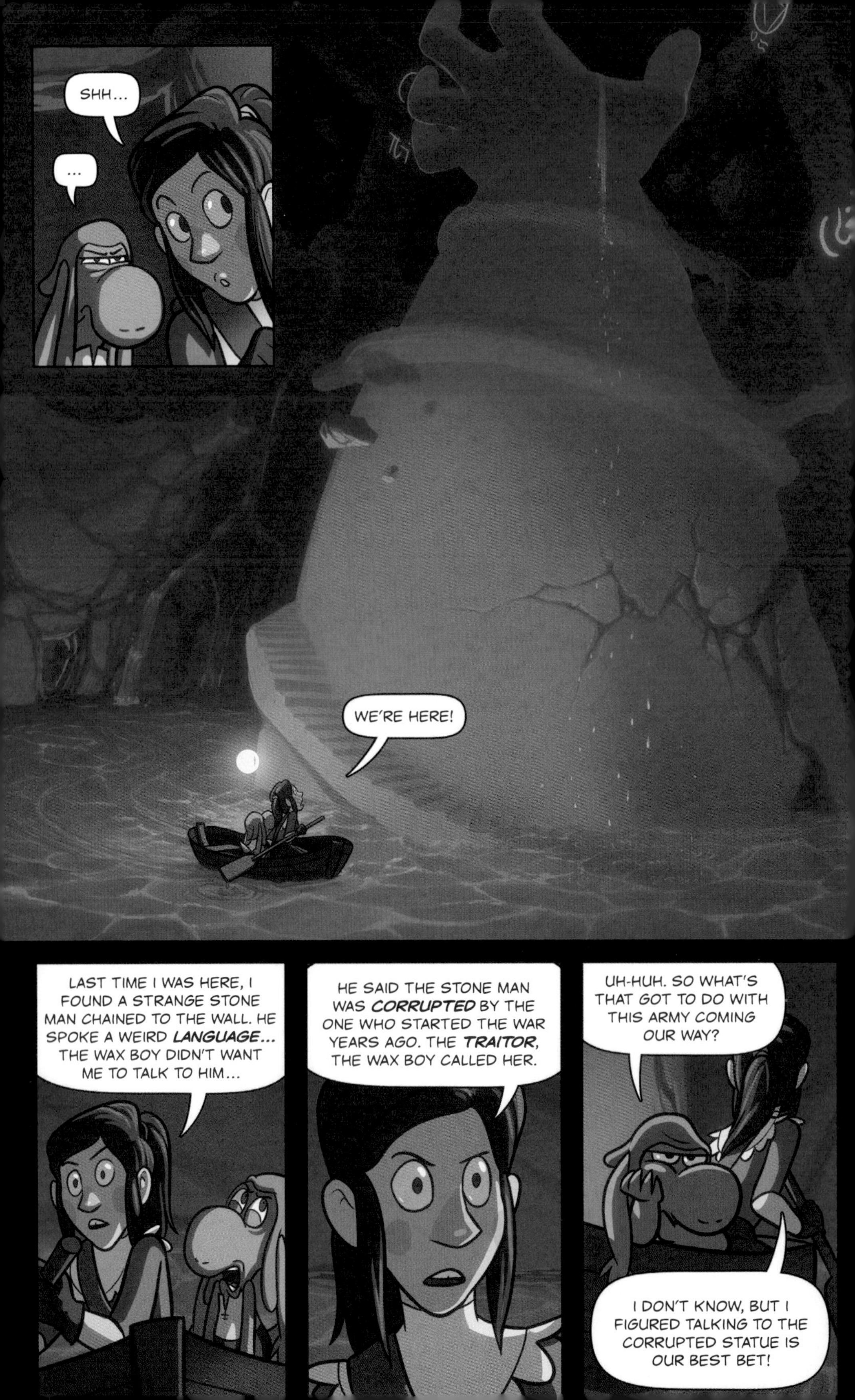
SHH...
...
WE'RE HERE!
LAST TIME I WAS HERE, I FOUND A STRANGE STONE MAN CHAINED TO THE WALL. HE SPOKE A WEIRD LANGUAGE... THE WAX BOY DIDN'T WANT ME TO TALK TO HIM...
HE SAID THE STONE MAN WAS CORRUPTED BY THE ONE WHO STARTED THE WAR YEARS AGO. THE TRAITOR, THE WAX BOY CALLED HER.
UH-HUH. SO WHAT'S THAT GOT TO DO WITH THIS ARMY COMING OUR WAY?
I DON'T KNOW, BUT I FIGURED TALKING TO THE CORRUPTED STATUE IS OUR BEST BET!

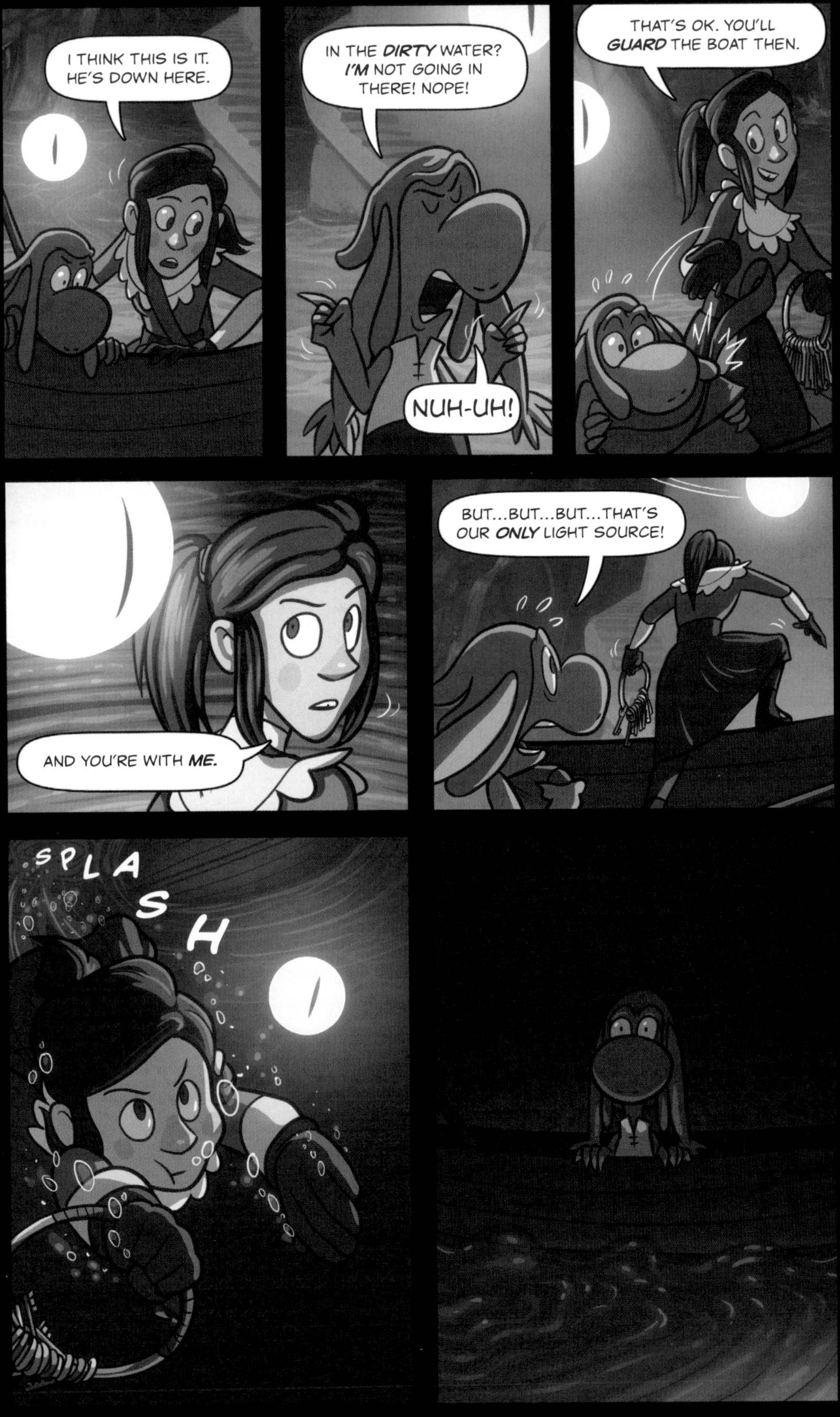
I THINK THIS IS IT. HE'S DOWN HERE.
IN THE DIRTY WATER? I'M NOT GOING IN THERE! NOPE!
NUH-UH!
THAT'S OK. YOU'LL GUARD THE BOAT THEN.
AND YOU'RE WITH ME.
BUT...BUT...BUT...THAT'S OUR ONLY LIGHT SOURCE!
SPLASH

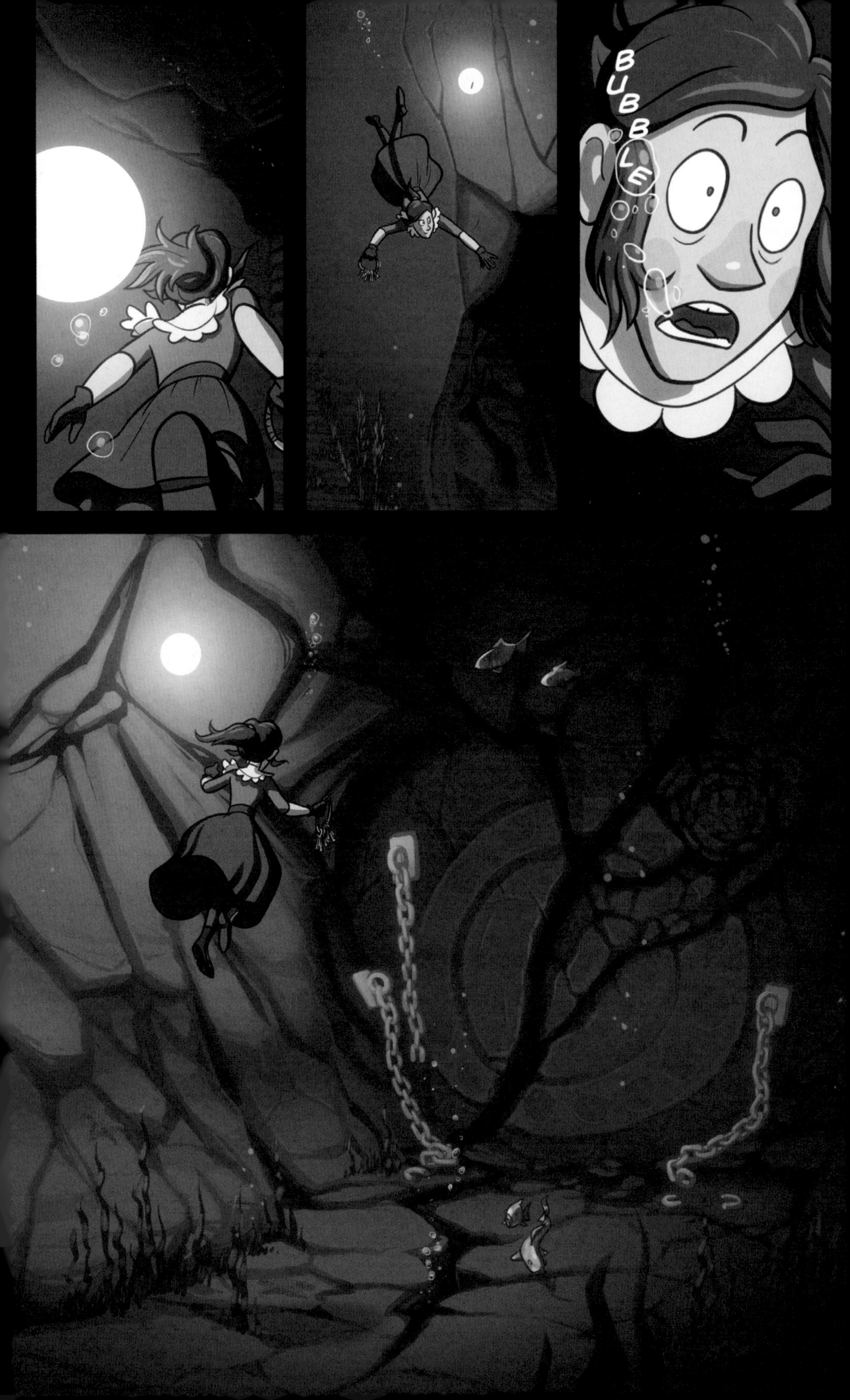
BUBBLE

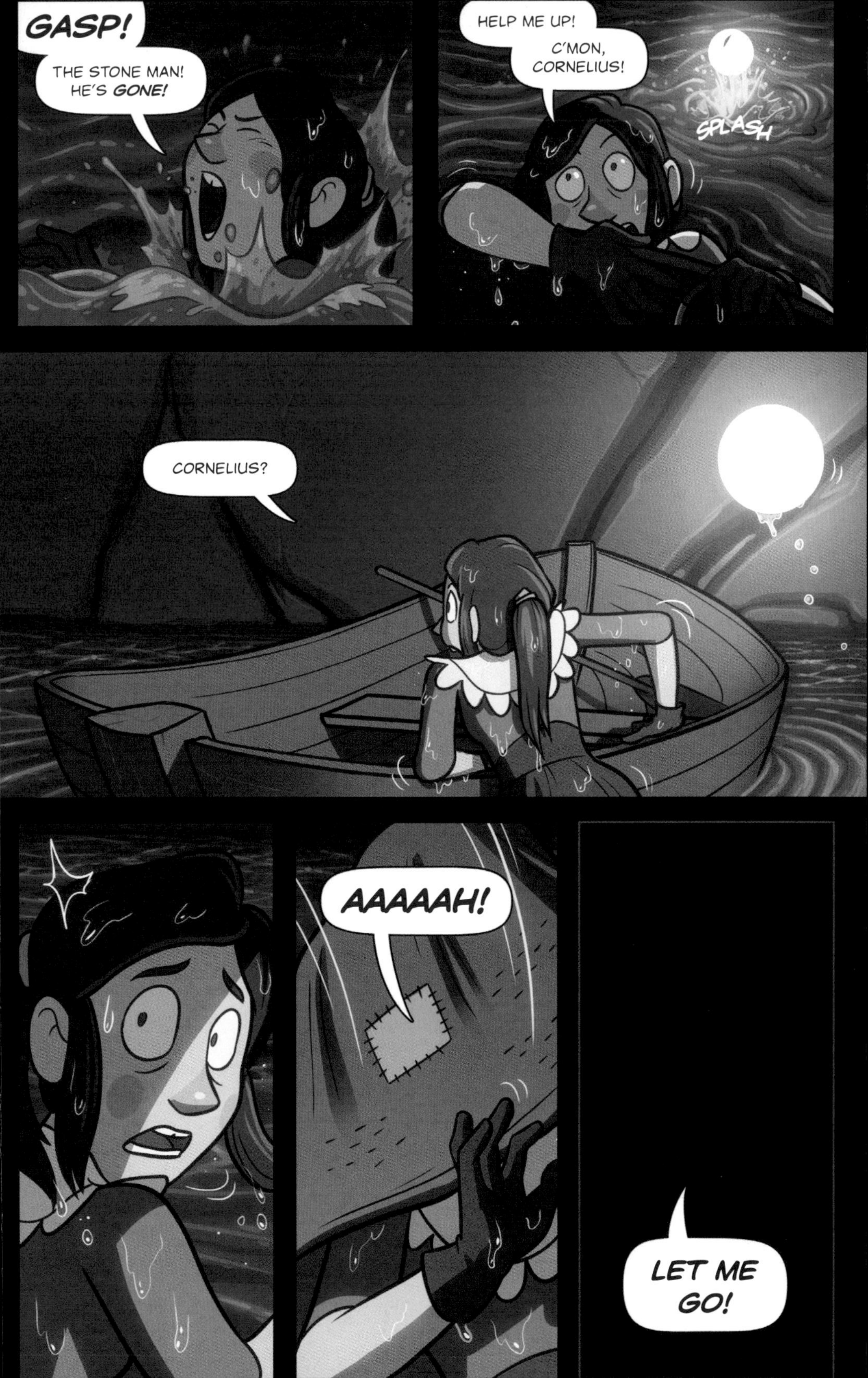
GASP!
THE STONE MAN! HE'S GONE!
HELP ME UP!
C'MON, CORNELIUS!
SPLASH
CORNELIUS?
AAAAAH!
LET ME GO!

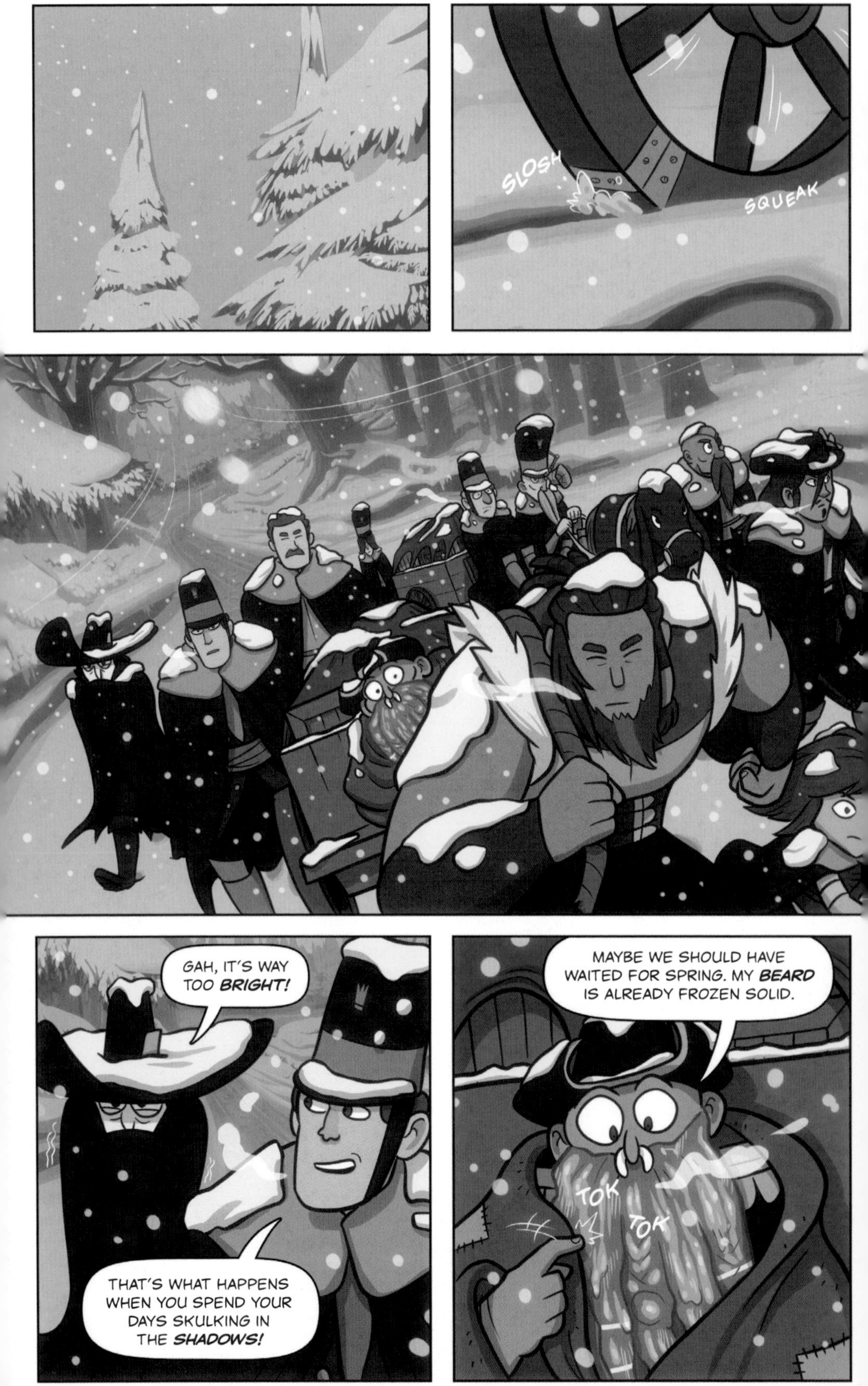
SLOSH
SQUEAK
GAH, IT'S WAY TOO BRIGHT!
THAT'S WHAT HAPPENS WHEN YOU SPEND YOUR DAYS SKULKING IN THE SHADOWS!
MAYBE WE SHOULD HAVE WAITED FOR SPRING. MY BEARD IS ALREADY FROZEN SOLID.
TOK
TOK

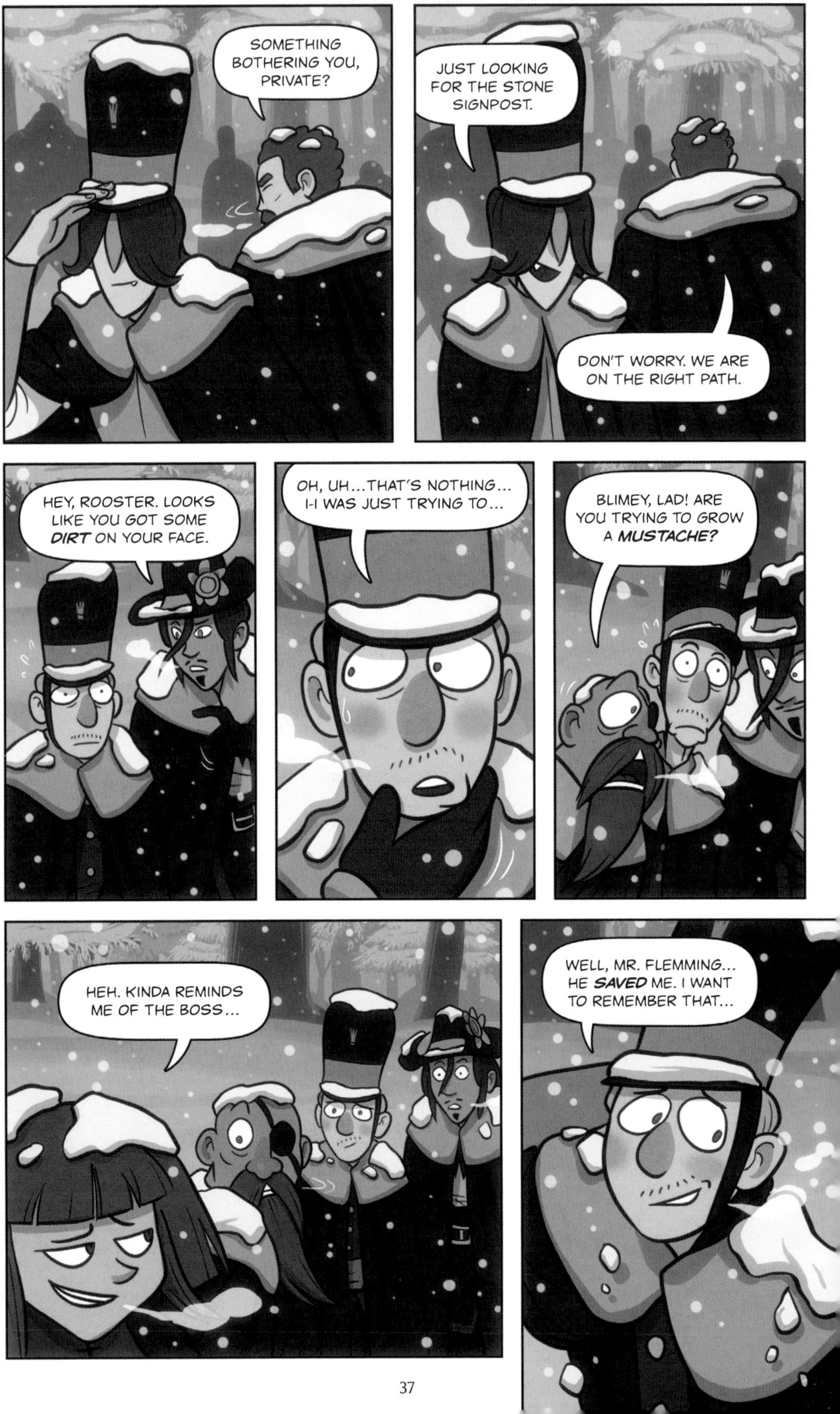
SOMETHING BOTHERING YOU, PRIVATE?
JUST LOOKING FOR THE STONE SIGNPOST.
DON'T WORRY. WE ARE ON THE RIGHT PATH.
HEY, ROOSTER. LOOKS LIKE YOU GOT SOME **DIRT** ON YOUR FACE.
OH, UH...THAT'S NOTHING... I-I WAS JUST TRYING TO...
BLIMEY, LAD! ARE YOU TRYING TO GROW A **MUSTACHE?**
HEH. KINDA REMINDS ME OF THE BOSS...
WELL, MR. FLEMMING... HE **SAVED** ME. I WANT TO REMEMBER THAT...

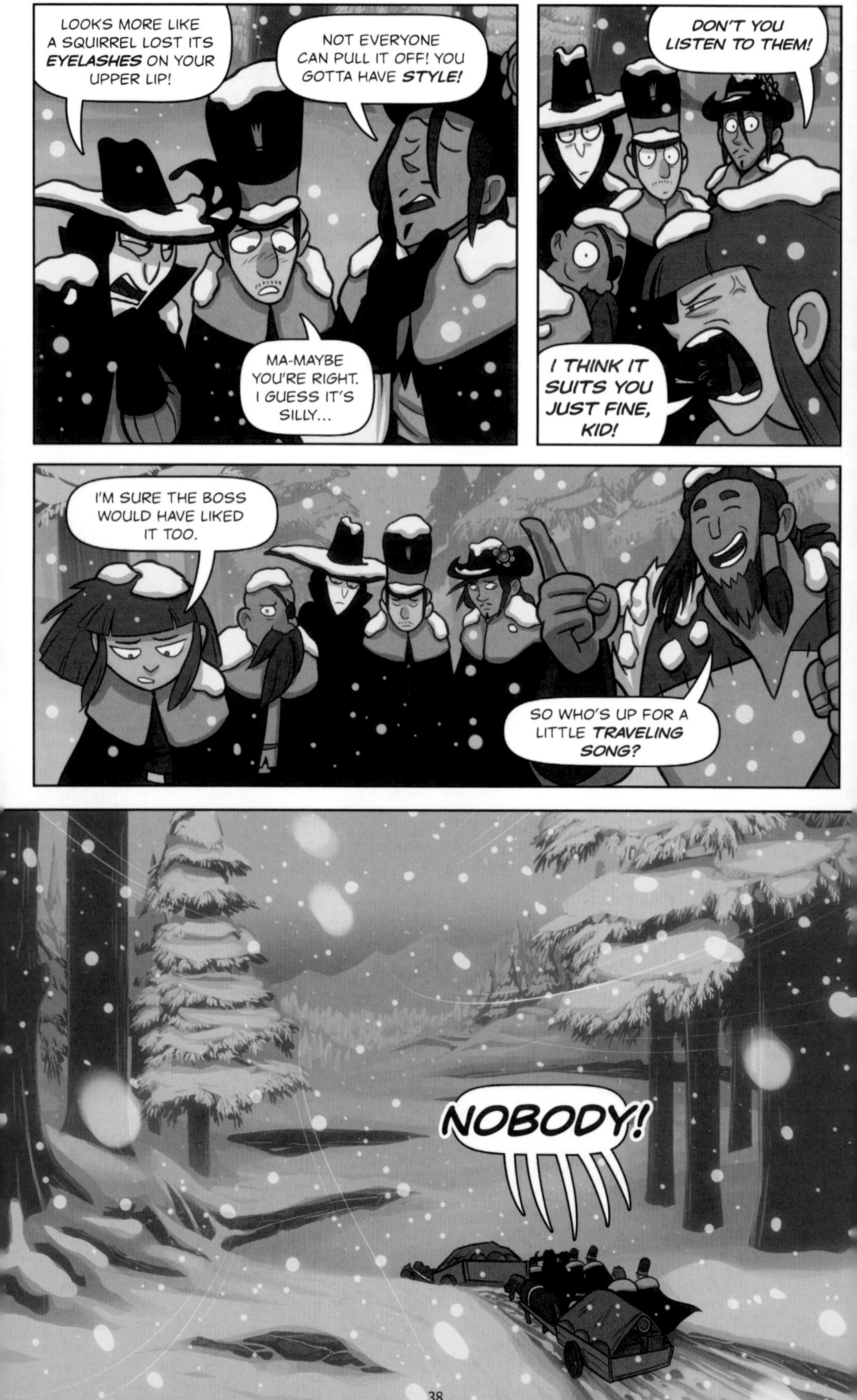
LOOKS MORE LIKE A SQUIRREL LOST ITS **EYELASHES** ON YOUR UPPER LIP!
NOT EVERYONE CAN PULL IT OFF! YOU GOTTA HAVE **STYLE!**
MA-MAYBE YOU'RE RIGHT. I GUESS IT'S SILLY...
DON'T YOU LISTEN TO THEM!
I THINK IT SUITS YOU JUST FINE, KID!
I'M SURE THE BOSS WOULD HAVE LIKED IT TOO.
SO WHO'S UP FOR A LITTLE **TRAVELING SONG?**
NOBODY!

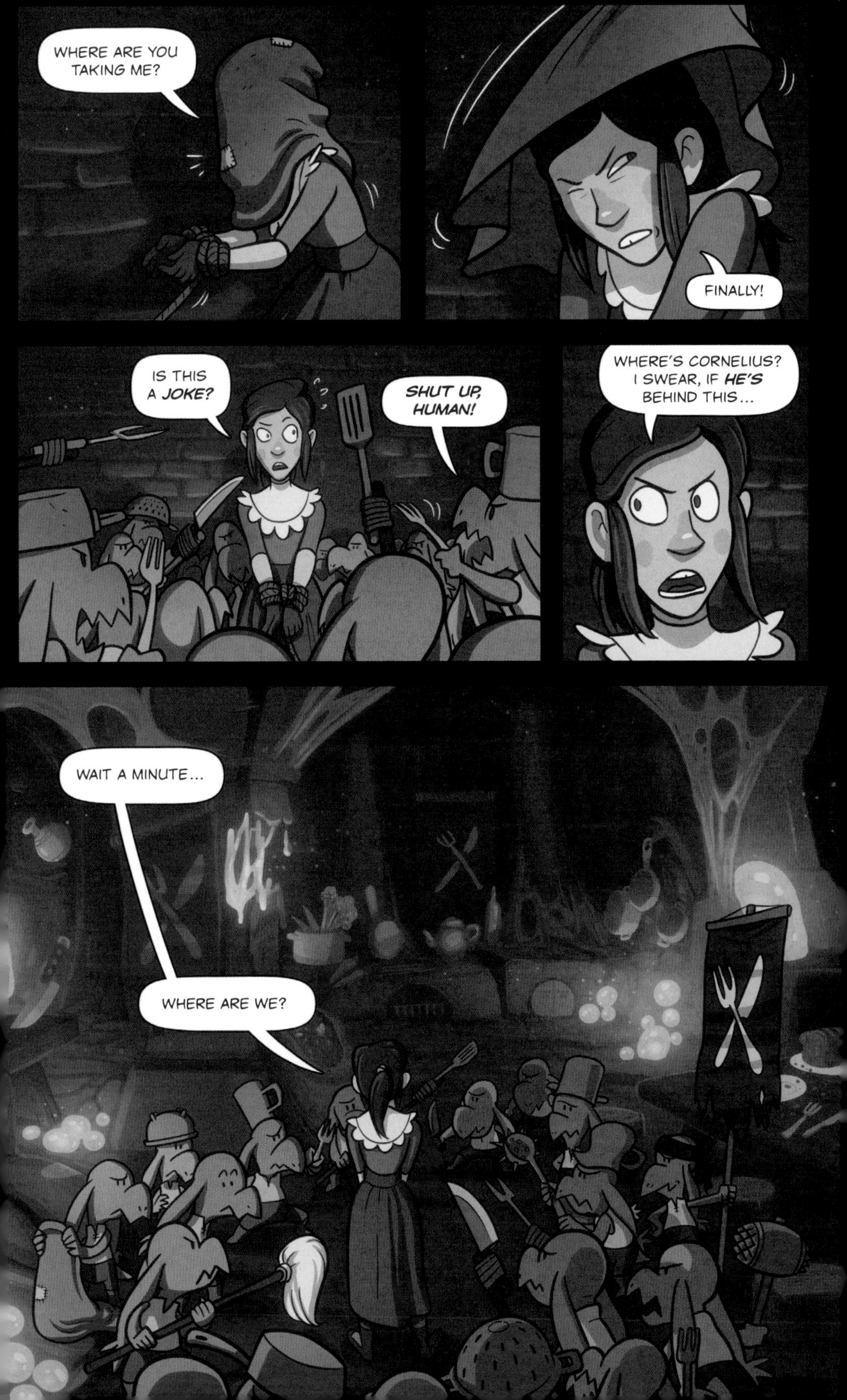
WHERE ARE YOU TAKING ME?
FINALLY!
IS THIS A *JOKE?*
SHUT UP, HUMAN!
WHERE'S CORNELIUS? I SWEAR, IF ***HE'S*** BEHIND THIS...
WAIT A MINUTE...
WHERE ARE WE?

THAT'S NOT THE KITCHEN I REMEMBER...

AND THOSE *WALLS*...

PEFFFFRRT

...DON'T LOOK VERY *HEALTHY*.

HENRIETTA!

CORNELIUS!

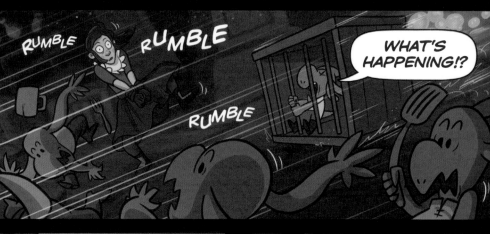

RUMBLE

RUMBLE

RUMBLE

WHAT'S HAPPENING!?

I THINK I KNOW WHAT THIS IS! IT'S WHAT HAPPENS TO *ROOMS* THAT AREN'T *NEEDED* ANYMORE.

HISSSS

IF THE *MAGIC* ISN'T RETURNED TO THE *GRAVEYARD*, THEY TURN...

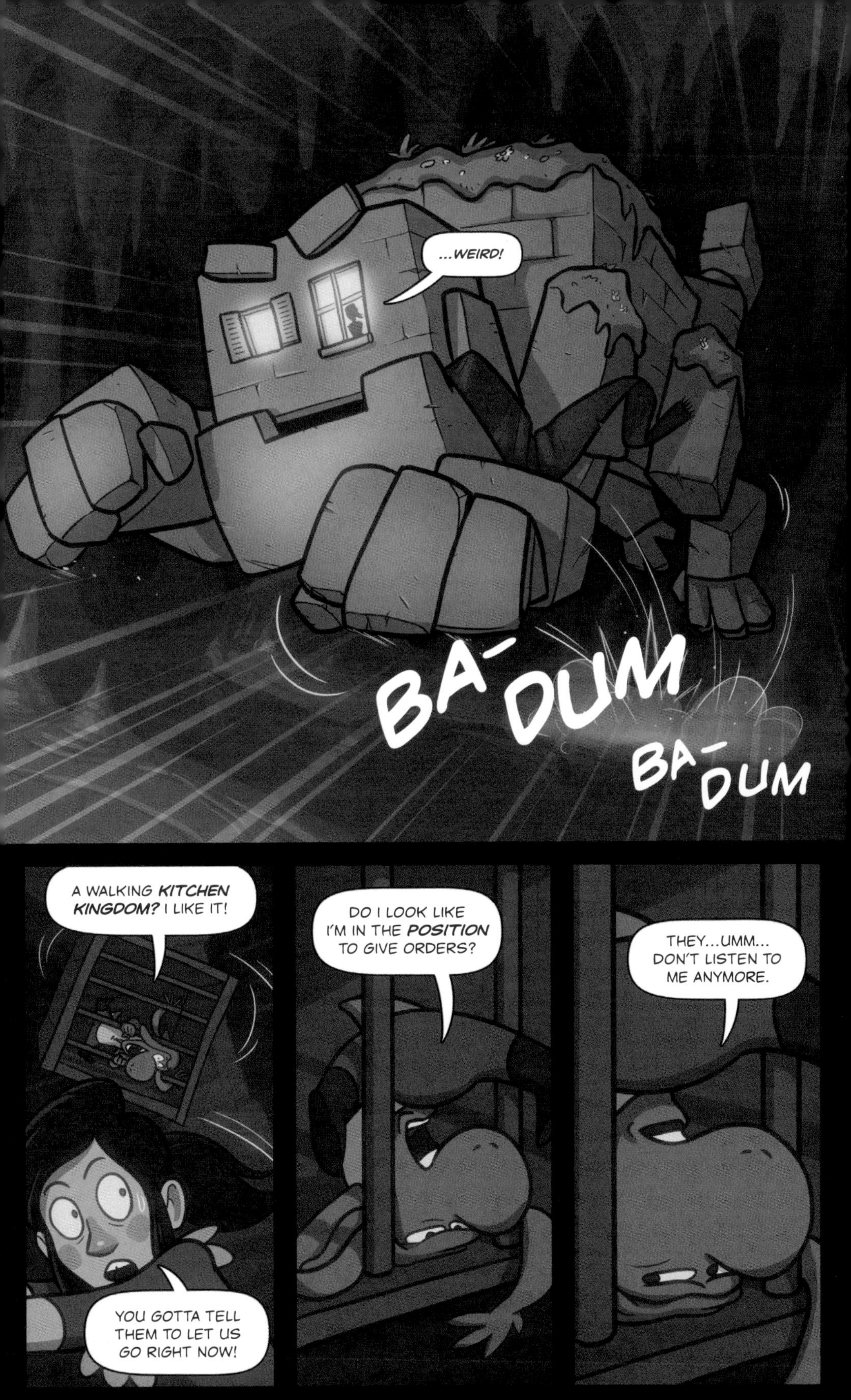
...WEIRD!
BA-DUM
BA-DUM
A WALKING KITCHEN KINGDOM? I LIKE IT!
YOU GOTTA TELL THEM TO LET US GO RIGHT NOW!
DO I LOOK LIKE I'M IN THE POSITION TO GIVE ORDERS?
THEY...UMM... DON'T LISTEN TO ME ANYMORE.

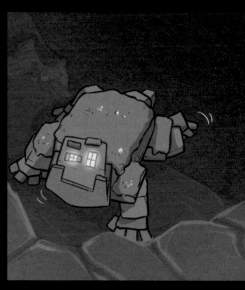
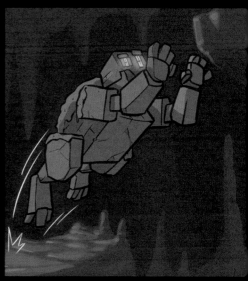

THE KOBOLDS HAVE A *NEW* KING NOW!

WAM

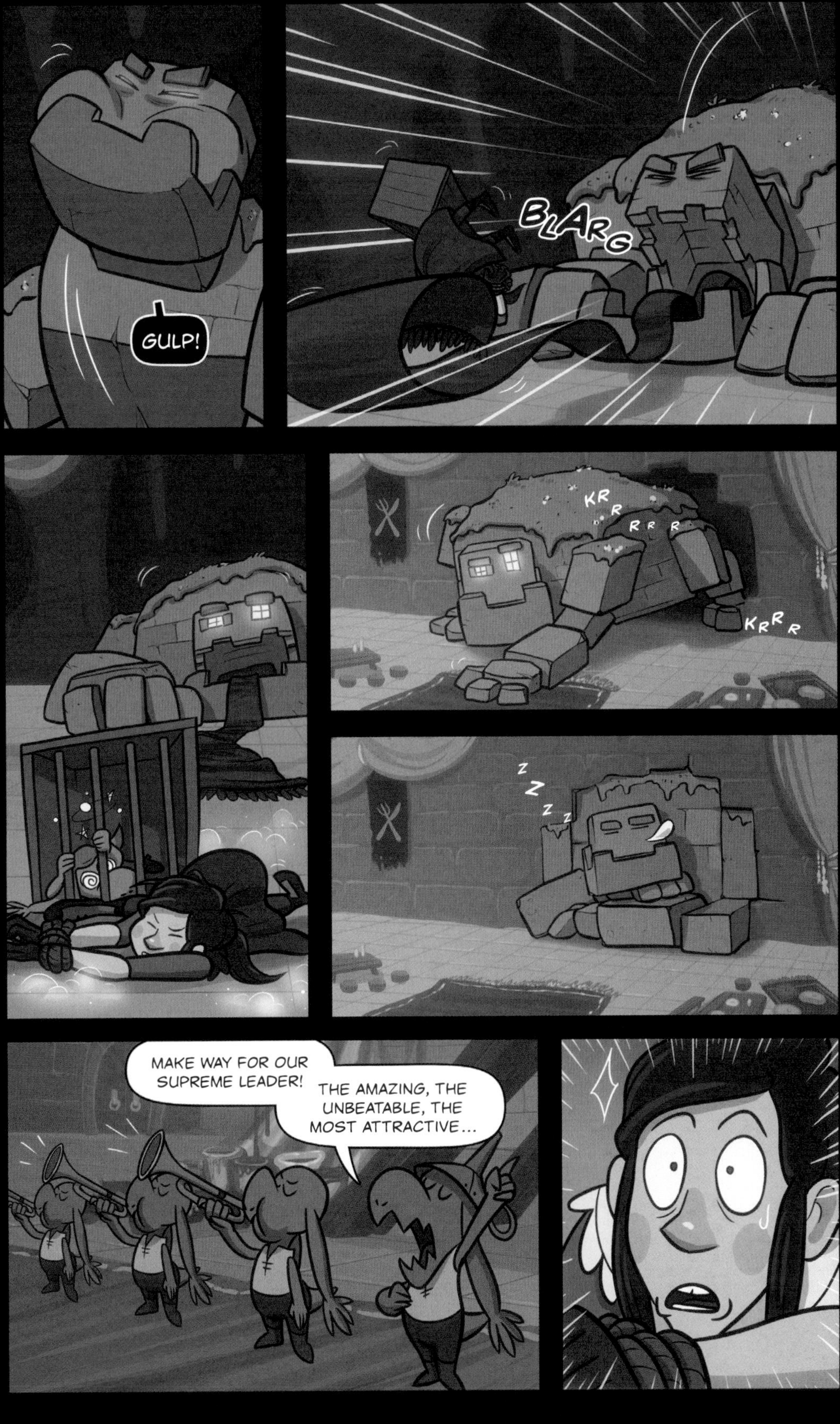
GULP!
BLARG
KRR
RRR
KRRR
Z Z Z Z
MAKE WAY FOR OUR SUPREME LEADER!
THE AMAZING, THE UNBEATABLE, THE MOST ATTRACTIVE...

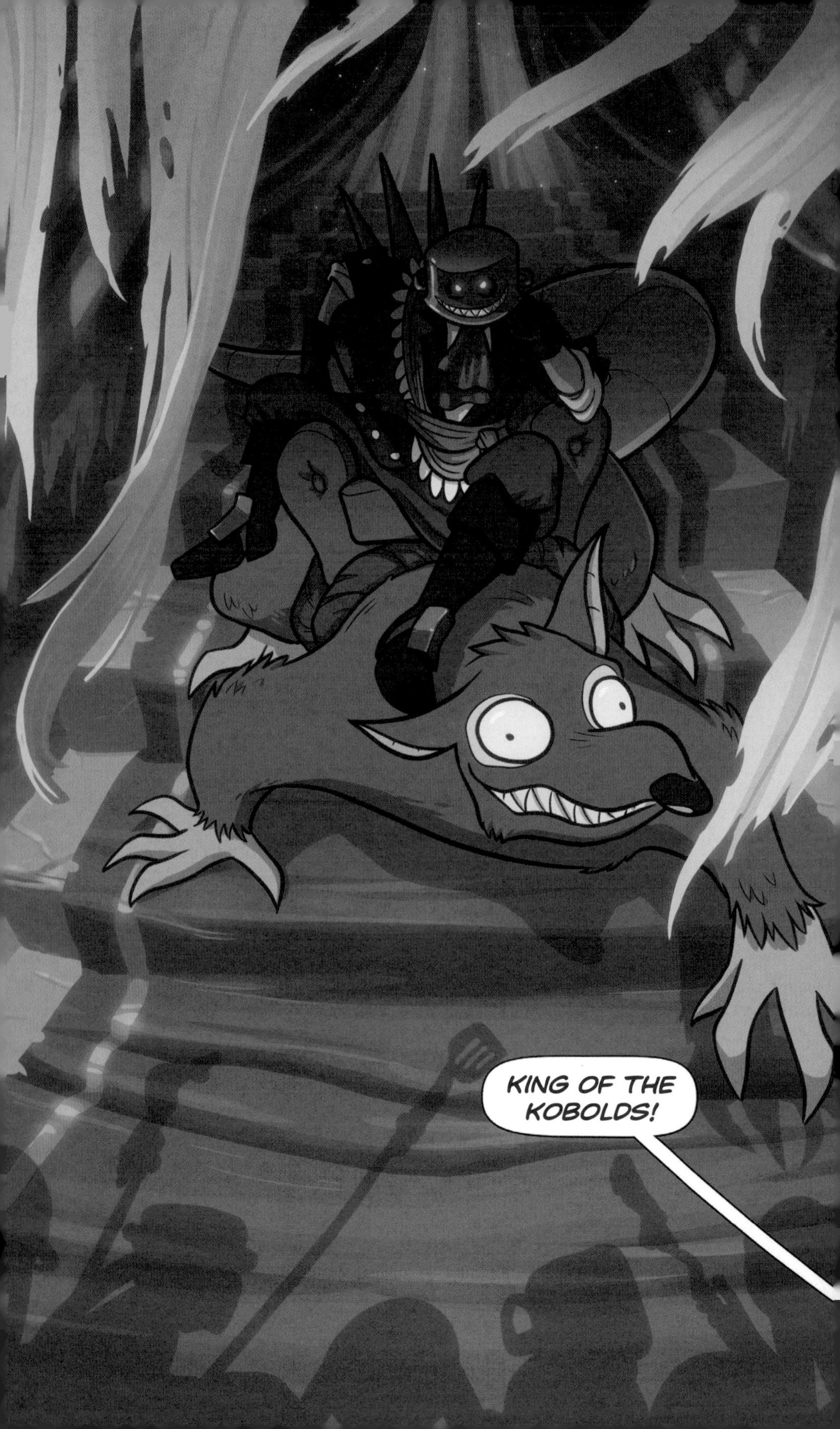
KING OF THE KOBOLDS!

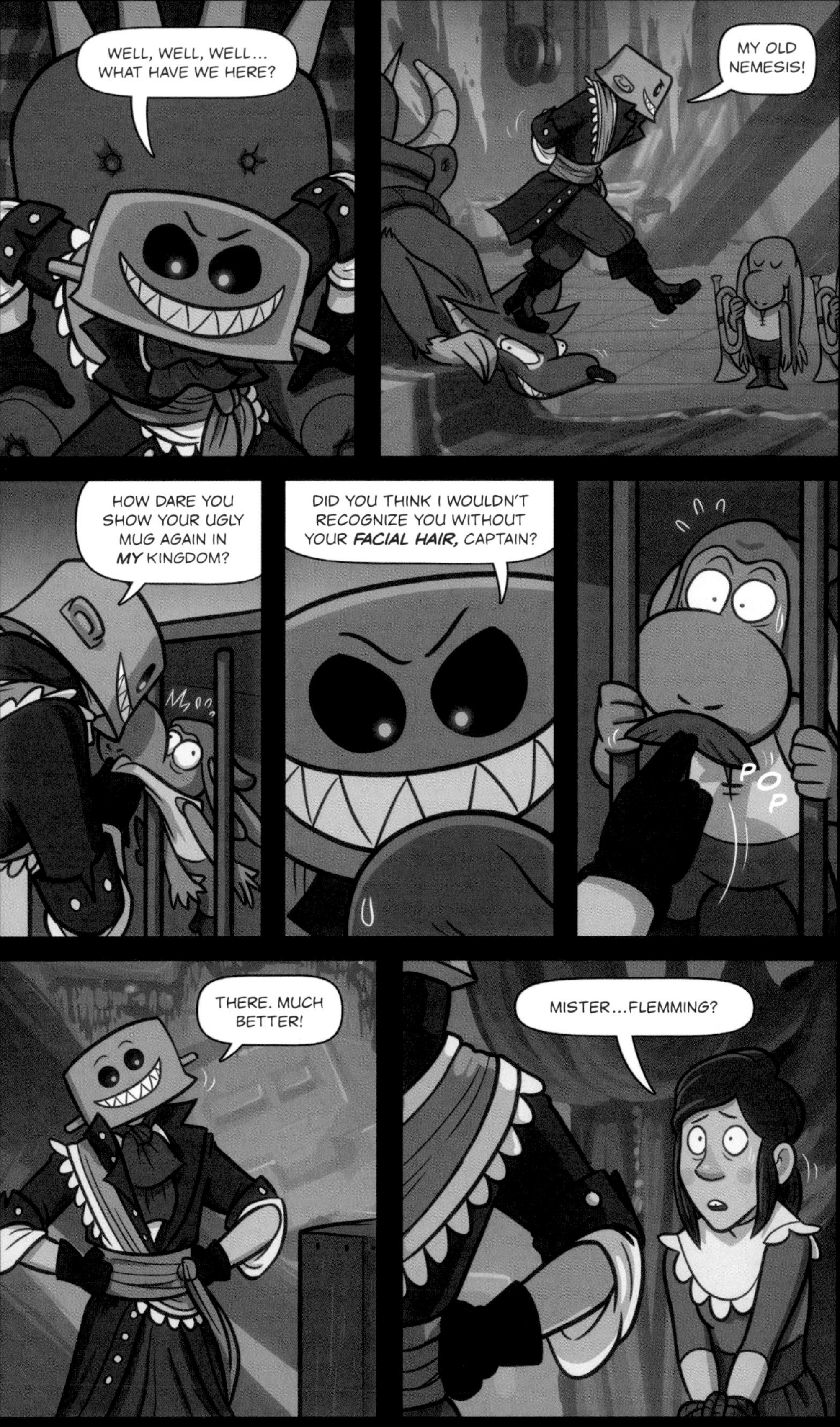
WELL, WELL, WELL...
WHAT HAVE WE HERE?
MY OLD NEMESIS!
HOW DARE YOU SHOW YOUR UGLY MUG AGAIN IN *MY* KINGDOM?
DID YOU THINK I WOULDN'T RECOGNIZE YOU WITHOUT YOUR ***FACIAL HAIR,*** CAPTAIN?
POP
THERE. MUCH BETTER!
MISTER...FLEMMING?

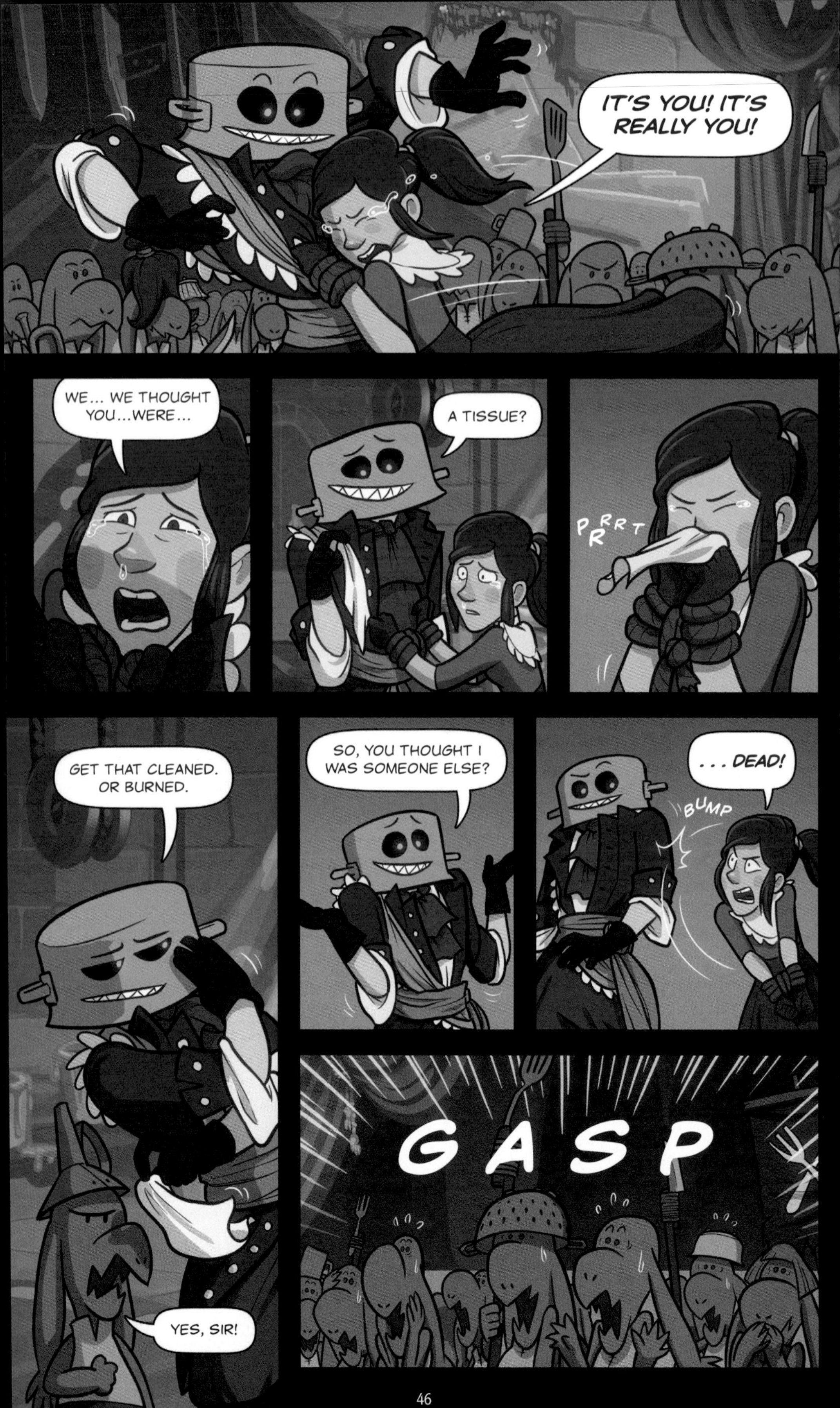
IT'S YOU! IT'S REALLY YOU!
WE... WE THOUGHT YOU...WERE...
A TISSUE?
PRRRT
GET THAT CLEANED. OR BURNED.
YES, SIR!
SO, YOU THOUGHT I WAS SOMEONE ELSE?
BUMP
. . . DEAD!
GASP

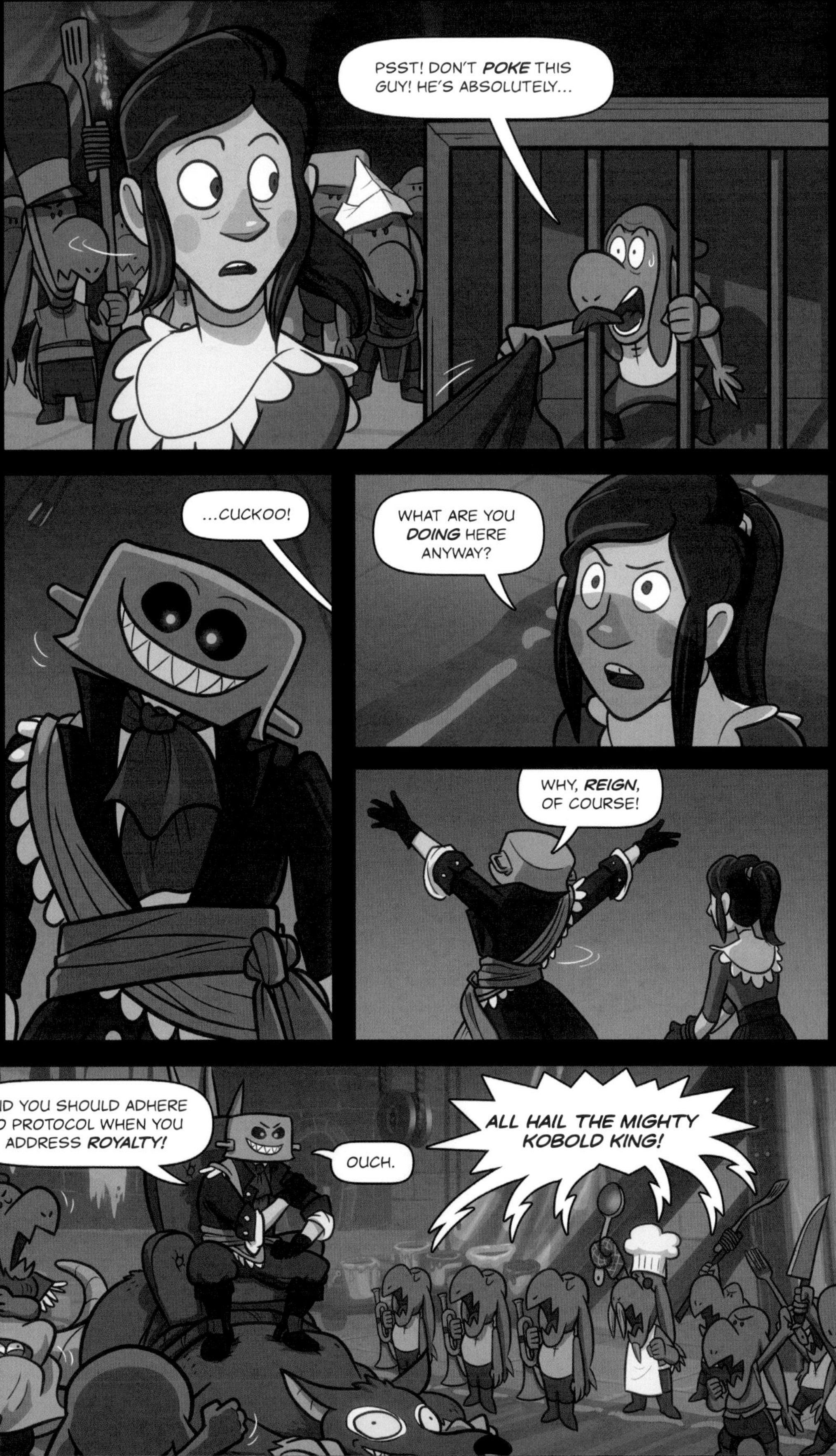
PSST! DON'T POKE THIS GUY! HE'S ABSOLUTELY...
...CUCKOO!
WHAT ARE YOU DOING HERE ANYWAY?
WHY, REIGN, OF COURSE!
ND YOU SHOULD ADHERE TO PROTOCOL WHEN YOU ADDRESS ROYALTY!
OUCH.
ALL HAIL THE MIGHTY KOBOLD KING!

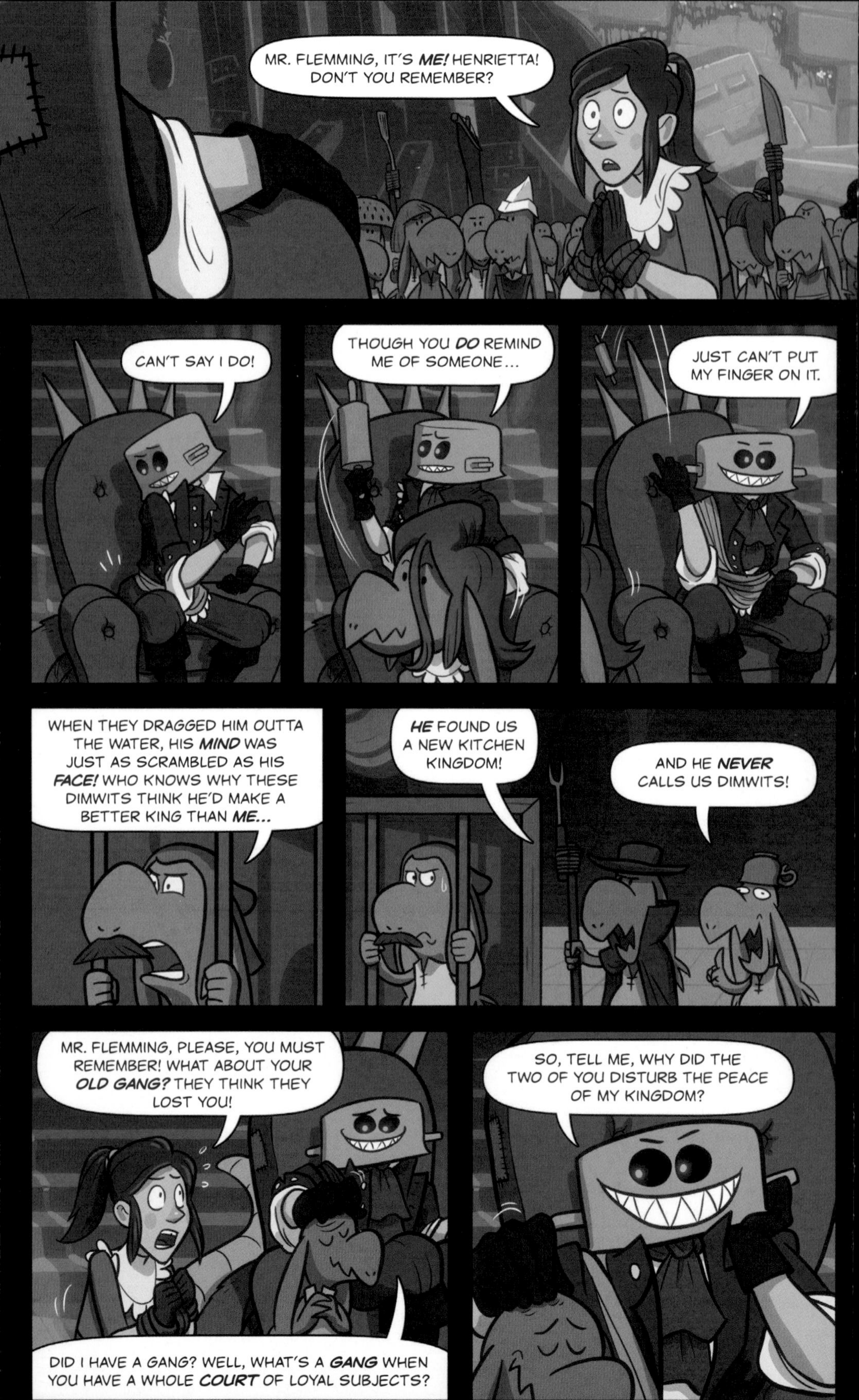
MR. FLEMMING, IT'S ME! HENRIETTA! DON'T YOU REMEMBER?
CAN'T SAY I DO!
THOUGH YOU DO REMIND ME OF SOMEONE...
JUST CAN'T PUT MY FINGER ON IT.
WHEN THEY DRAGGED HIM OUTTA THE WATER, HIS MIND WAS JUST AS SCRAMBLED AS HIS FACE! WHO KNOWS WHY THESE DIMWITS THINK HE'D MAKE A BETTER KING THAN ME...
HE FOUND US A NEW KITCHEN KINGDOM!
AND HE NEVER CALLS US DIMWITS!
MR. FLEMMING, PLEASE, YOU MUST REMEMBER! WHAT ABOUT YOUR OLD GANG? THEY THINK THEY LOST YOU!
DID I HAVE A GANG? WELL, WHAT'S A GANG WHEN YOU HAVE A WHOLE COURT OF LOYAL SUBJECTS?
SO, TELL ME, WHY DID THE TWO OF YOU DISTURB THE PEACE OF MY KINGDOM?

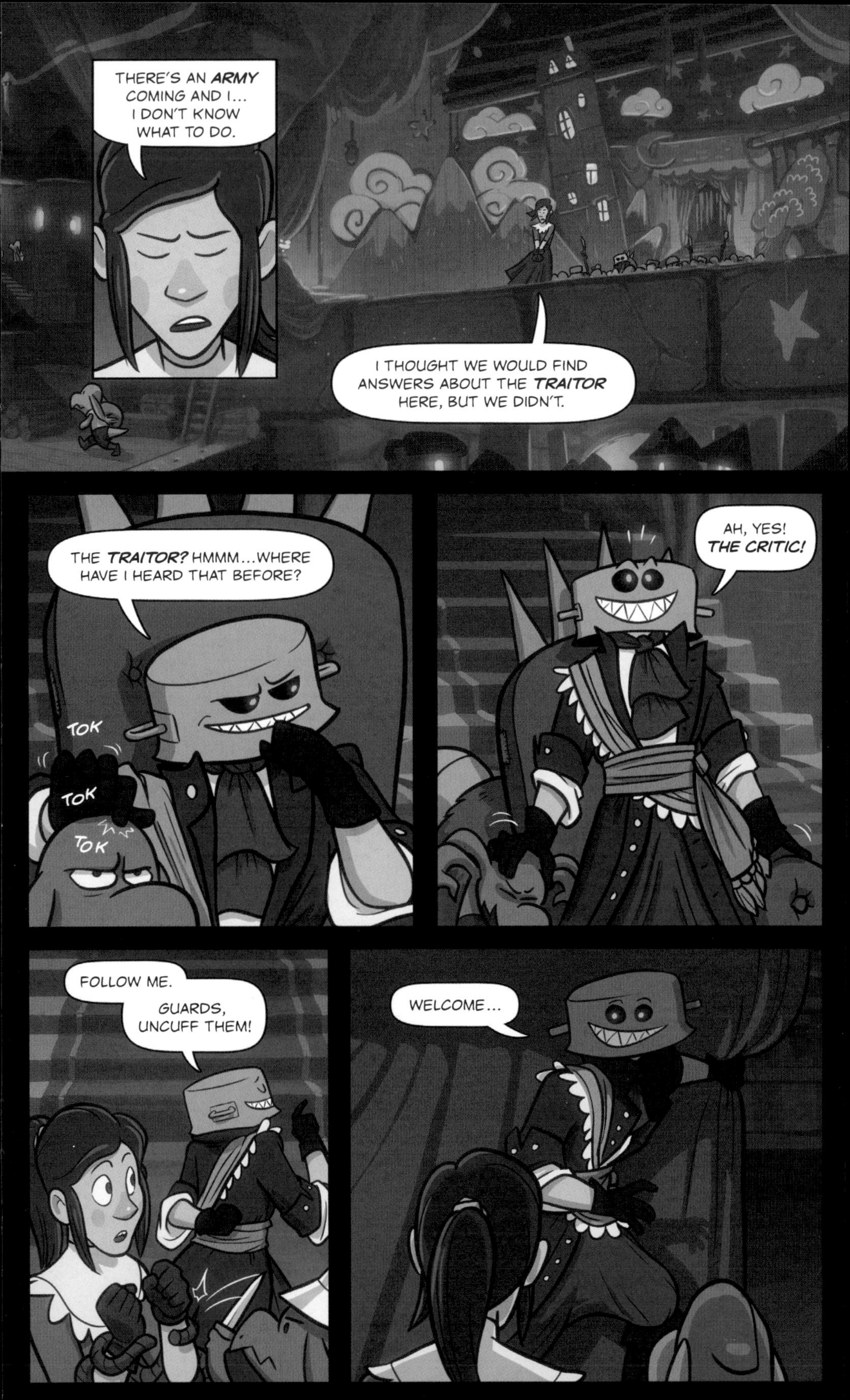
THERE'S AN **ARMY** COMING AND I... I DON'T KNOW WHAT TO DO.
I THOUGHT WE WOULD FIND ANSWERS ABOUT THE **TRAITOR** HERE, BUT WE DIDN'T.
THE **TRAITOR?** HMMM...WHERE HAVE I HEARD THAT BEFORE?
TOK
TOK
TOK
AH, YES! **THE CRITIC!**
FOLLOW ME.
GUARDS, UNCUFF THEM!
WELCOME...

...TO MY PRIVATE LAIR!

HERE I THINK DEEP ROYAL THOUGHTS...

...AND WORK ON MY 12-ACT *PLAY!*

IT'S ABOUT TWO *LEADERS,* ONE A BANDIT AND ONE A SOLDIER, ONCE TRUSTED FRIENDS, NOW MORTAL *ENEMIES...*

DESTINED TO FIGHT AND *DIE* BY EACH OTHER'S BLADE...

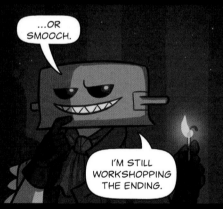

...OR SMOOCH.

I'M STILL WORKSHOPPING THE ENDING.

UH, THAT... SOUNDS GREAT!

YEAH...VERY... UH...DRAMATIC!

OH, *STOP* IT! YOU'RE MUCH KINDER THAN THE CRITIC!

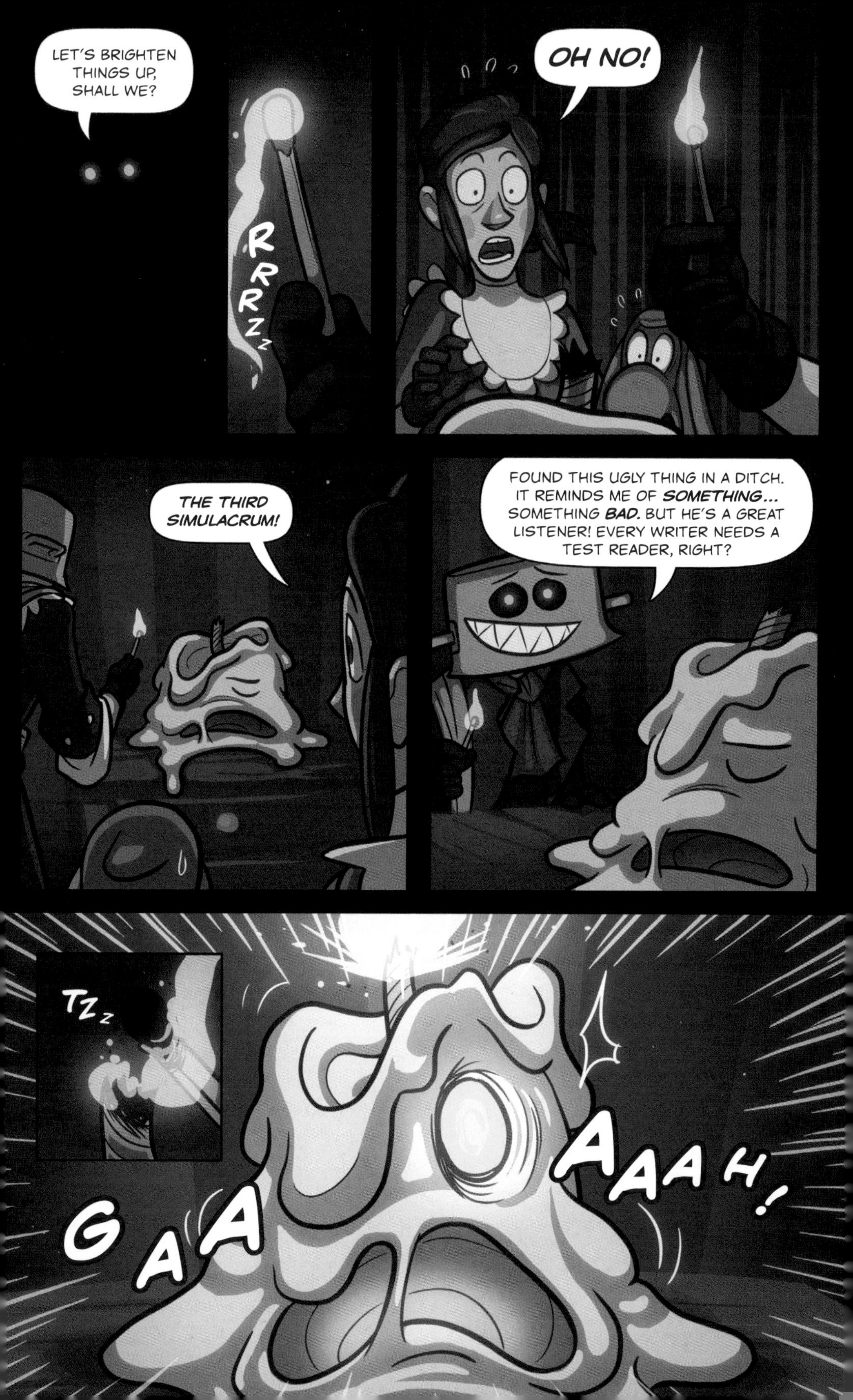
LET'S BRIGHTEN THINGS UP, SHALL WE?
RRRZZ
OH NO!
THE THIRD SIMULACRUM!
FOUND THIS UGLY THING IN A DITCH. IT REMINDS ME OF SOMETHING... SOMETHING BAD. BUT HE'S A GREAT LISTENER! EVERY WRITER NEEDS A TEST READER, RIGHT?
TZZ
GAAAAAH!

HENRIETTA. SO NICE TO SEE YOU AGAIN.

WISH I COULD SAY THE SAME.

DON'T TRY ANYTHING STUPID OR YOU'LL BE ASLEEP FOR GOOD!

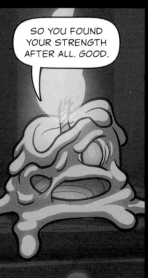

SO YOU FOUND YOUR STRENGTH AFTER ALL. GOOD.

SOMETHING HAS HAPPENED, HASN'T IT? WHY ELSE WOULD YOU RISK WAKING ME AGAIN?

THERE'S AN ARMY OF STONE MEN ON ITS WAY. THEY'RE ALL SPEAKING LIKE THE CORRUPTED ONE.

THAT'S... IMPOSSIBLE!

FATHER DEFEATED HER!

I NEED YOU TO TELL ME *EVERYTHING* YOU KNOW ABOUT THE TRAITOR.

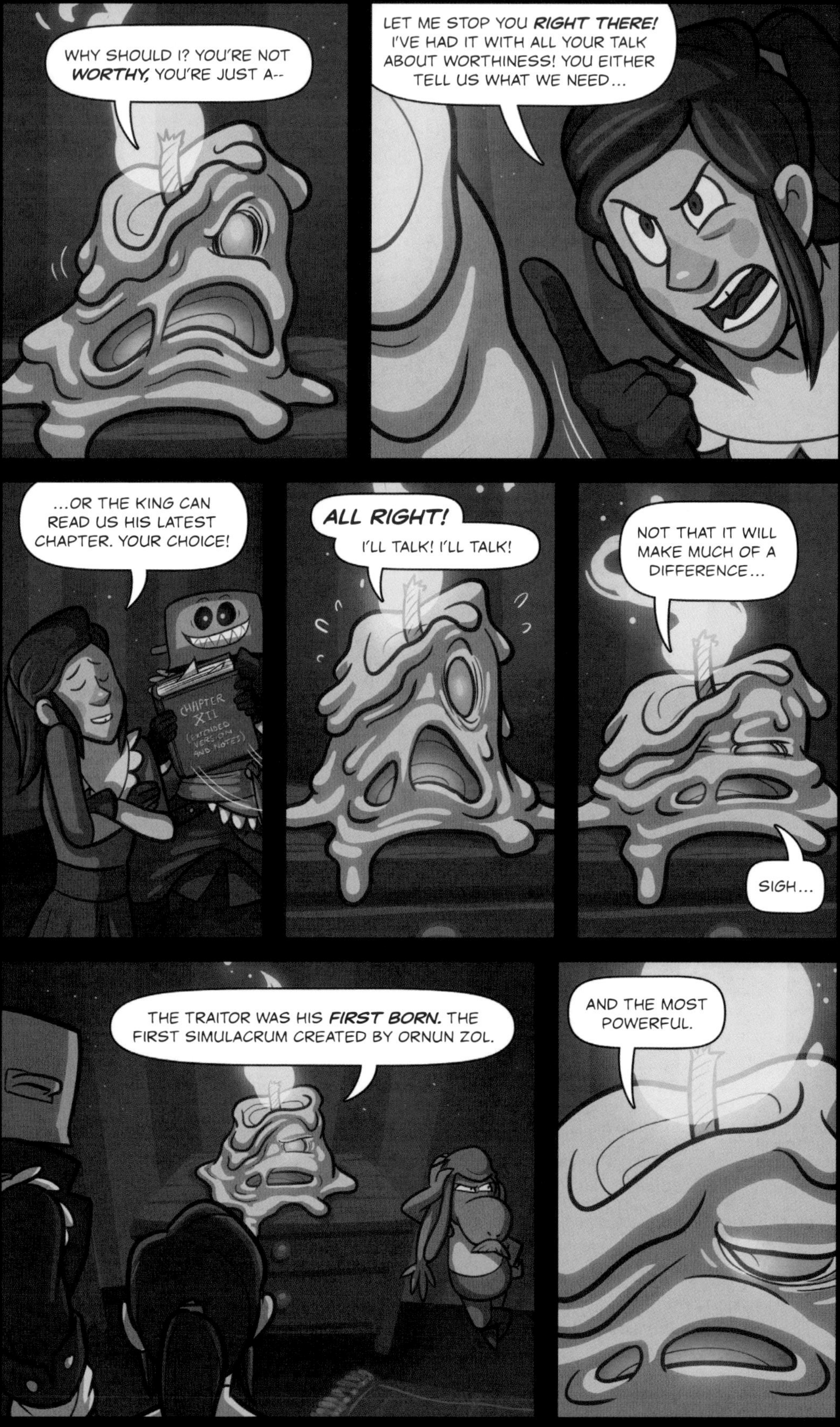
WHY SHOULD I? YOU'RE NOT **WORTHY,** YOU'RE JUST A--
LET ME STOP YOU **RIGHT THERE!** I'VE HAD IT WITH ALL YOUR TALK ABOUT WORTHINESS! YOU EITHER TELL US WHAT WE NEED...
...OR THE KING CAN READ US HIS LATEST CHAPTER. YOUR CHOICE!
CHAPTER XII (EXTENDED VERSION AND NOTES)
ALL RIGHT!
I'LL TALK! I'LL TALK!
NOT THAT IT WILL MAKE MUCH OF A DIFFERENCE...
SIGH...
THE TRAITOR WAS HIS **FIRST BORN.** THE FIRST SIMULACRUM CREATED BY ORNUN ZOL.
AND THE MOST POWERFUL.

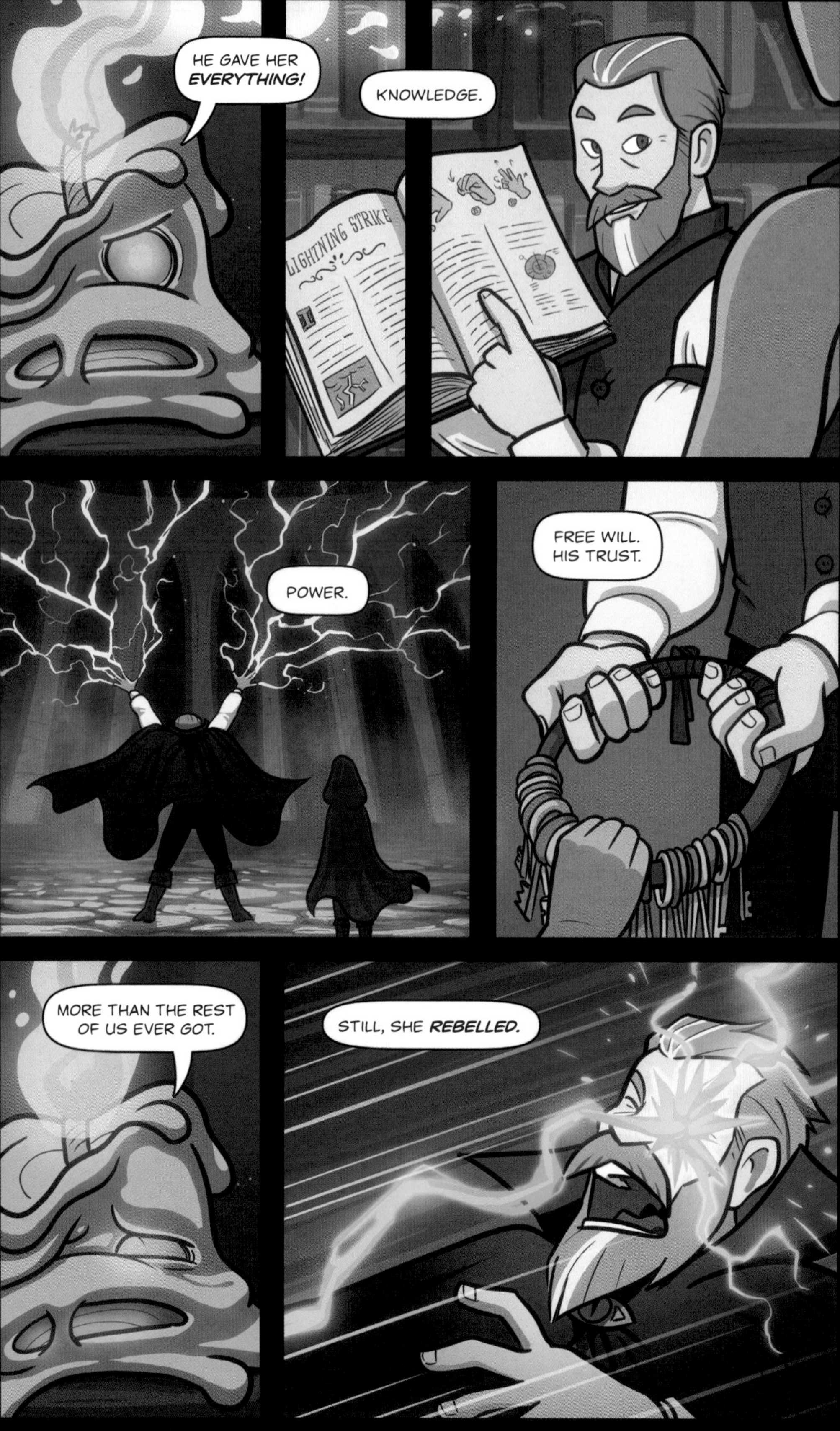
HE GAVE HER *EVERYTHING!*
KNOWLEDGE.
LIGHTNING STRIKE
POWER.
FREE WILL. HIS TRUST.
MORE THAN THE REST OF US EVER GOT.
STILL, SHE *REBELLED.*

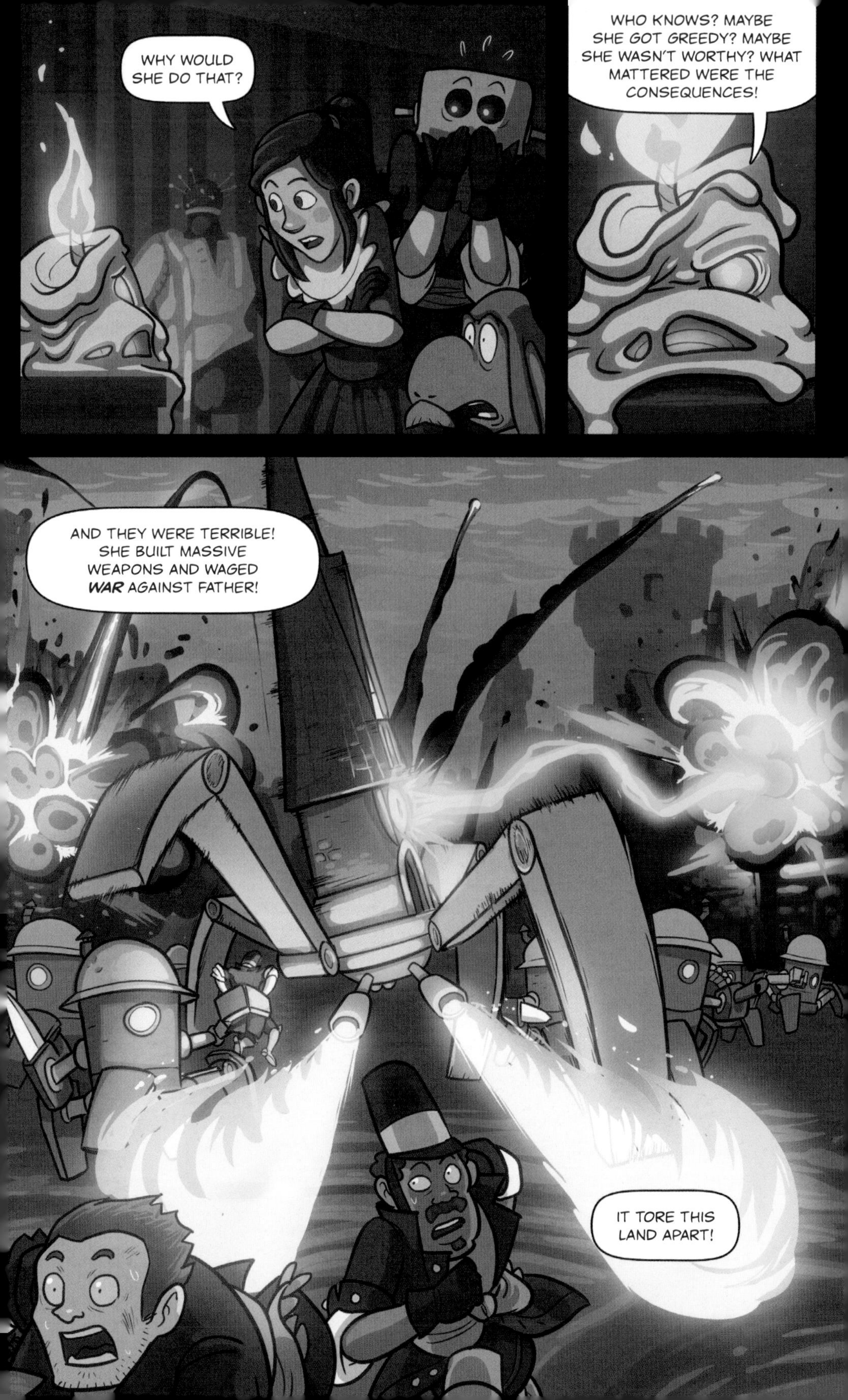
WHY WOULD SHE DO THAT?
WHO KNOWS? MAYBE SHE GOT GREEDY? MAYBE SHE WASN'T WORTHY? WHAT MATTERED WERE THE CONSEQUENCES!
AND THEY WERE TERRIBLE! SHE BUILT MASSIVE WEAPONS AND WAGED *WAR* AGAINST FATHER!
IT TORE THIS LAND APART!

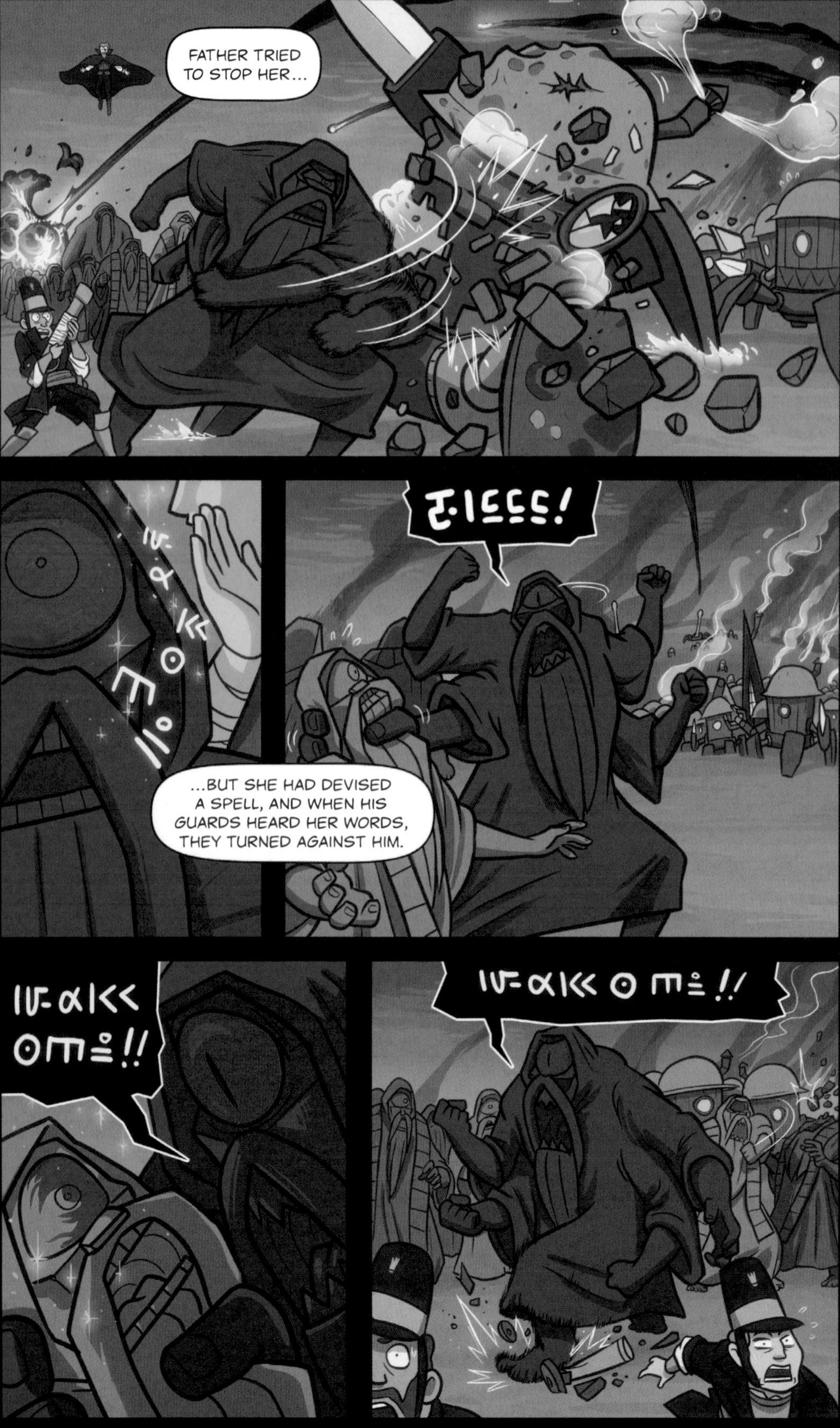
FATHER TRIED TO STOP HER...
...BUT SHE HAD DEVISED A SPELL, AND WHEN HIS GUARDS HEARD HER WORDS, THEY TURNED AGAINST HIM.

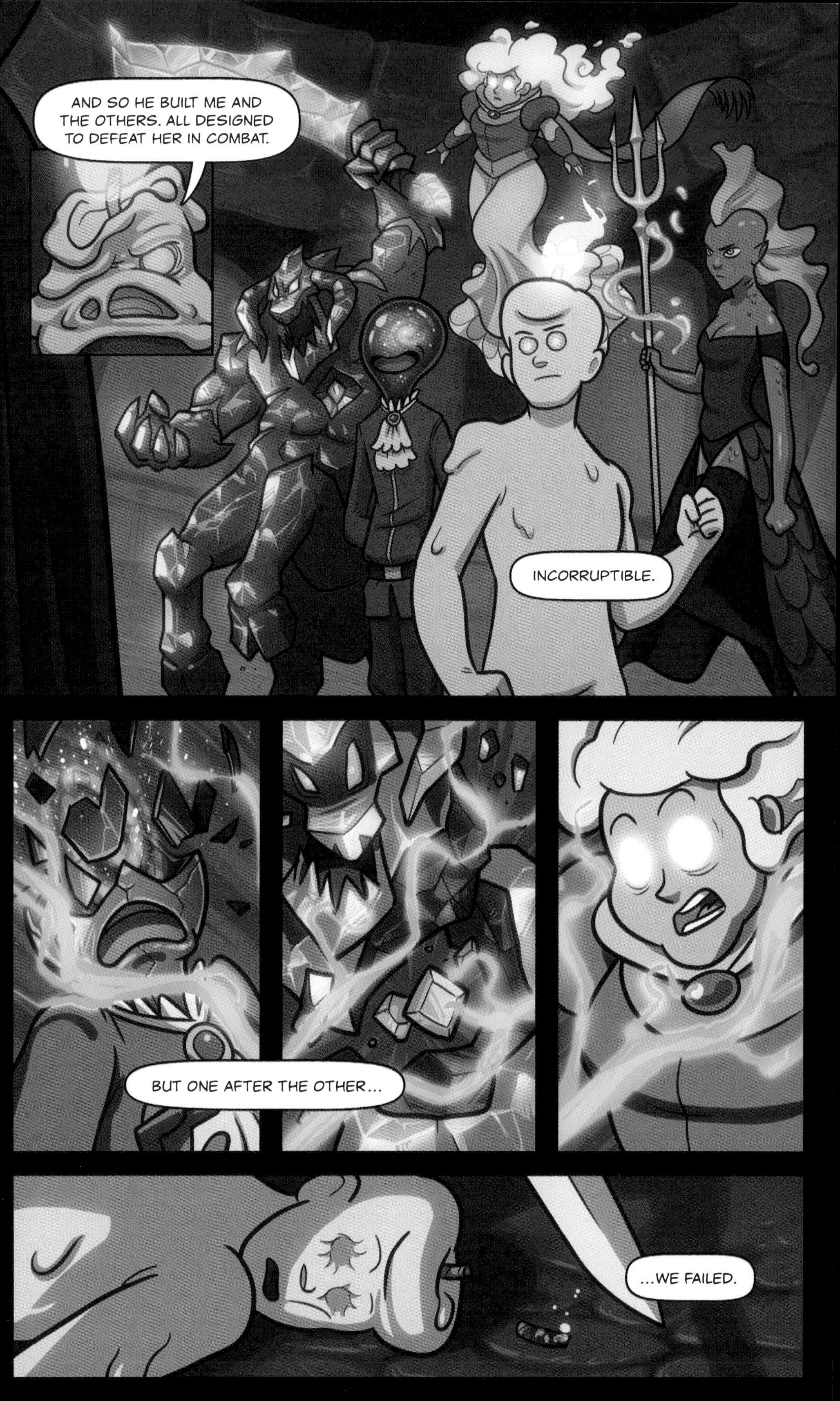
AND SO HE BUILT ME AND THE OTHERS. ALL DESIGNED TO DEFEAT HER IN COMBAT.
INCORRUPTIBLE.
BUT ONE AFTER THE OTHER...
...WE FAILED.

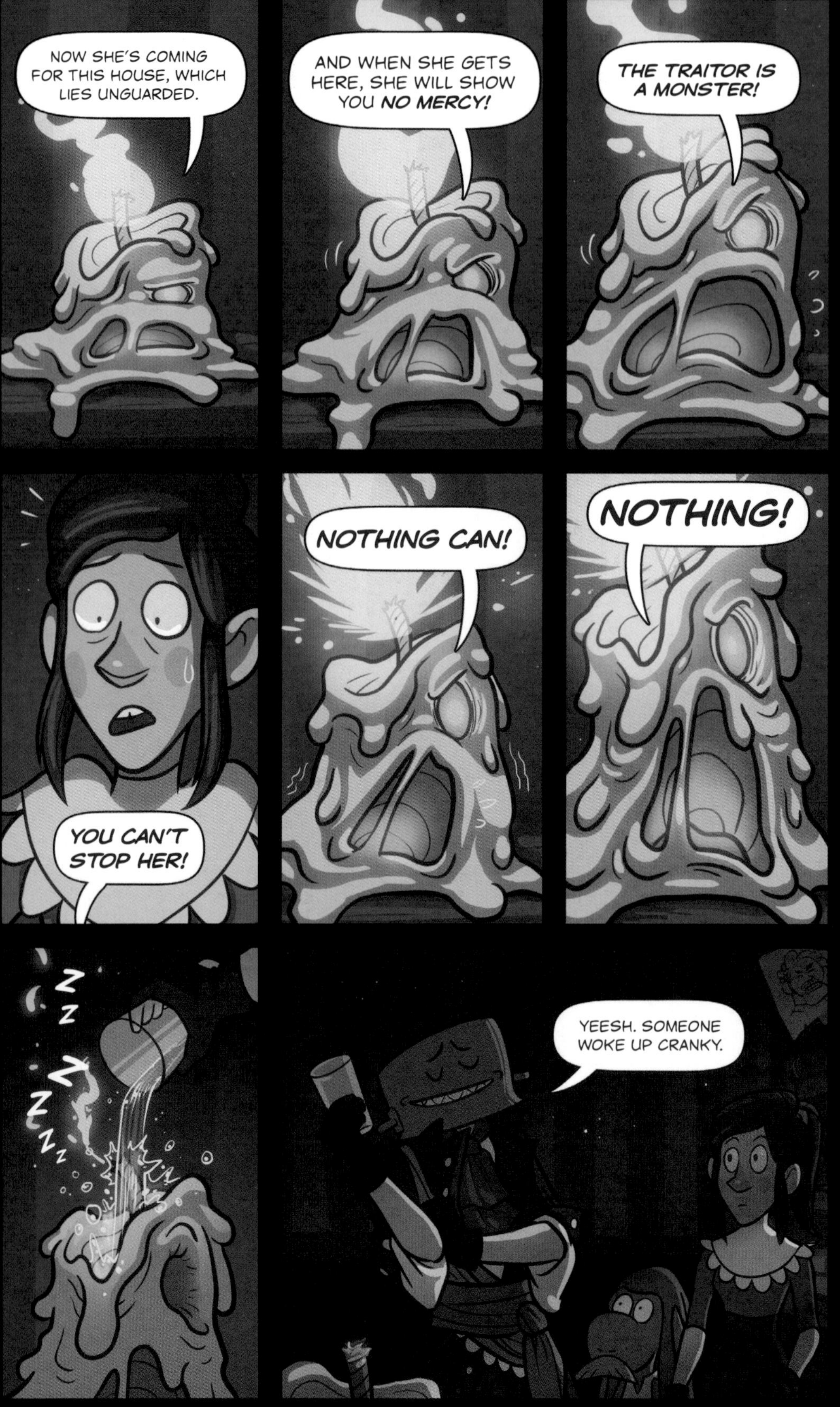
NOW SHE'S COMING FOR THIS HOUSE, WHICH LIES UNGUARDED.
AND WHEN SHE GETS HERE, SHE WILL SHOW YOU NO MERCY!
THE TRAITOR IS A MONSTER!
YOU CAN'T STOP HER!
NOTHING CAN!
NOTHING!
YEESH. SOMEONE WOKE UP CRANKY.

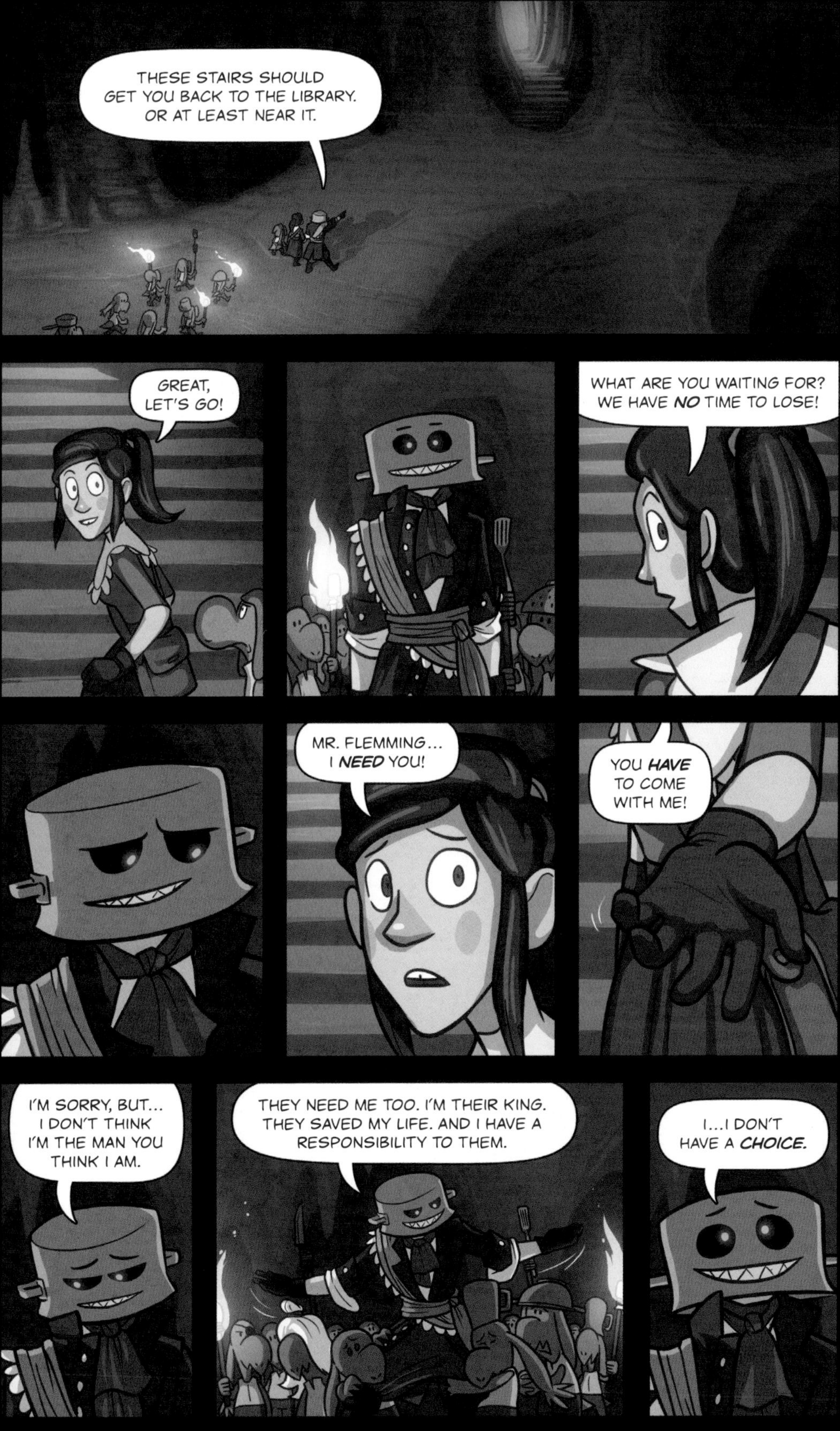
THESE STAIRS SHOULD GET YOU BACK TO THE LIBRARY. OR AT LEAST NEAR IT.
GREAT, LET'S GO!
WHAT ARE YOU WAITING FOR? WE HAVE *NO* TIME TO LOSE!
MR. FLEMMING... I *NEED* YOU!
YOU *HAVE* TO COME WITH ME!
I'M SORRY, BUT... I DON'T THINK I'M THE MAN YOU THINK I AM.
THEY NEED ME TOO. I'M THEIR KING. THEY SAVED MY LIFE. AND I HAVE A RESPONSIBILITY TO THEM.
I...I DON'T HAVE A *CHOICE.*

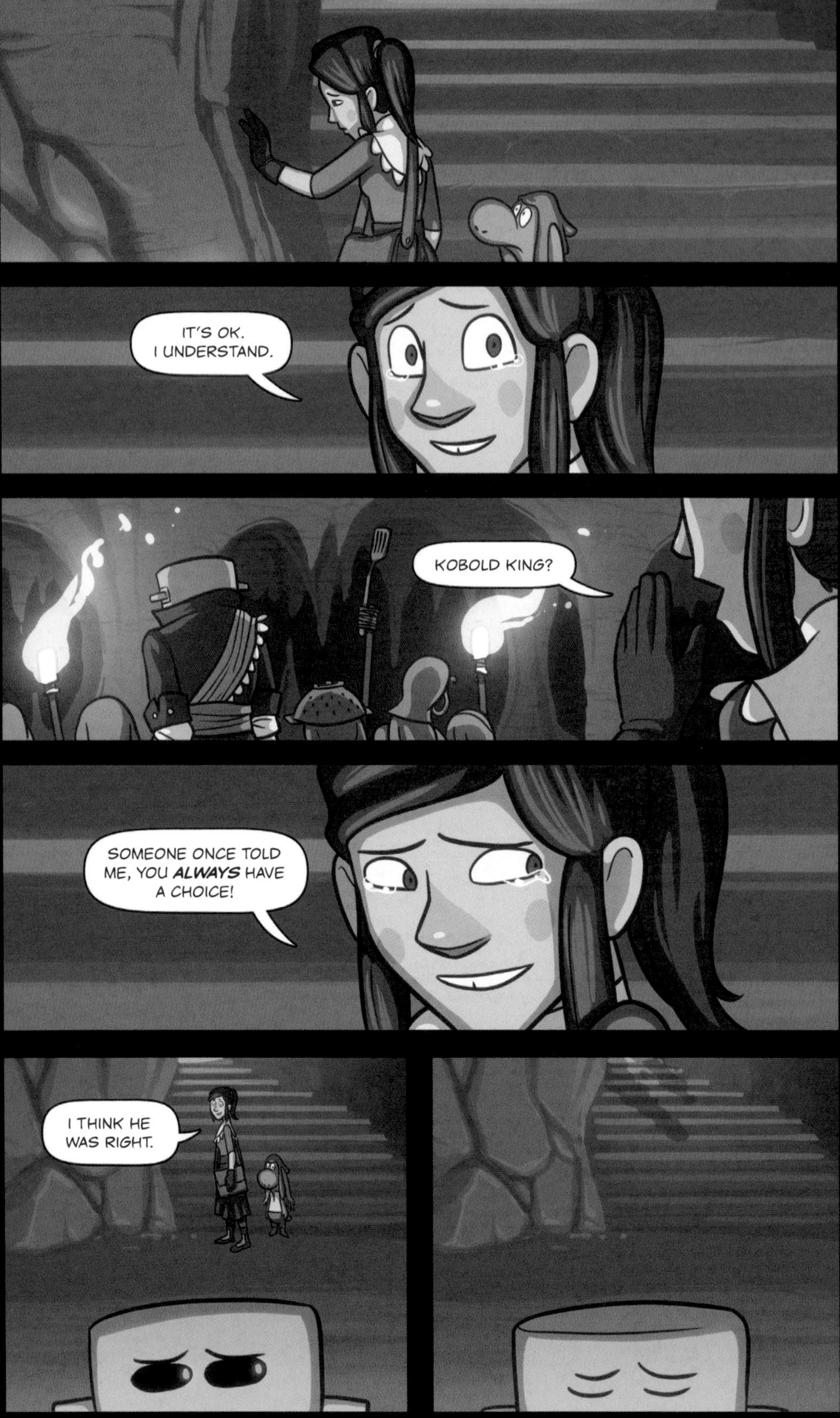
IT'S OK. I UNDERSTAND.
KOBOLD KING?
SOMEONE ONCE TOLD ME, YOU ALWAYS HAVE A CHOICE!
I THINK HE WAS RIGHT.

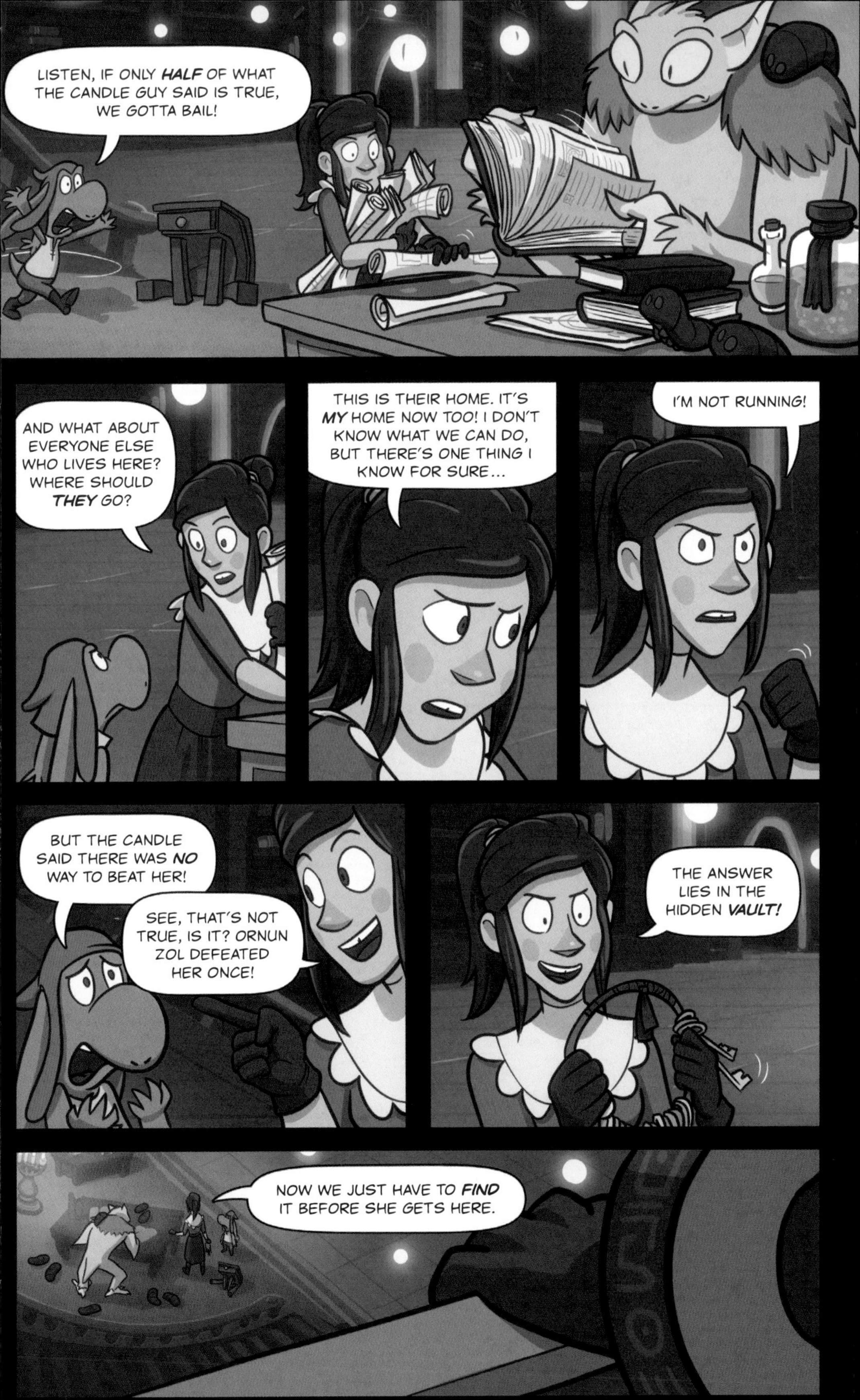
LISTEN, IF ONLY HALF OF WHAT THE CANDLE GUY SAID IS TRUE, WE GOTTA BAIL!
AND WHAT ABOUT EVERYONE ELSE WHO LIVES HERE? WHERE SHOULD THEY GO?
THIS IS THEIR HOME. IT'S MY HOME NOW TOO! I DON'T KNOW WHAT WE CAN DO, BUT THERE'S ONE THING I KNOW FOR SURE...
I'M NOT RUNNING!
BUT THE CANDLE SAID THERE WAS NO WAY TO BEAT HER!
SEE, THAT'S NOT TRUE, IS IT? ORNUN ZOL DEFEATED HER ONCE!
THE ANSWER LIES IN THE HIDDEN VAULT!
NOW WE JUST HAVE TO FIND IT BEFORE SHE GETS HERE.

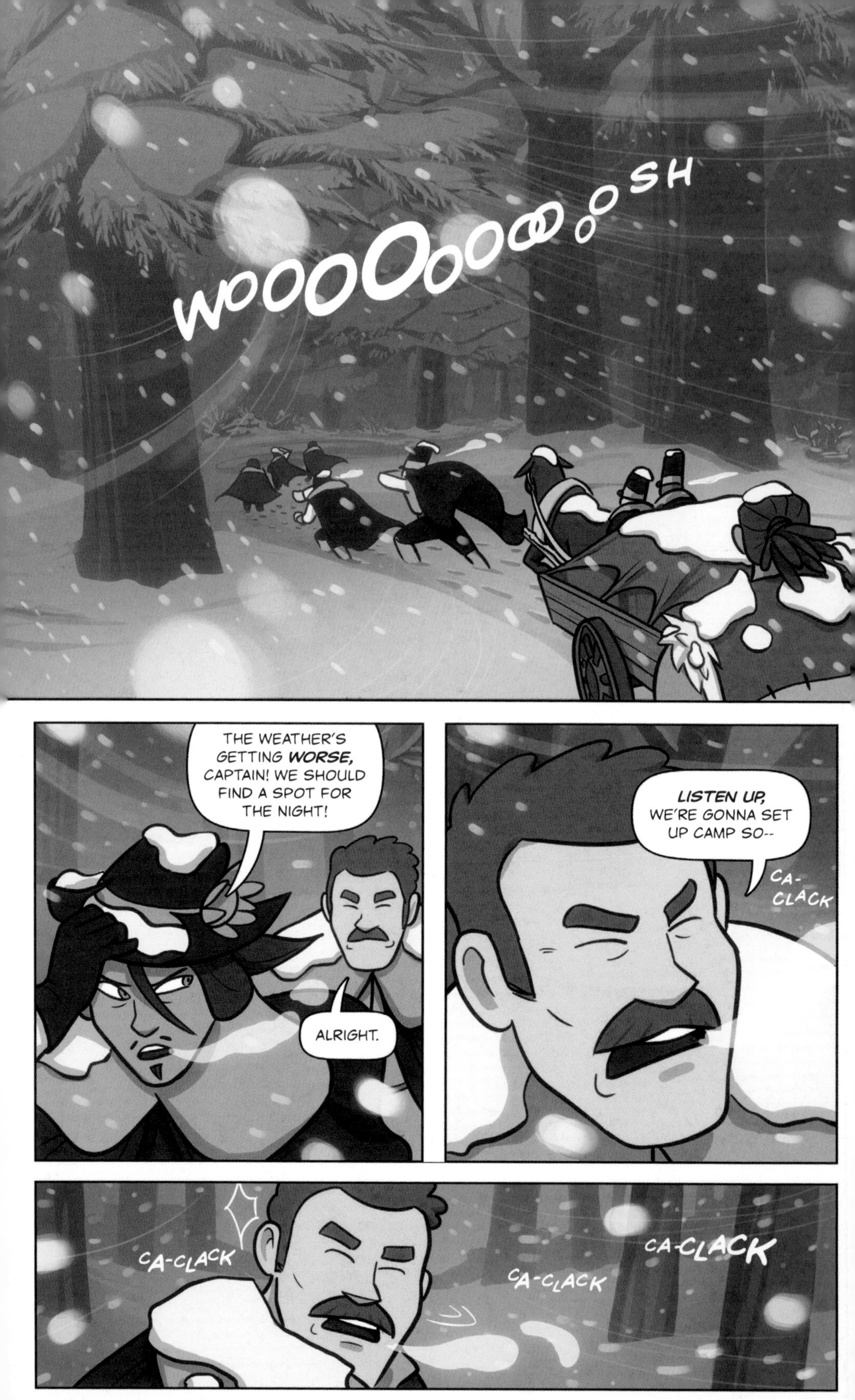
WOOOOooooo°°SH
THE WEATHER'S GETTING **WORSE,** CAPTAIN! WE SHOULD FIND A SPOT FOR THE NIGHT!
ALRIGHT.
LISTEN UP, WE'RE GONNA SET UP CAMP SO--
CA-CLACK
CA-CLACK
CA-CLACK
CA-CLACK

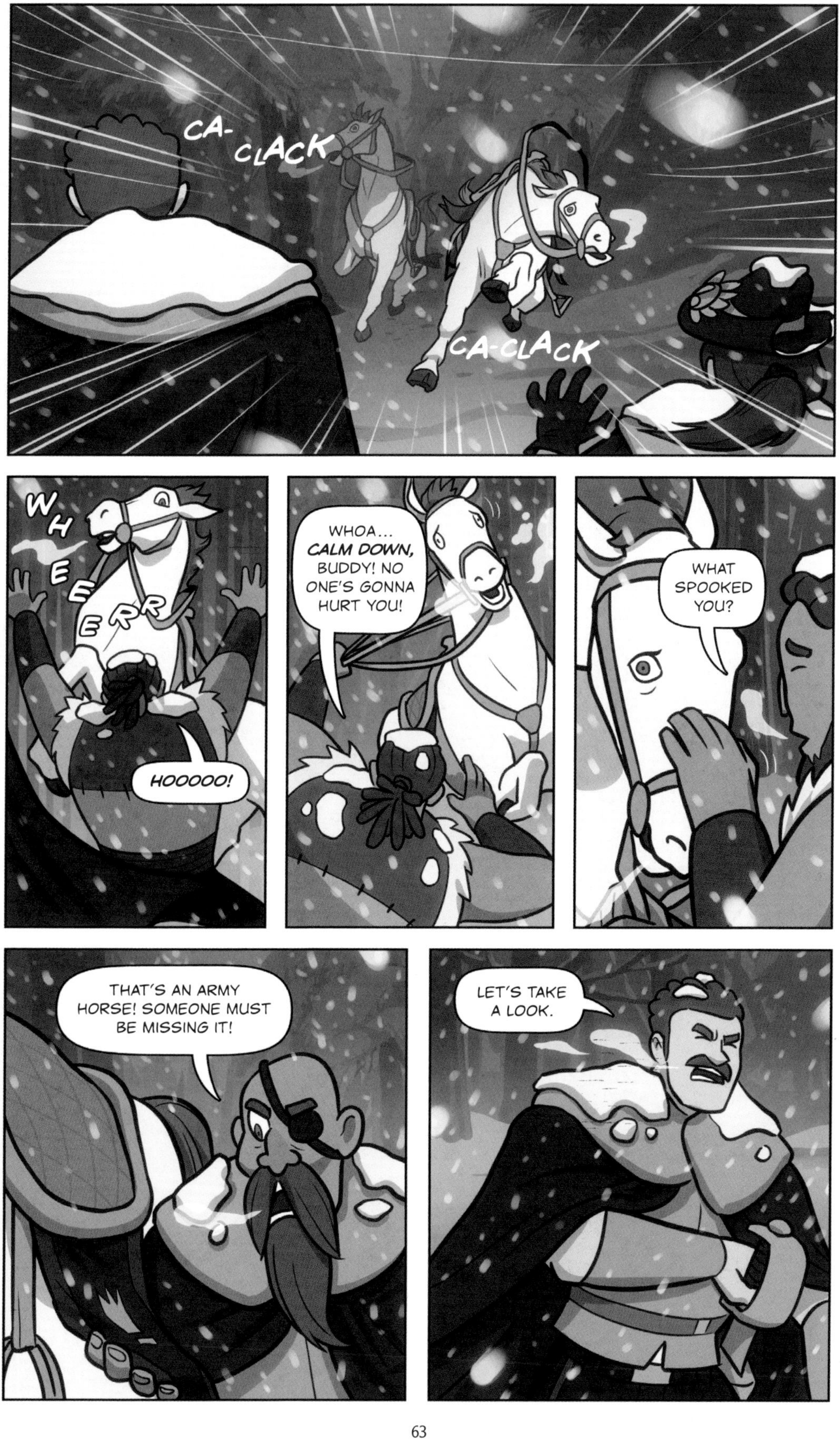
CA-CLACK
CA-CLACK
WHEEERR
HOOOOO!
WHOA... **CALM DOWN,** BUDDY! NO ONE'S GONNA HURT YOU!
WHAT SPOOKED YOU?
THAT'S AN ARMY HORSE! SOMEONE MUST BE MISSING IT!
LET'S TAKE A LOOK.

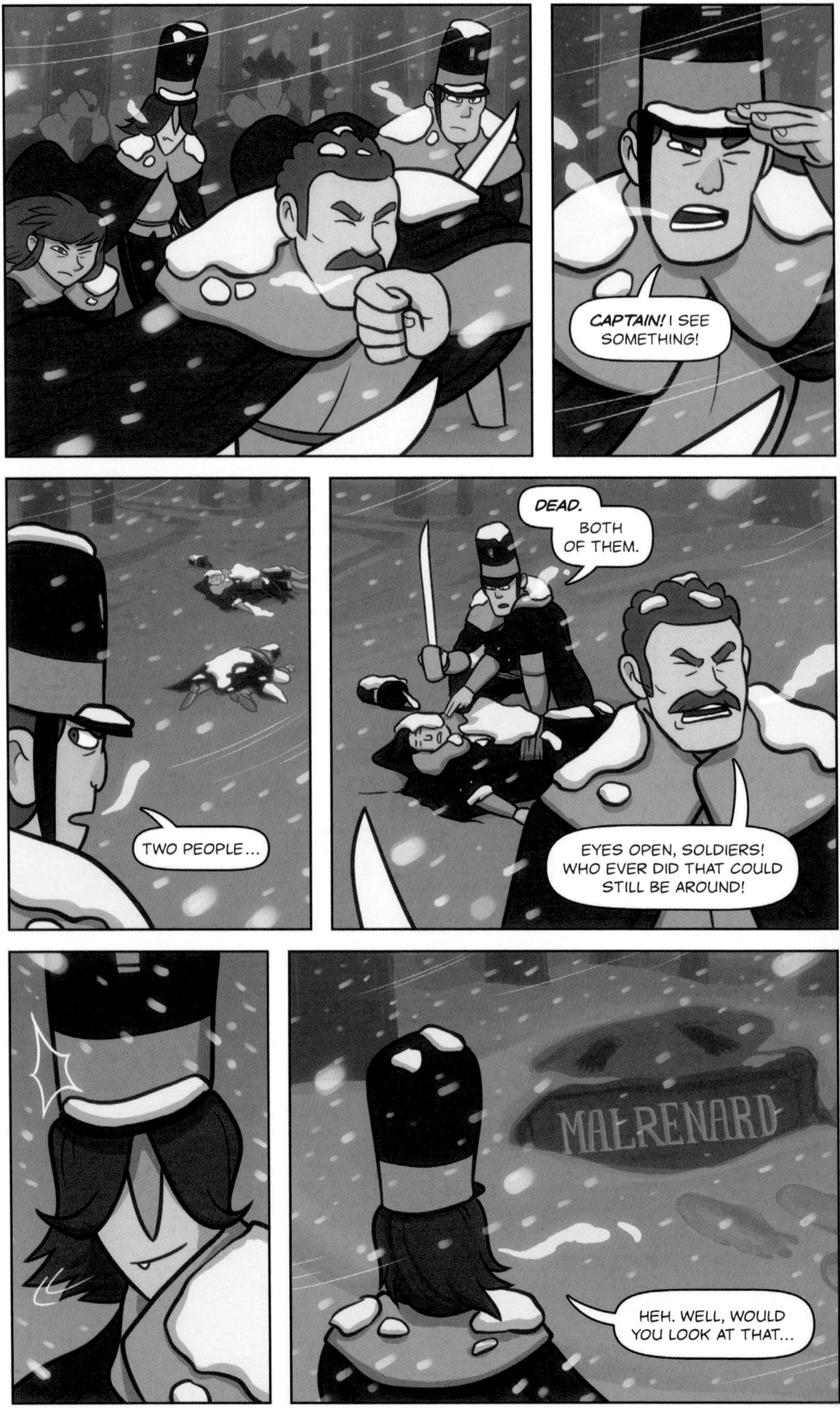
CAPTAIN! I SEE SOMETHING!
TWO PEOPLE...
DEAD. BOTH OF THEM.
EYES OPEN, SOLDIERS! WHO EVER DID THAT COULD STILL BE AROUND!
MALRENARD
HEH. WELL, WOULD YOU LOOK AT THAT...

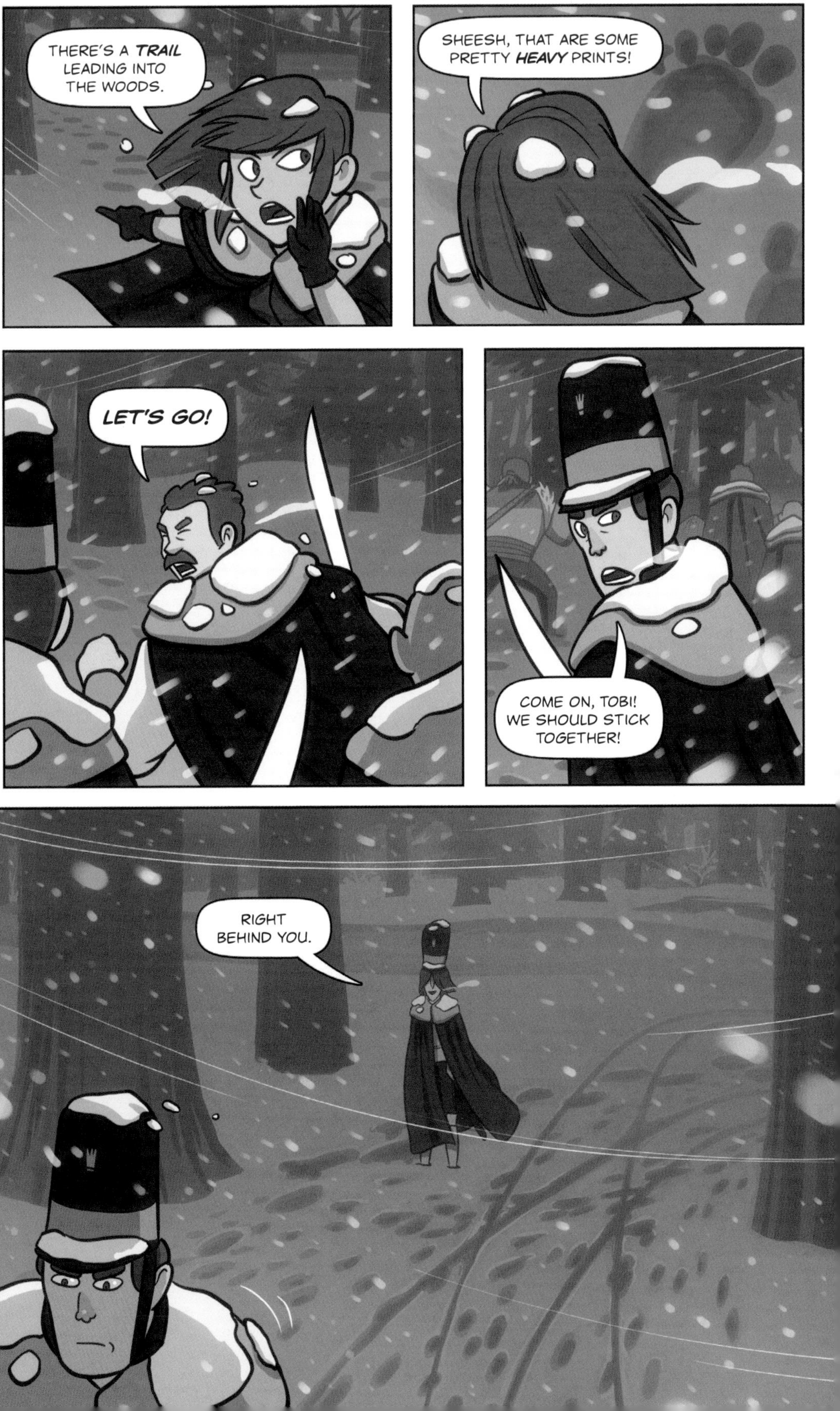
THERE'S A **TRAIL** LEADING INTO THE WOODS.
SHEESH, THAT ARE SOME PRETTY **HEAVY** PRINTS!
LET'S GO!
COME ON, TOBI! WE SHOULD STICK TOGETHER!
RIGHT BEHIND YOU.

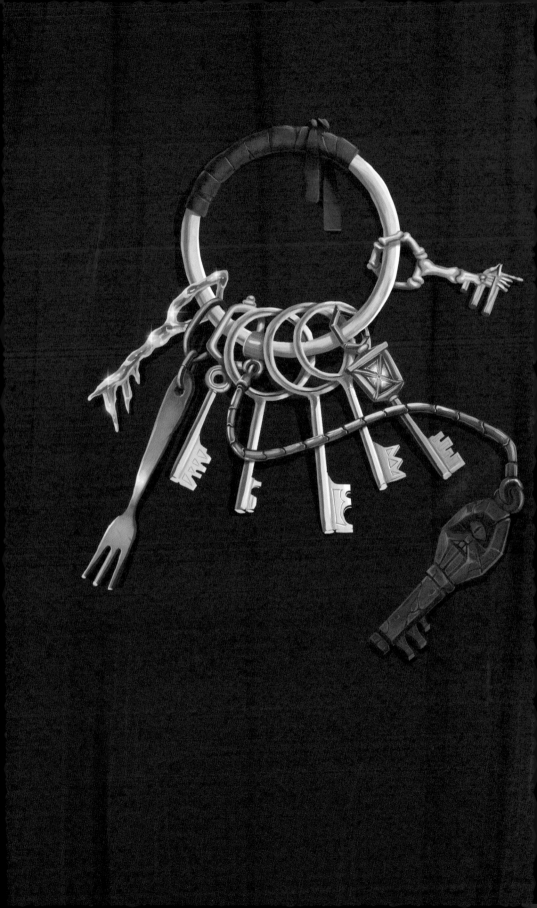

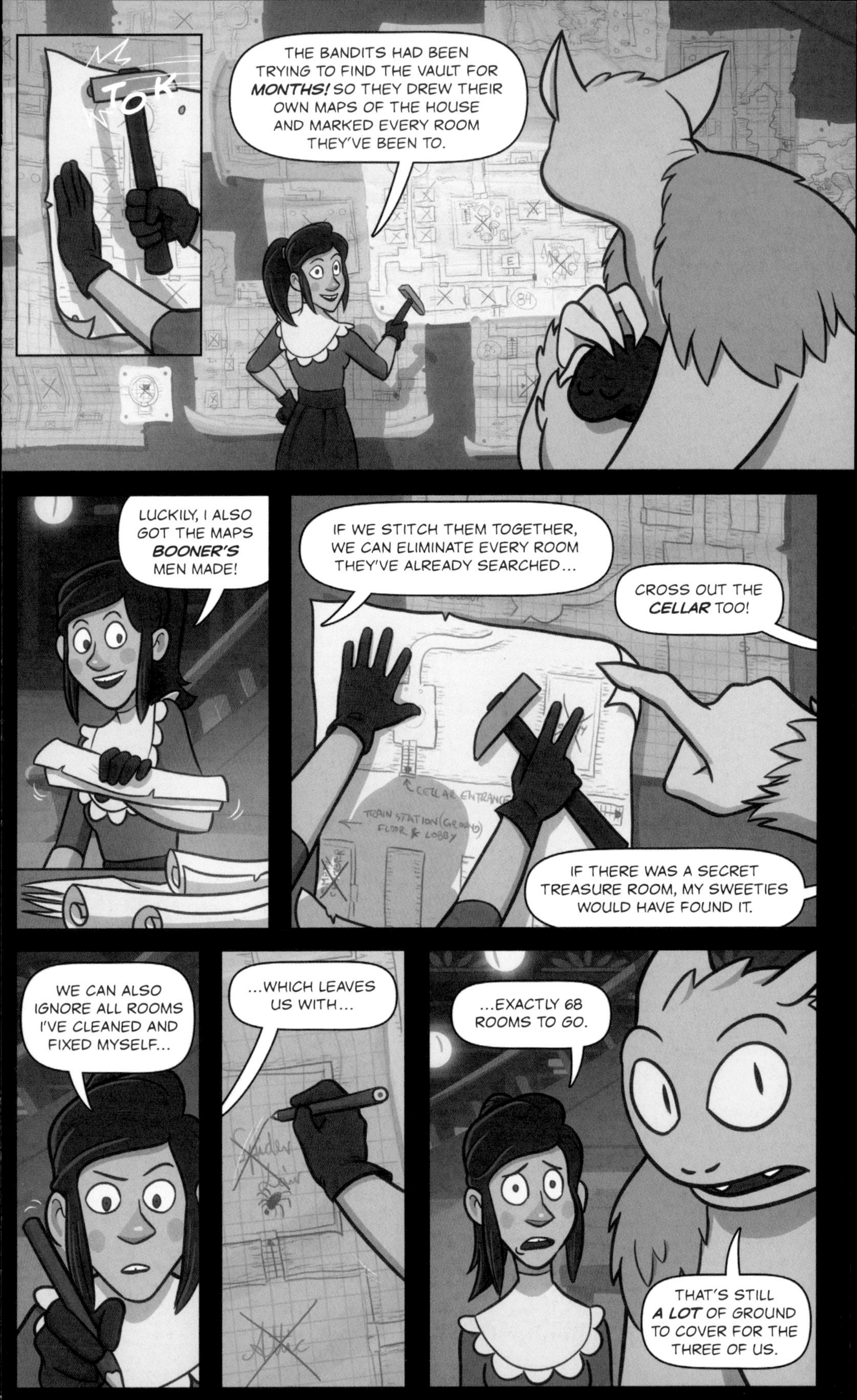
TOK
THE BANDITS HAD BEEN TRYING TO FIND THE VAULT FOR MONTHS! SO THEY DREW THEIR OWN MAPS OF THE HOUSE AND MARKED EVERY ROOM THEY'VE BEEN TO.
84
LUCKILY, I ALSO GOT THE MAPS BOONER'S MEN MADE!
IF WE STITCH THEM TOGETHER, WE CAN ELIMINATE EVERY ROOM THEY'VE ALREADY SEARCHED...
CROSS OUT THE CELLAR TOO!
CELLAR ENTRANCE
TRAIN STATION (GROUND) FLOOR & LOBBY
IF THERE WAS A SECRET TREASURE ROOM, MY SWEETIES WOULD HAVE FOUND IT.
WE CAN ALSO IGNORE ALL ROOMS I'VE CLEANED AND FIXED MYSELF...
...WHICH LEAVES US WITH...
Spider Lair
Attic
...EXACTLY 68 ROOMS TO GO.
THAT'S STILL A LOT OF GROUND TO COVER FOR THE THREE OF US.

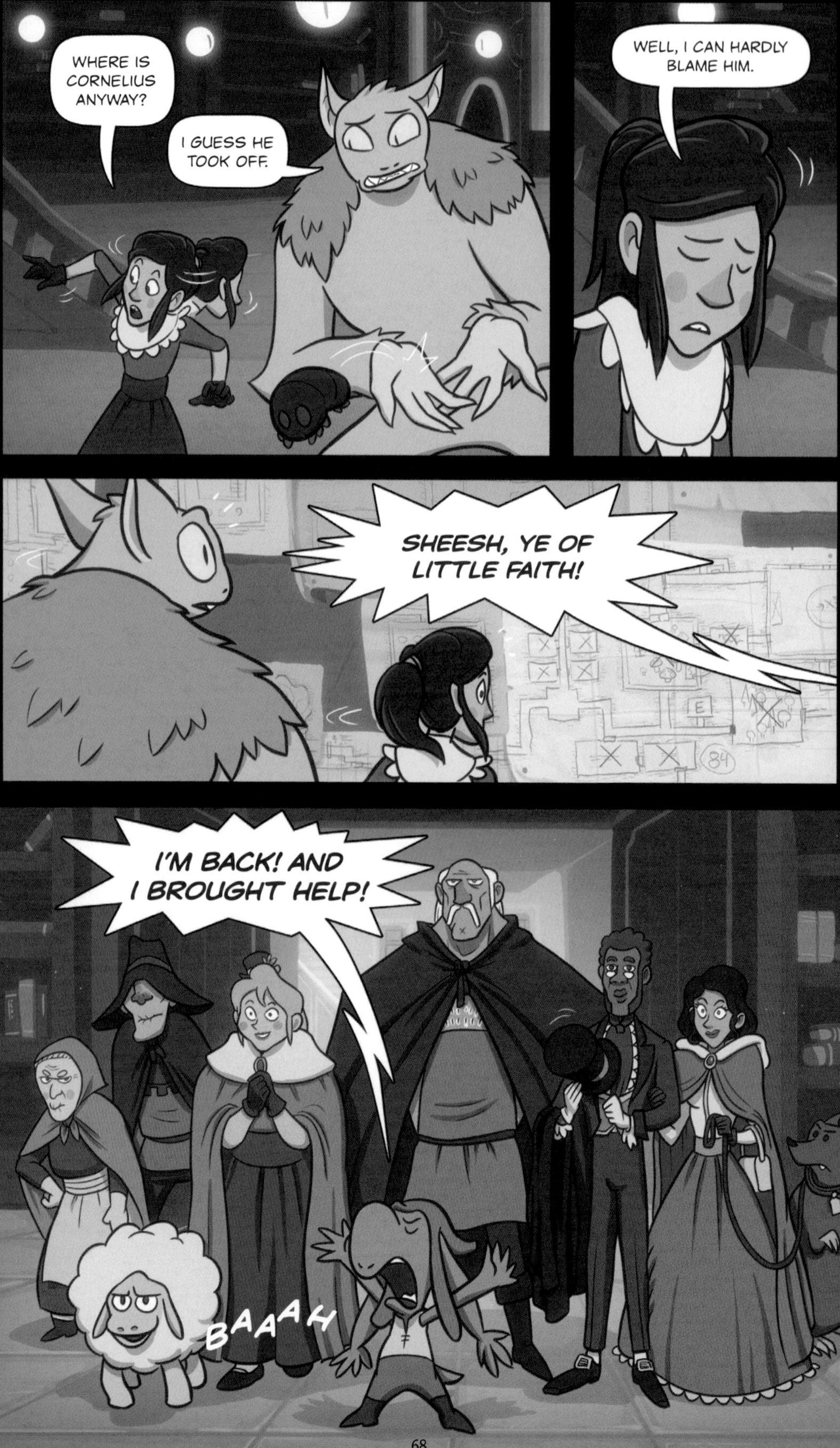
WHERE IS CORNELIUS ANYWAY?
I GUESS HE TOOK OFF.
WELL, I CAN HARDLY BLAME HIM.
SHEESH, YE OF LITTLE FAITH!
84
I'M BACK! AND I BROUGHT HELP!
BAAAH

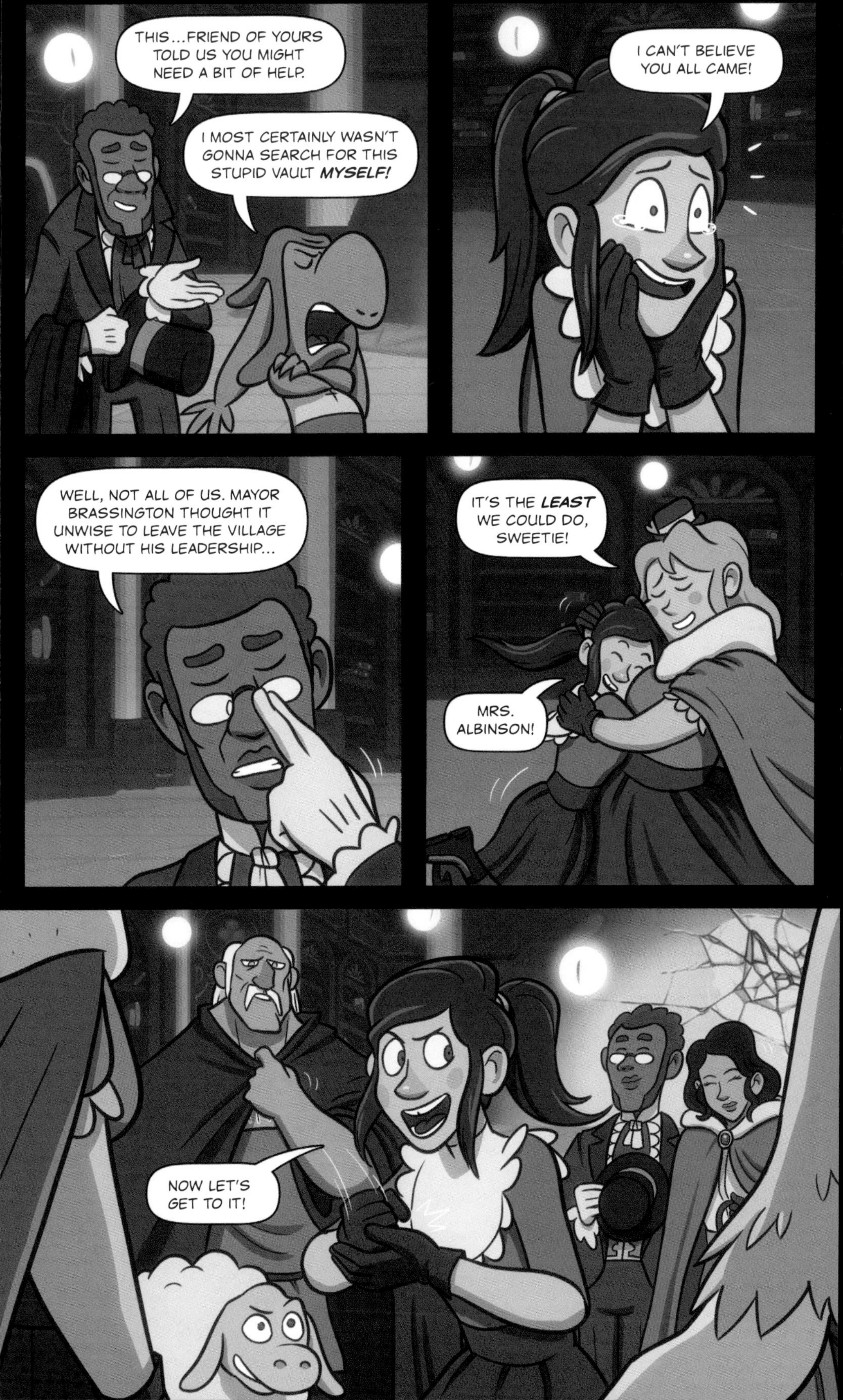
THIS...FRIEND OF YOURS TOLD US YOU MIGHT NEED A BIT OF HELP.
I MOST CERTAINLY WASN'T GONNA SEARCH FOR THIS STUPID VAULT ***MYSELF!***
I CAN'T BELIEVE YOU ALL CAME!
WELL, NOT ALL OF US. MAYOR BRASSINGTON THOUGHT IT UNWISE TO LEAVE THE VILLAGE WITHOUT HIS LEADERSHIP...
IT'S THE ***LEAST*** WE COULD DO, SWEETIE!
MRS. ALBINSON!
NOW LET'S GET TO IT!

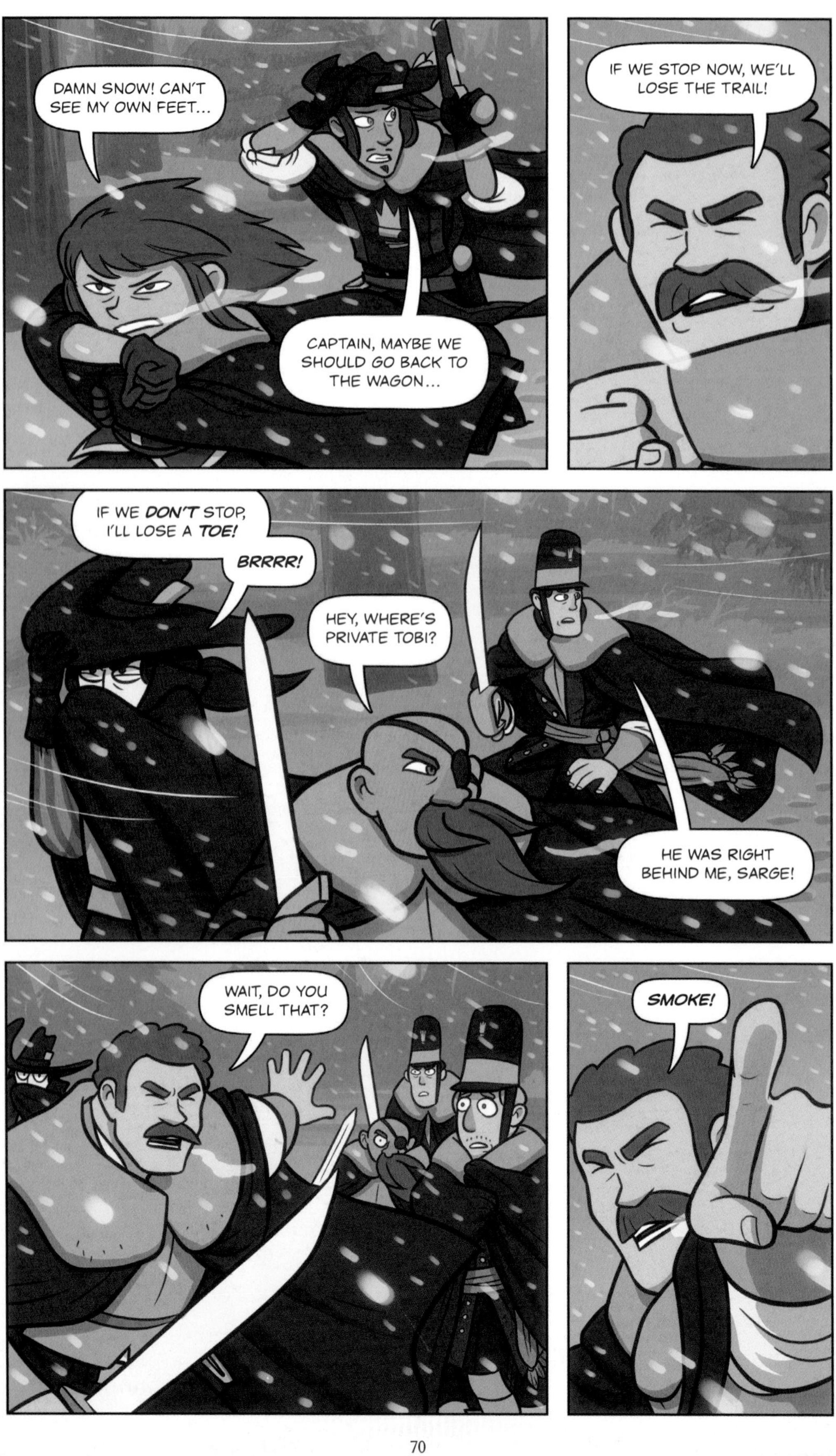
DAMN SNOW! CAN'T SEE MY OWN FEET...
CAPTAIN, MAYBE WE SHOULD GO BACK TO THE WAGON...
IF WE STOP NOW, WE'LL LOSE THE TRAIL!
IF WE *DON'T* STOP, I'LL LOSE A *TOE!*
BRRRR!
HEY, WHERE'S PRIVATE TOBI?
HE WAS RIGHT BEHIND ME, SARGE!
WAIT, DO YOU SMELL THAT?
SMOKE!

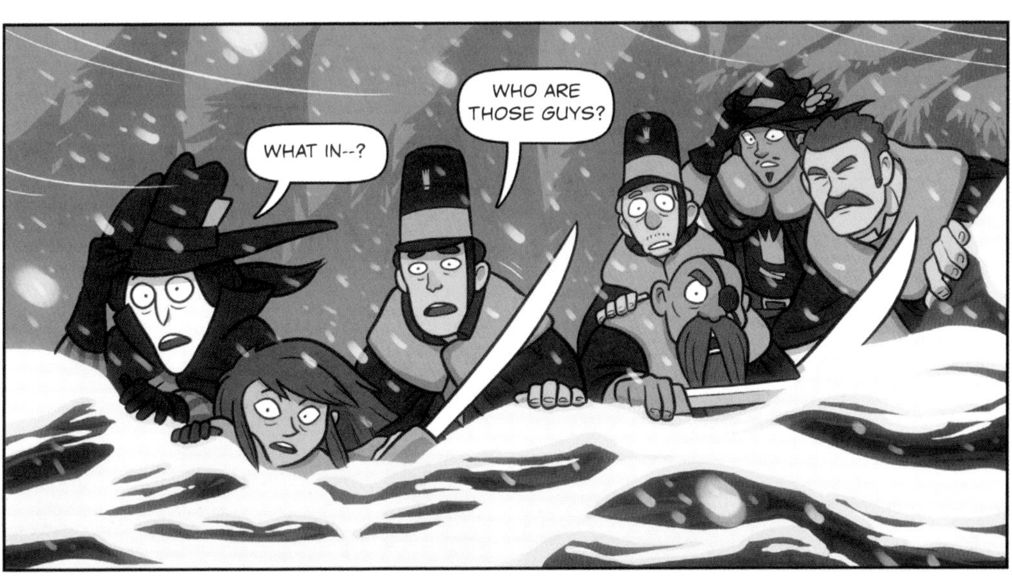
WHAT IN--?
WHO ARE THOSE GUYS?
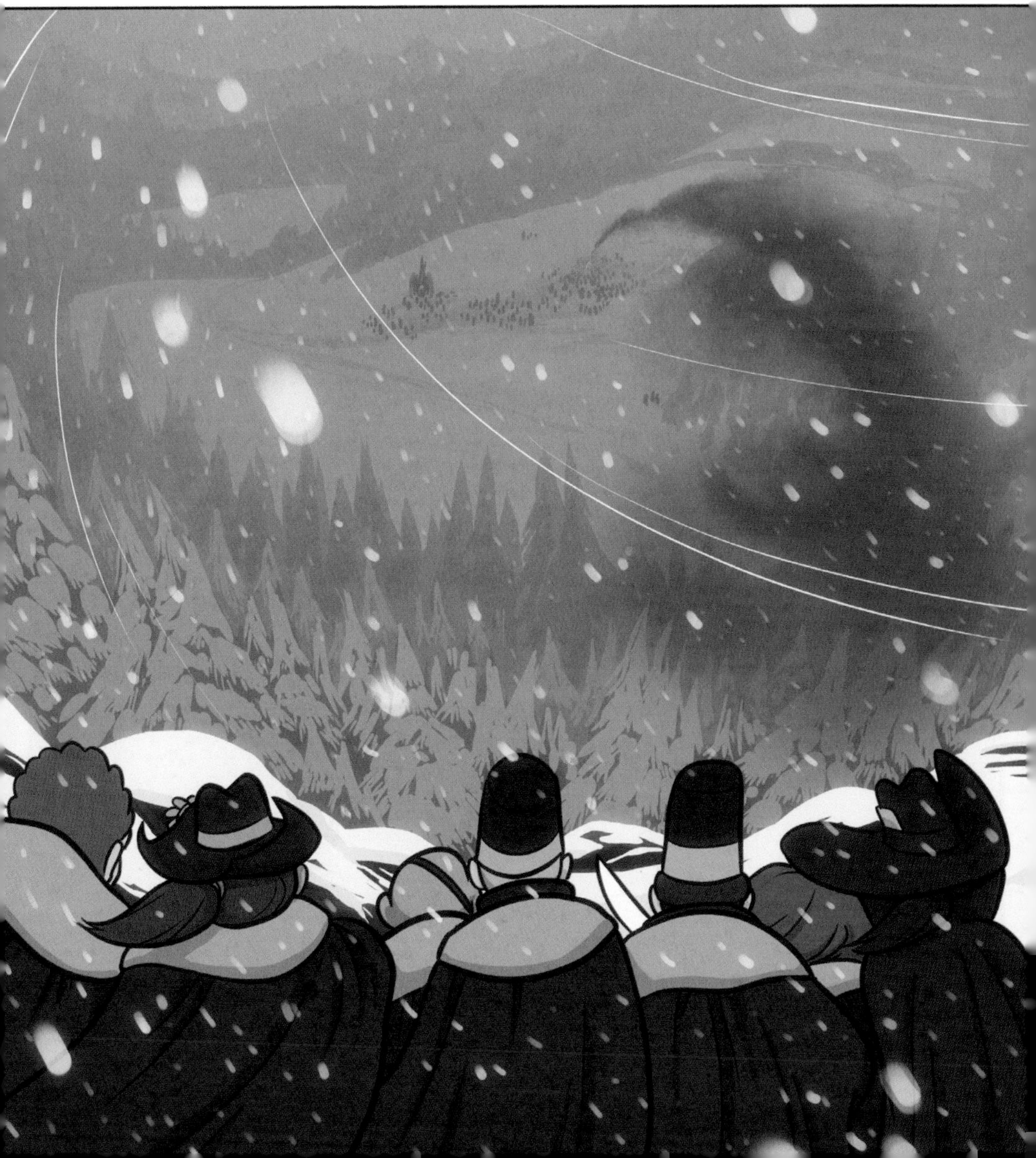

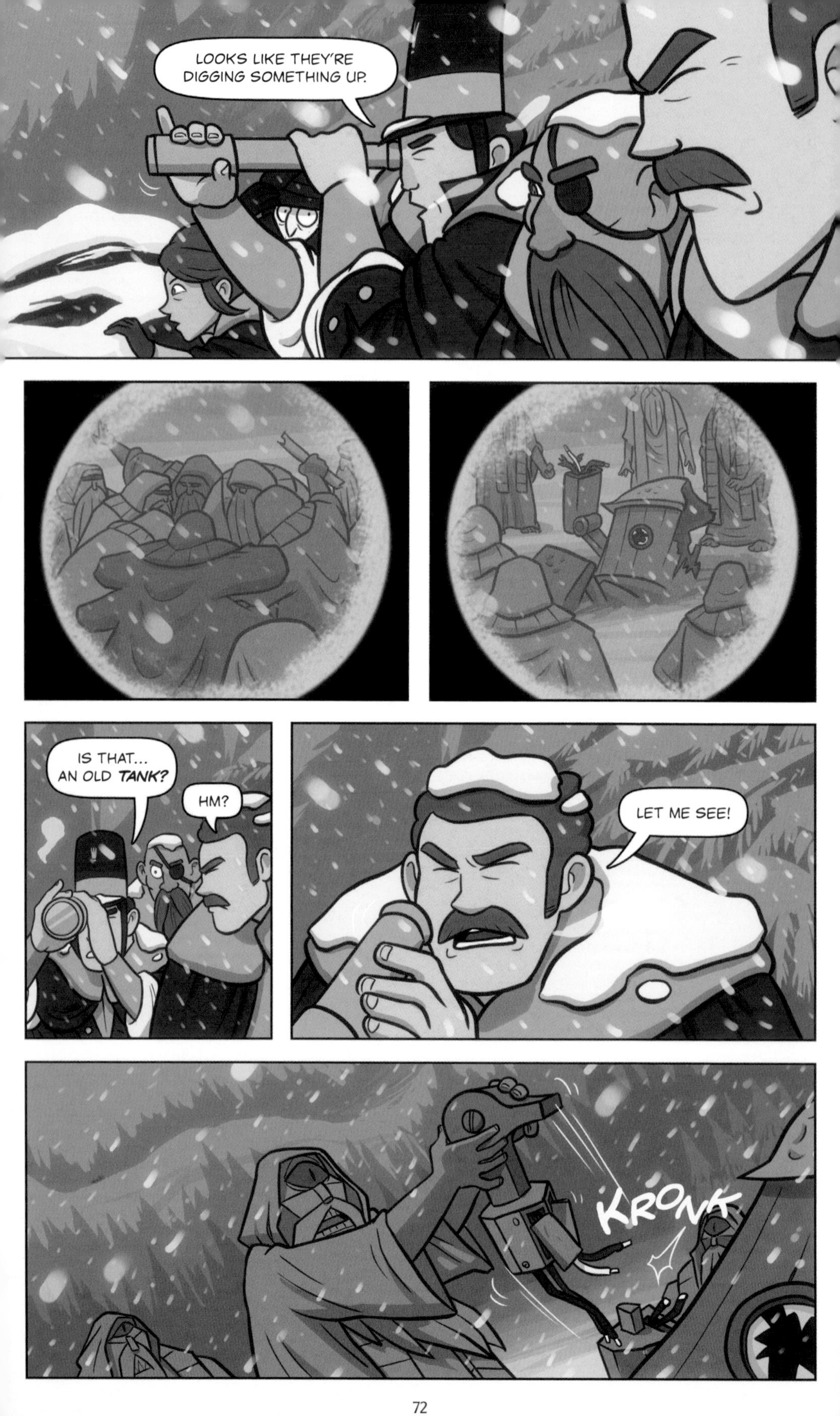
LOOKS LIKE THEY'RE DIGGING SOMETHING UP.
IS THAT... AN OLD TANK?
HM?
LET ME SEE!
KRONK

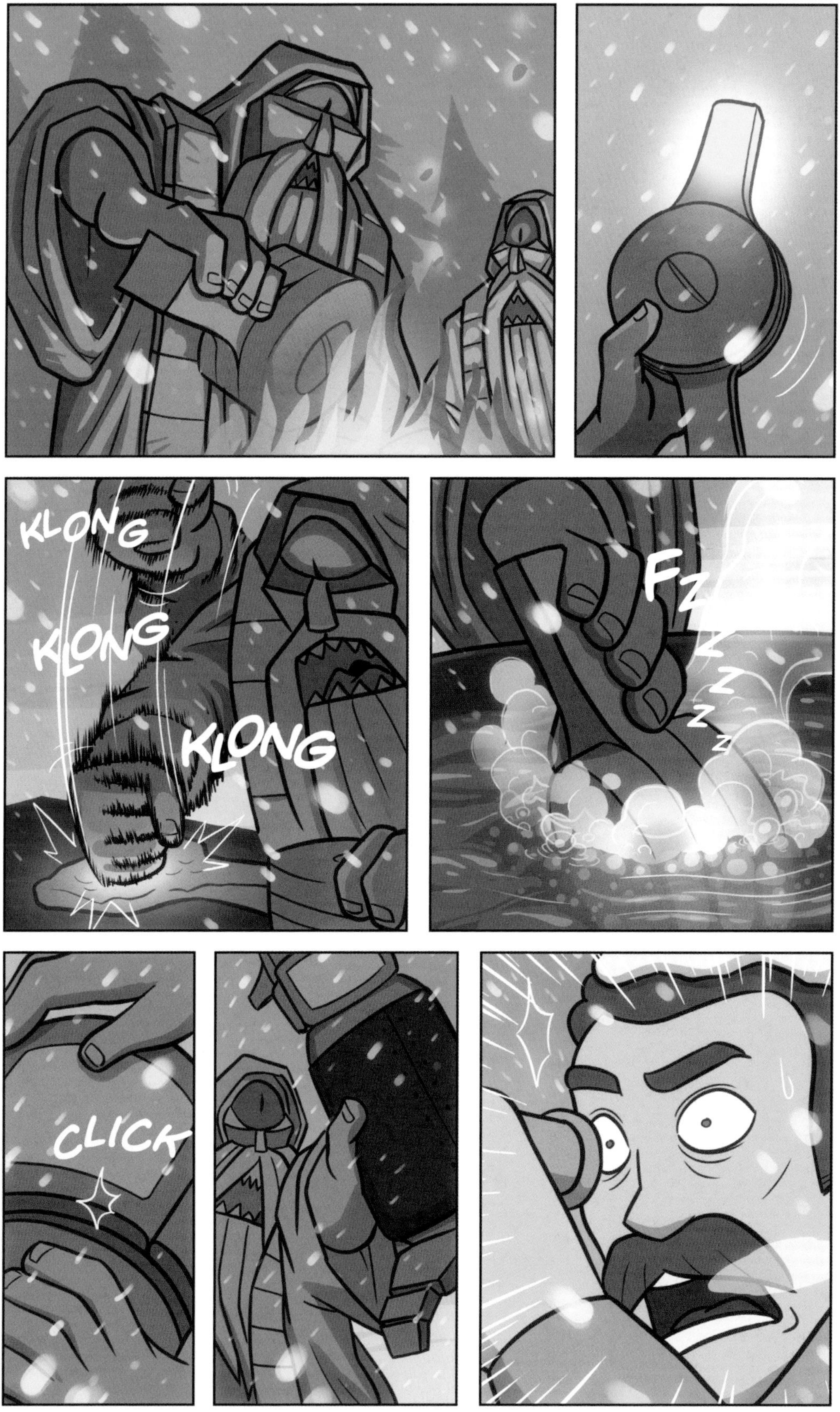
KLONG
KLONG
KLONG
FZZZZZ
CLICK

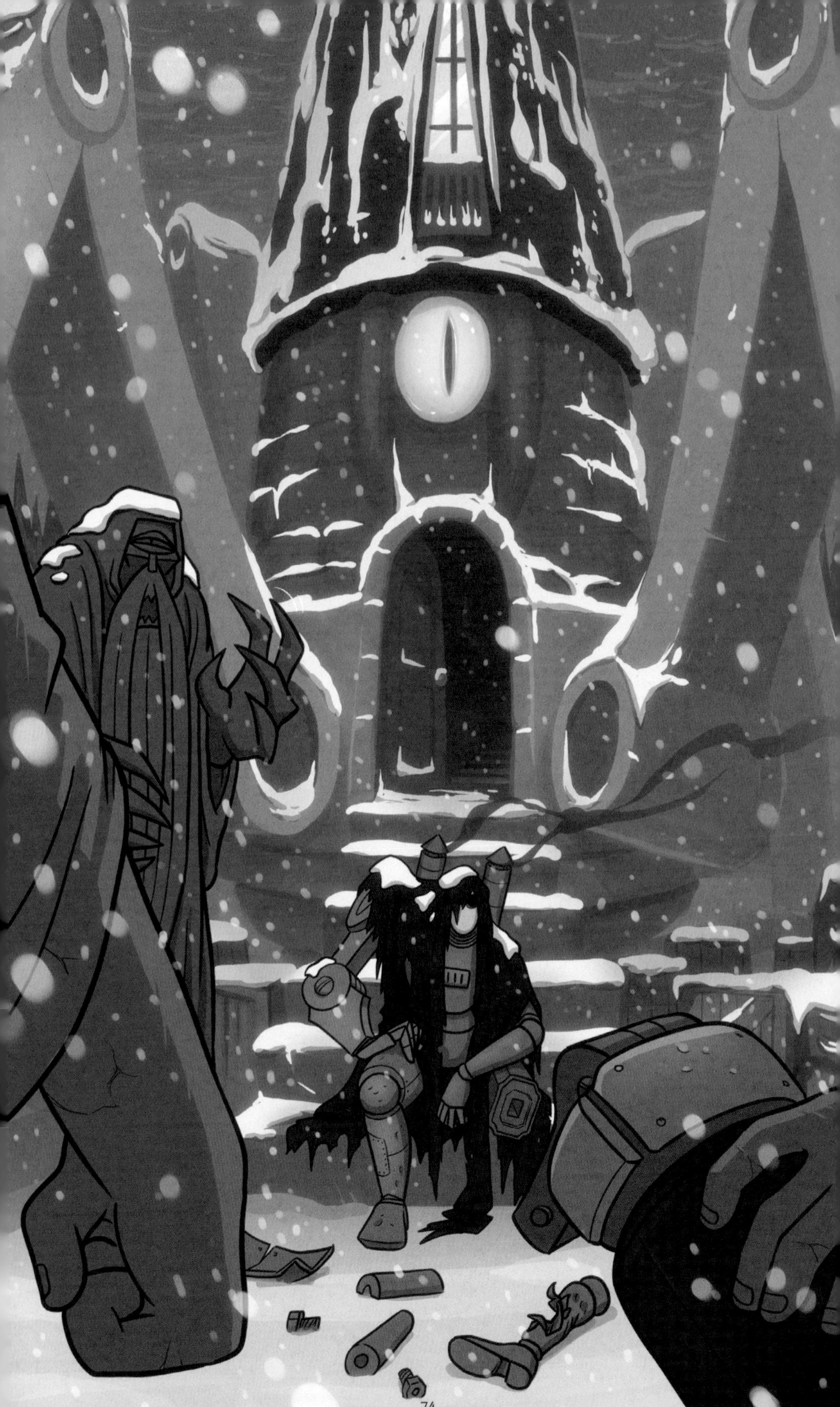

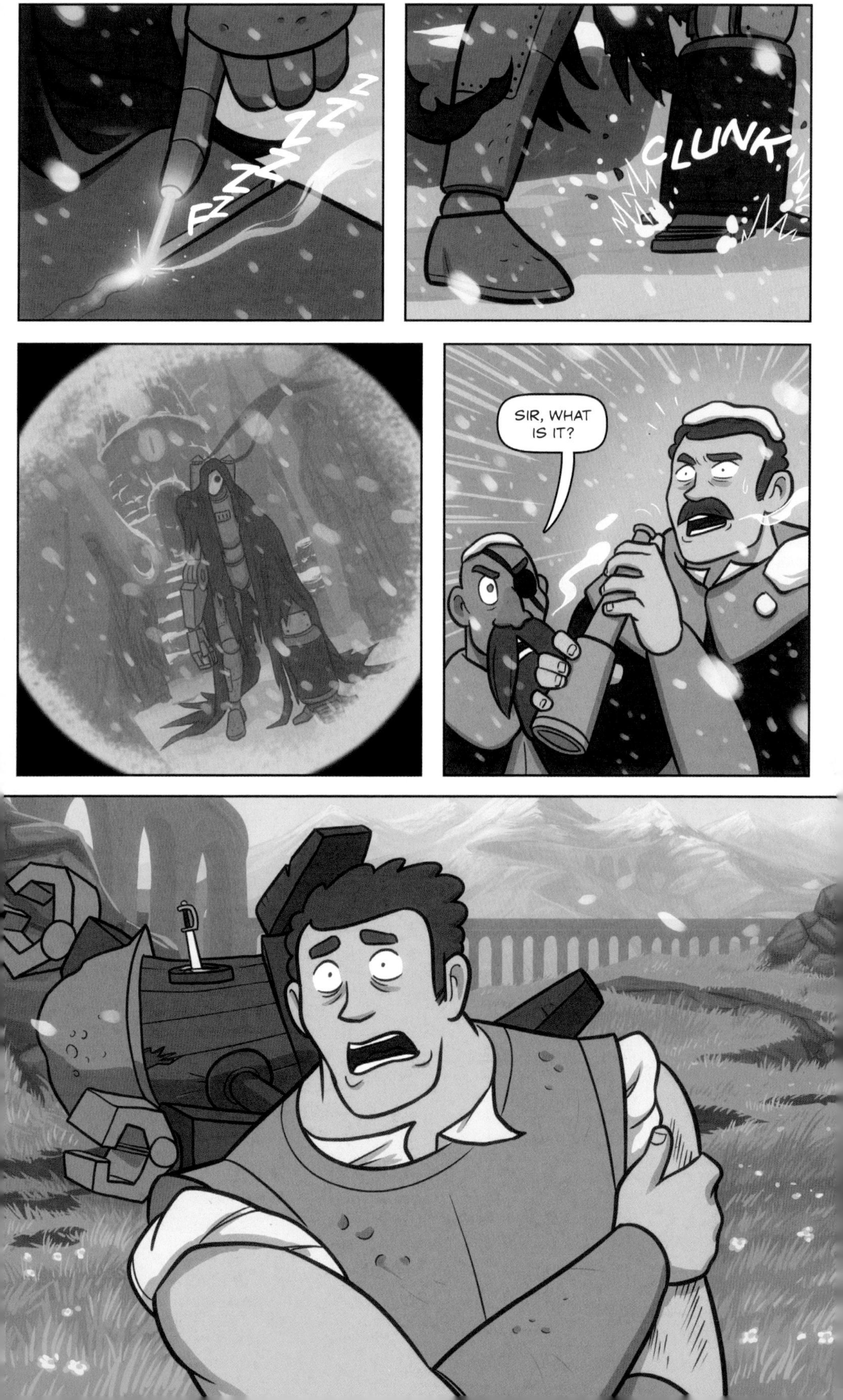
FZZZZZZ
CLUNK
SIR, WHAT IS IT?

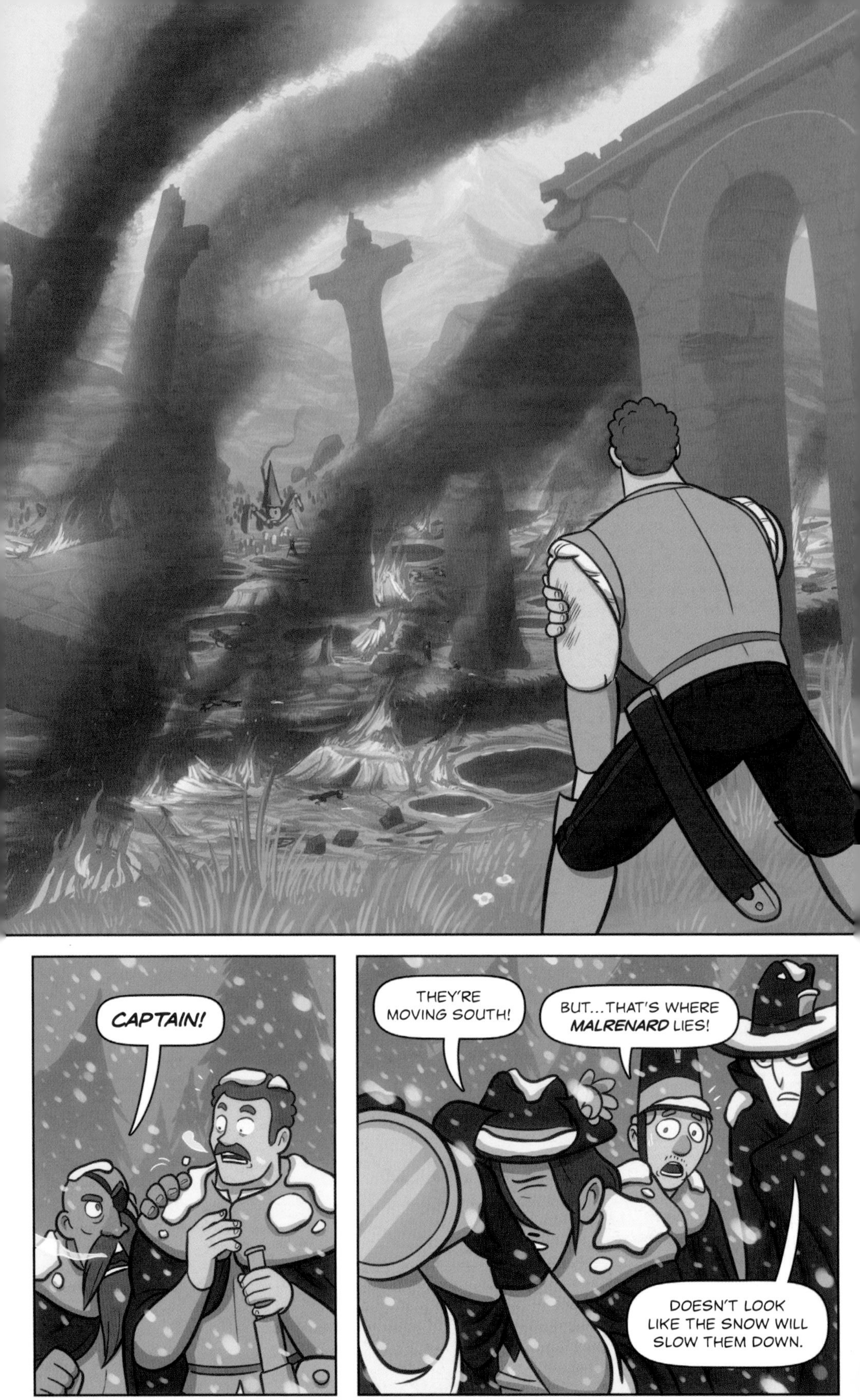
CAPTAIN!
THEY'RE MOVING SOUTH!
BUT...THAT'S WHERE MALRENARD LIES!
DOESN'T LOOK LIKE THE SNOW WILL SLOW THEM DOWN.

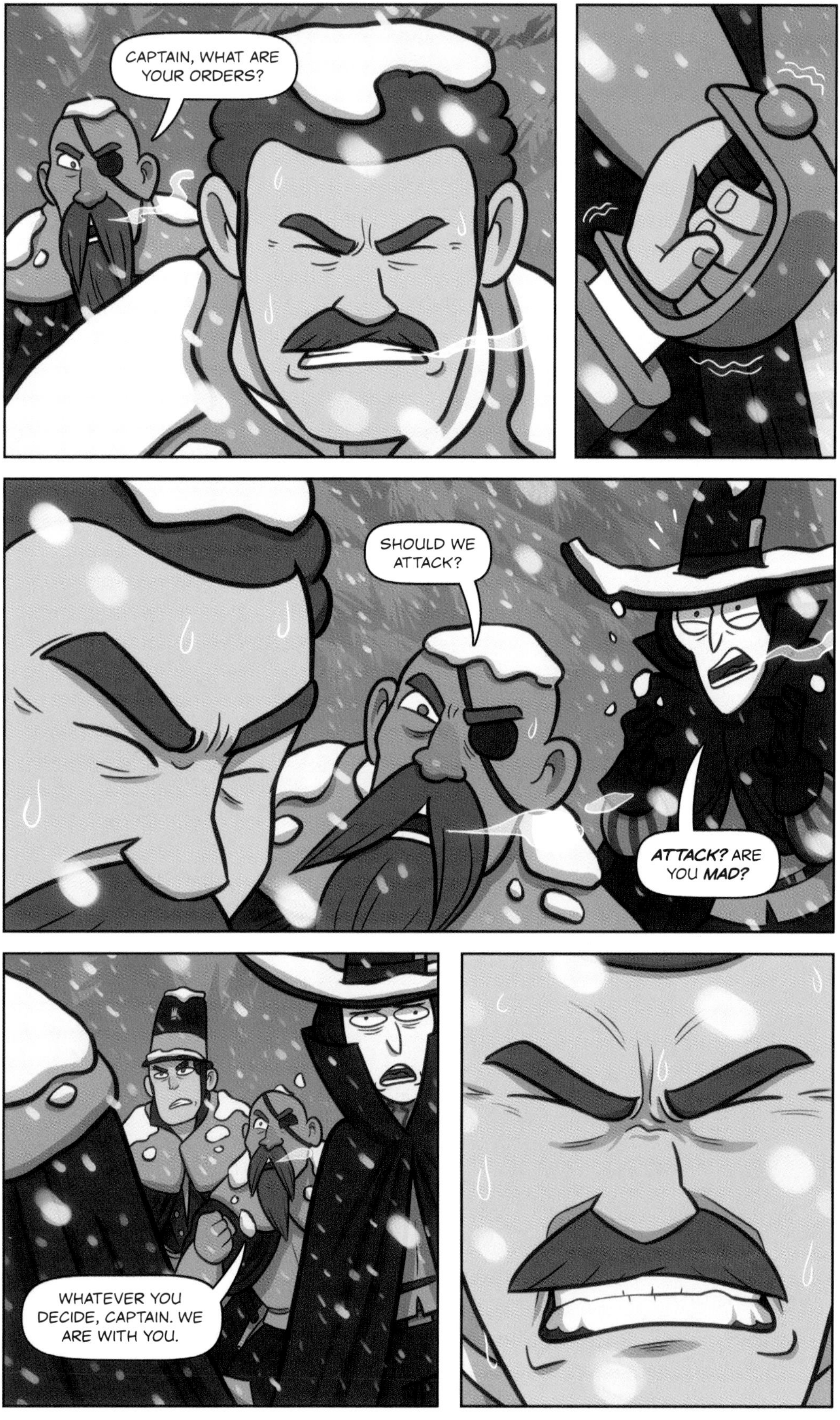
CAPTAIN, WHAT ARE YOUR ORDERS?
SHOULD WE ATTACK?
ATTACK? ARE YOU MAD?
WHATEVER YOU DECIDE, CAPTAIN. WE ARE WITH YOU.

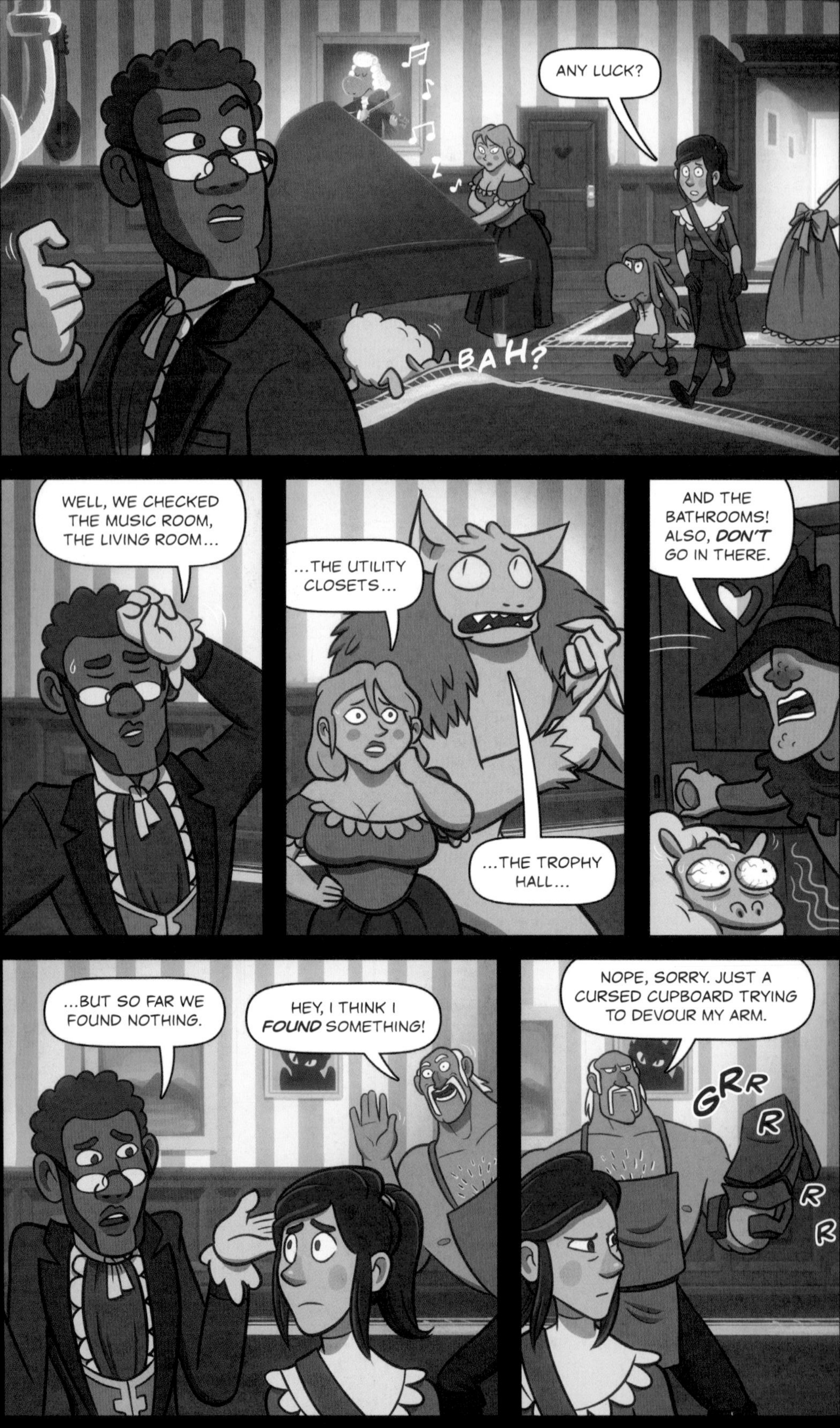
ANY LUCK?
BAH?
WELL, WE CHECKED THE MUSIC ROOM, THE LIVING ROOM...
...THE UTILITY CLOSETS...
...THE TROPHY HALL...
AND THE BATHROOMS! ALSO, **DON'T** GO IN THERE.
...BUT SO FAR WE FOUND NOTHING.
HEY, I THINK I **FOUND** SOMETHING!
NOPE, SORRY. JUST A CURSED CUPBOARD TRYING TO DEVOUR MY ARM.
GRRRRR

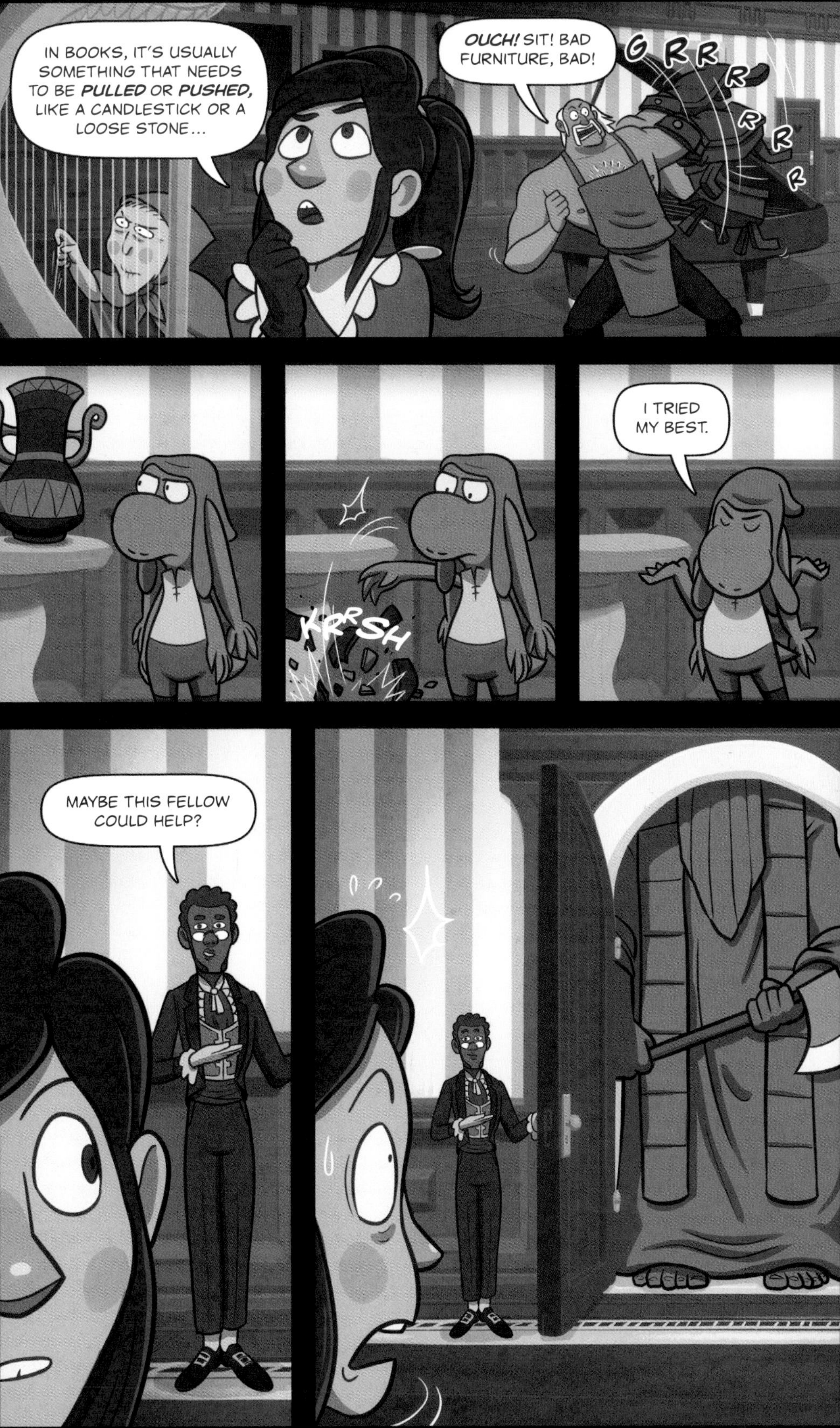

IN BOOKS, IT'S USUALLY SOMETHING THAT NEEDS TO BE ***PULLED*** OR ***PUSHED,*** LIKE A CANDLESTICK OR A LOOSE STONE...
OUCH! SIT! BAD FURNITURE, BAD!
GRRRRRRR
KRRSH
I TRIED MY BEST.
MAYBE THIS FELLOW COULD HELP?

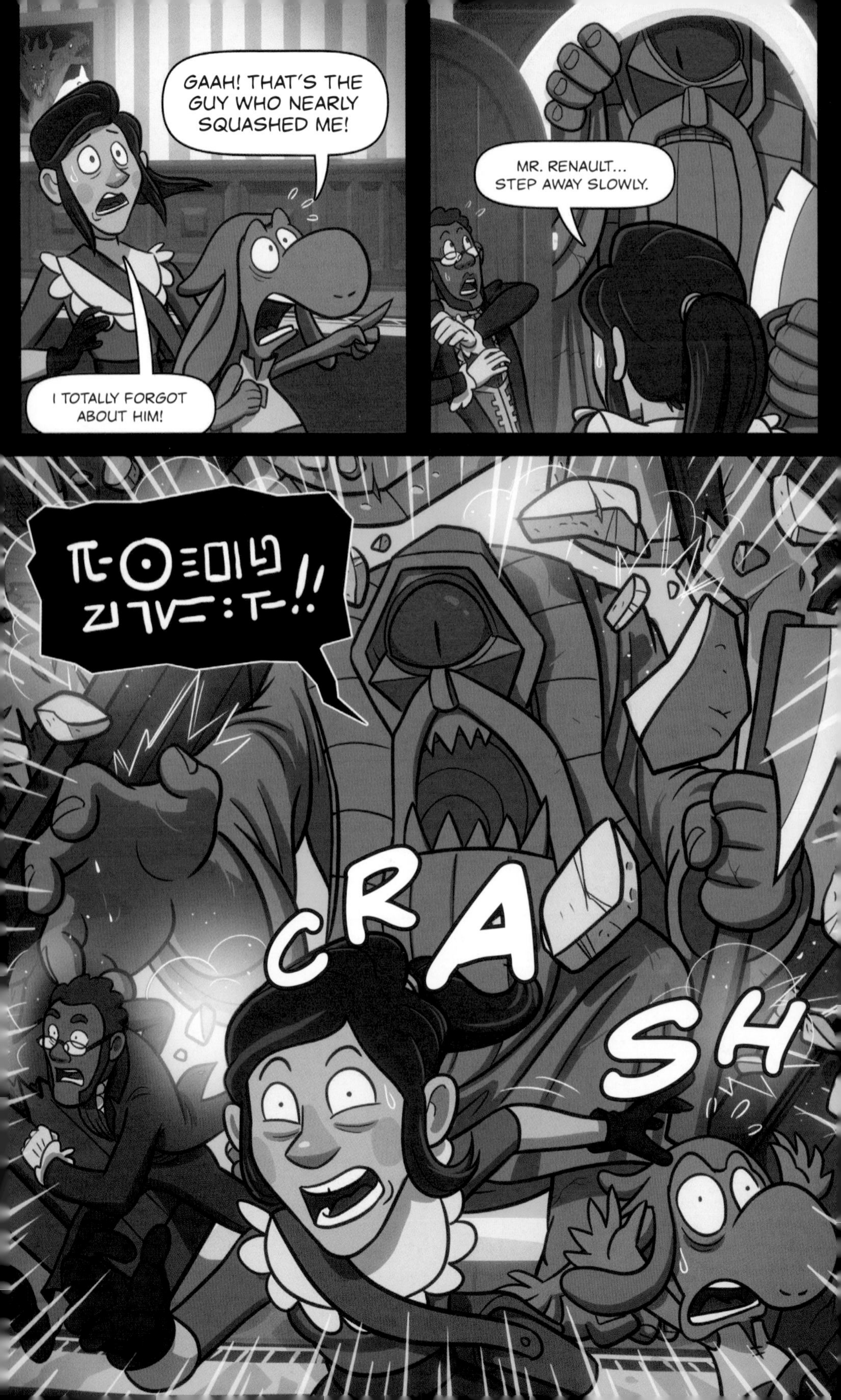
GAAH! THAT'S THE GUY WHO NEARLY SQUASHED ME!
I TOTALLY FORGOT ABOUT HIM!
MR. RENAULT... STEP AWAY SLOWLY.
CRASH

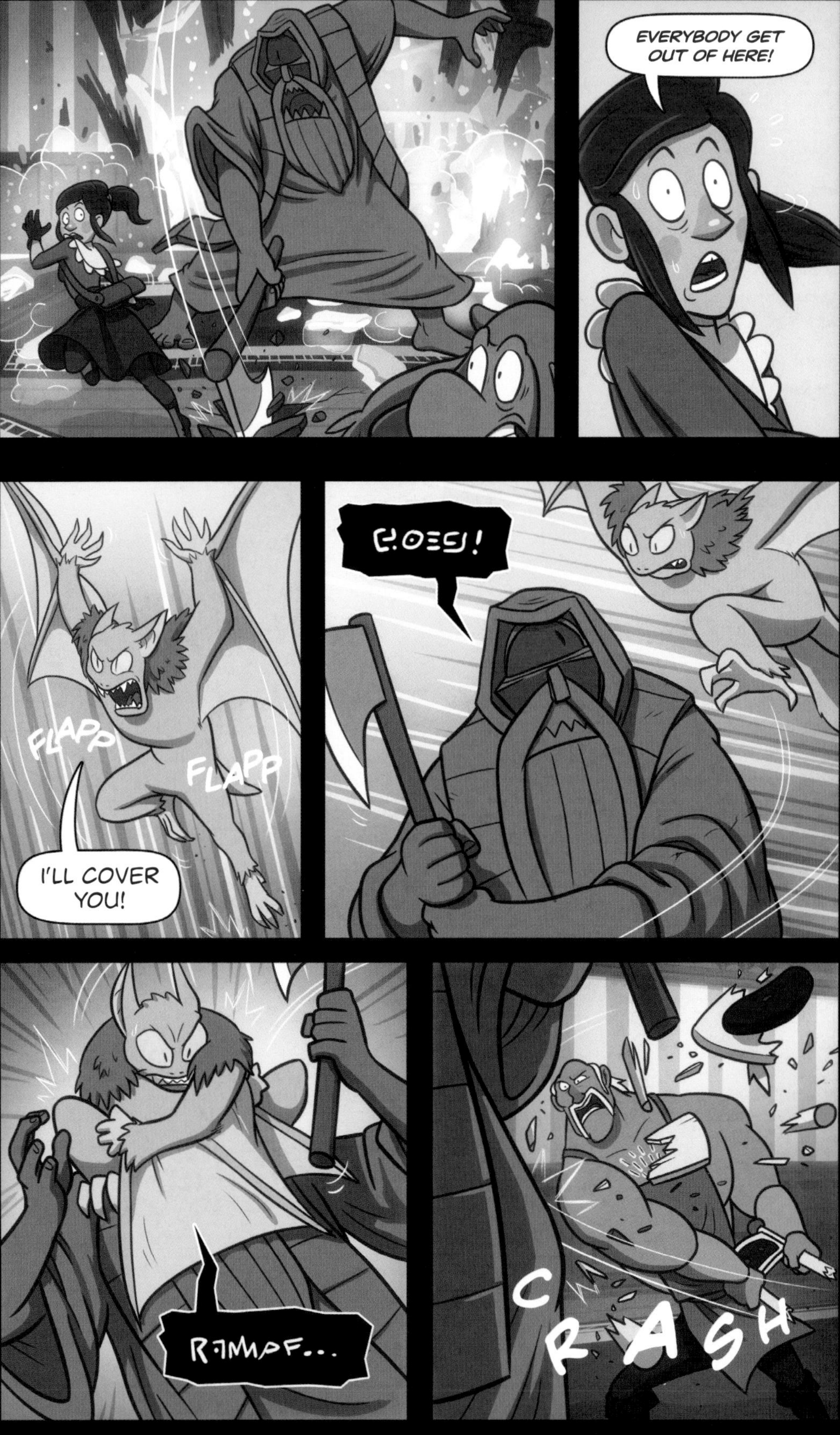
EVERYBODY GET OUT OF HERE!
FLAPP
FLAPP
I'LL COVER YOU!
CRASH

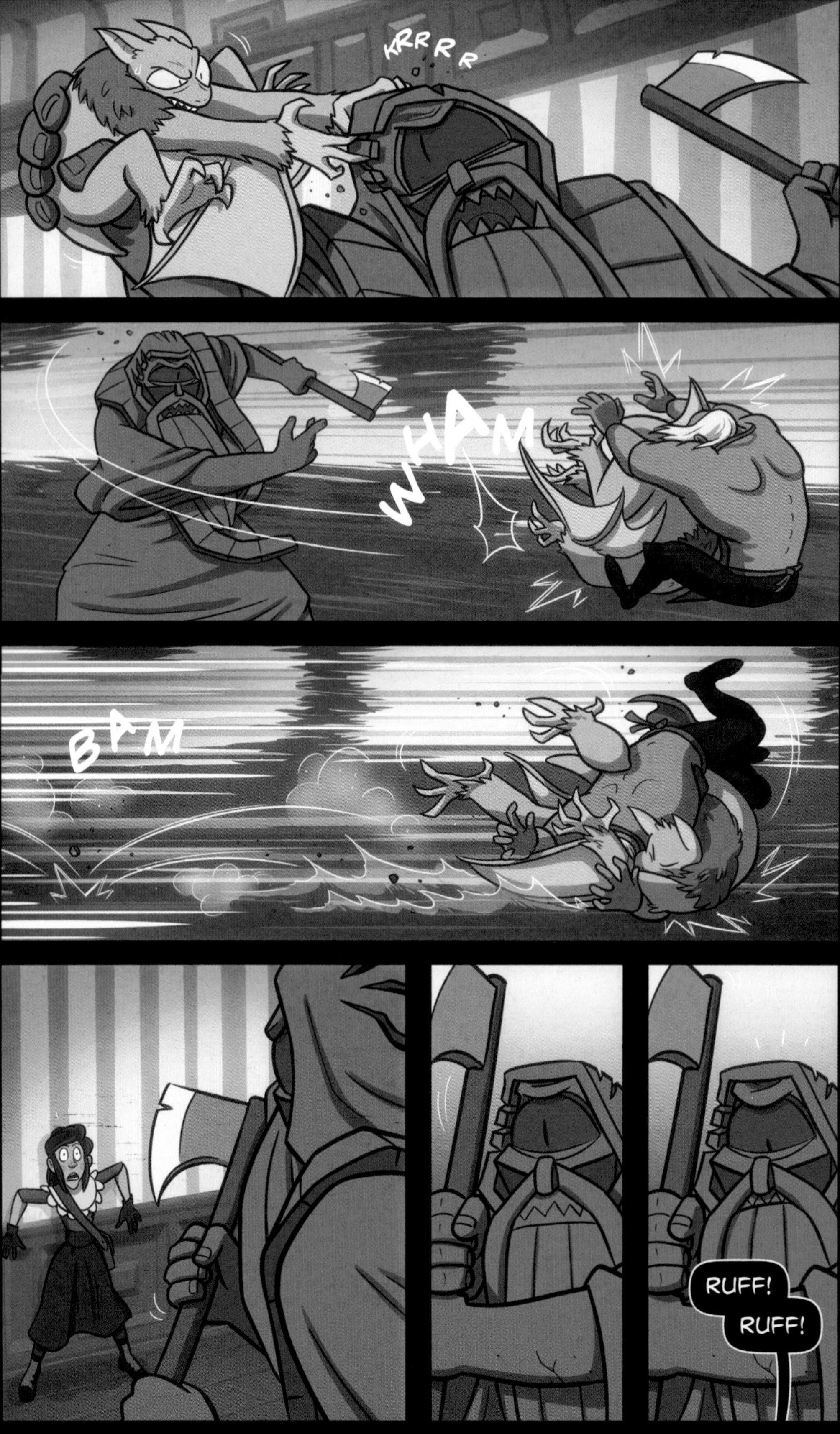
KRRRR
WHAM
BAM
RUFF!
RUFF!

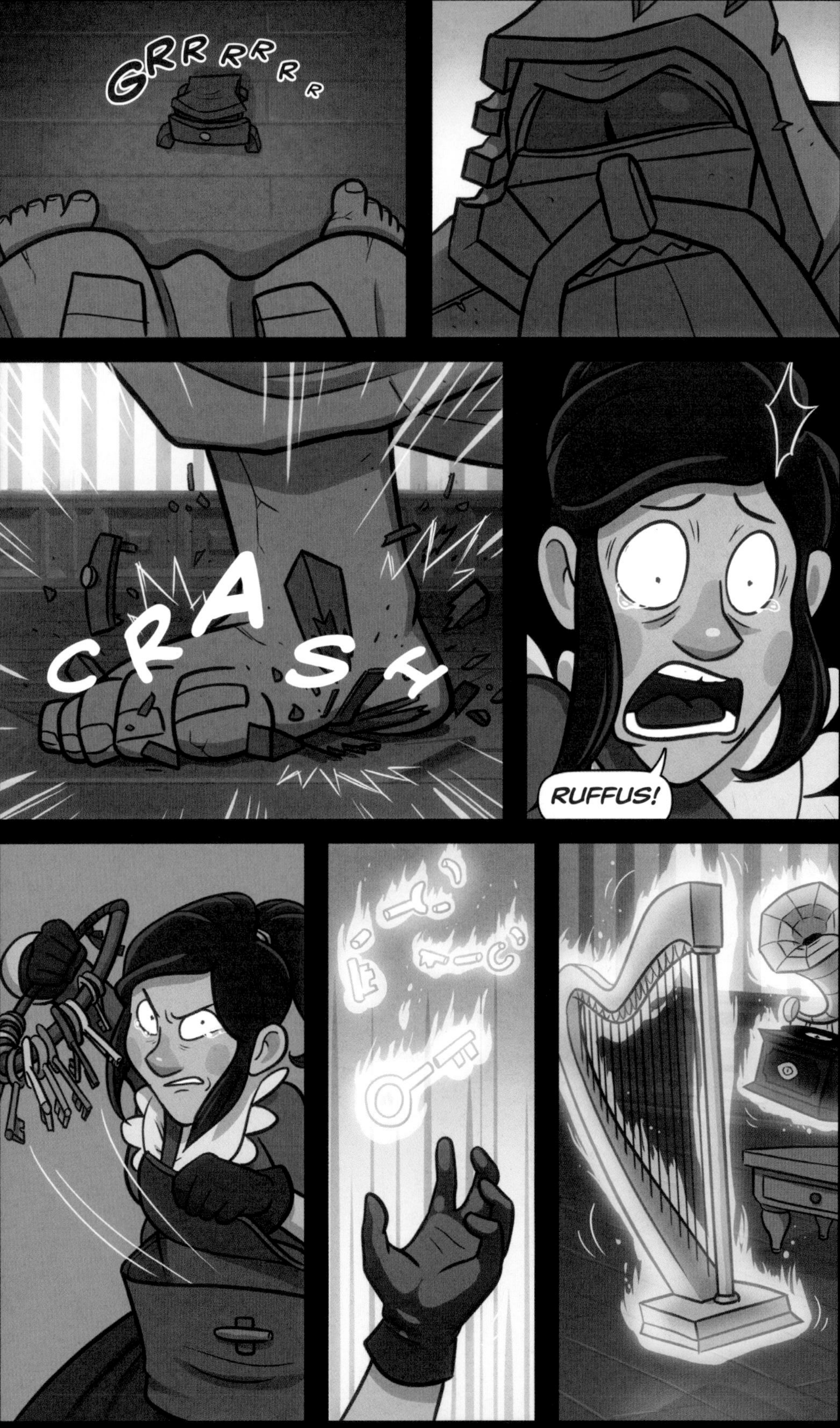
GRRRRRRR
CRASH
RUFFUS!

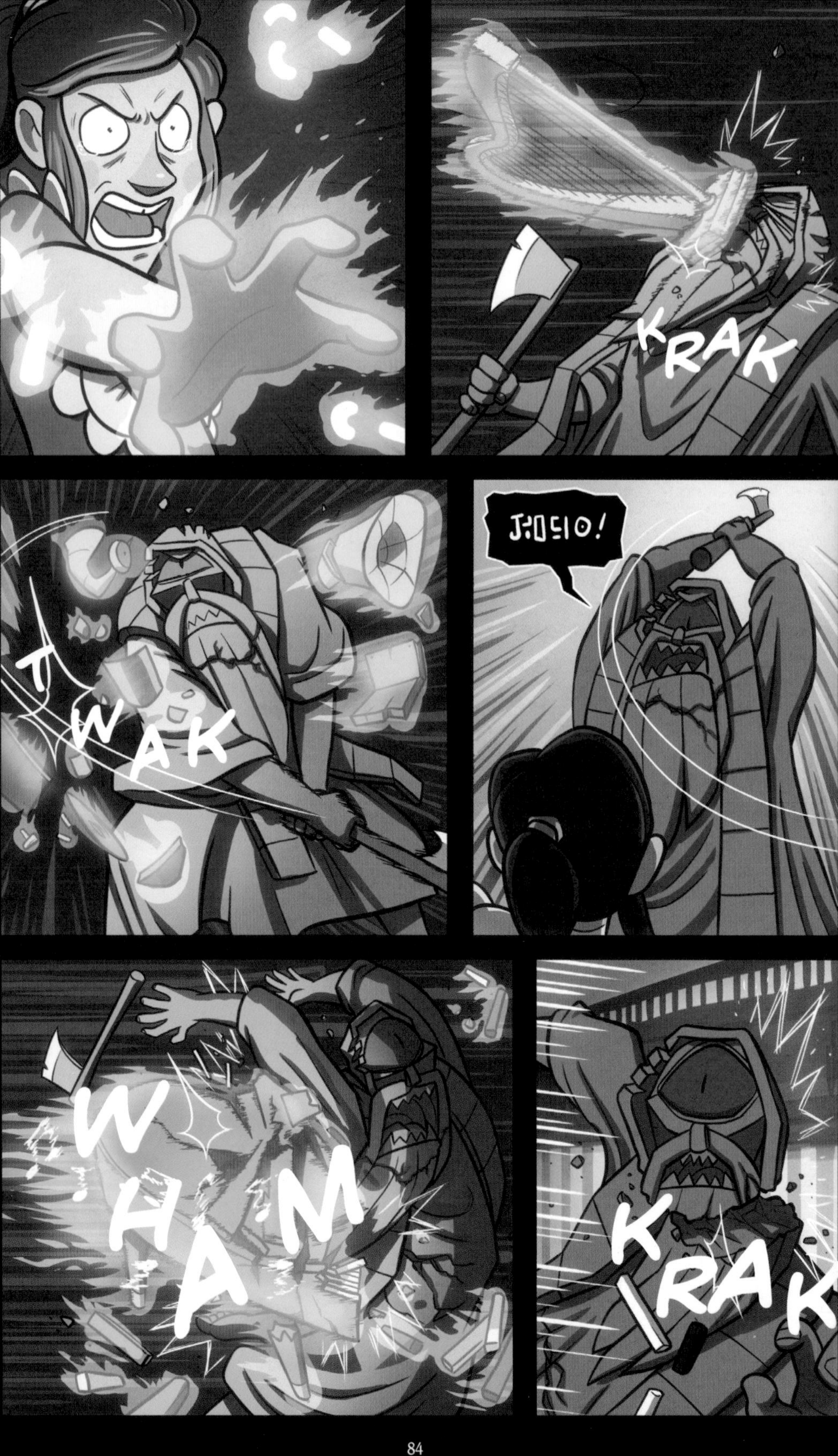
KRAK
TWAK
WHAM
KRAK

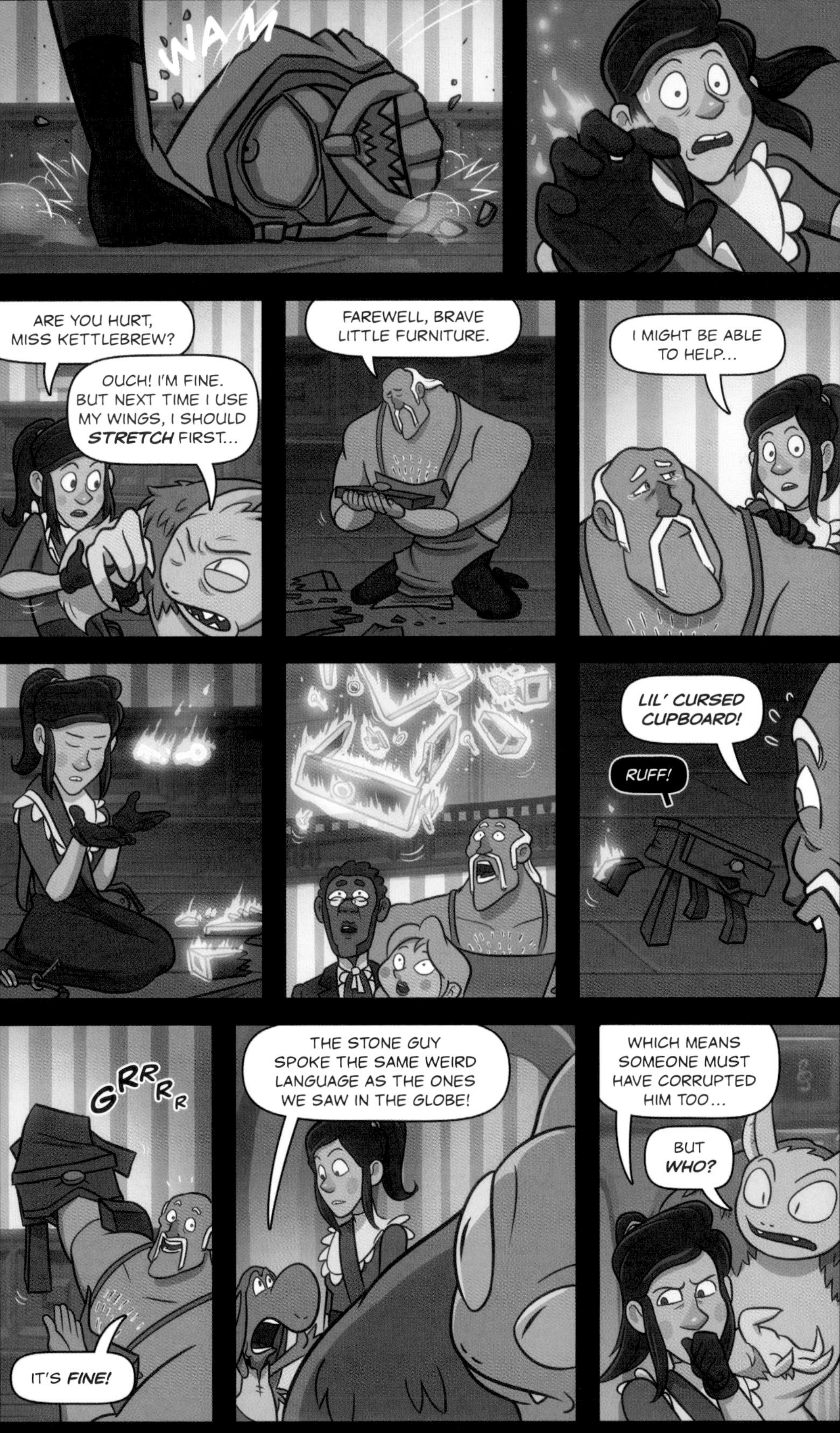
WAM
ARE YOU HURT, MISS KETTLEBREW?
OUCH! I'M FINE. BUT NEXT TIME I USE MY WINGS, I SHOULD STRETCH FIRST...
FAREWELL, BRAVE LITTLE FURNITURE.
I MIGHT BE ABLE TO HELP...
LIL' CURSED CUPBOARD!
RUFF!
GRRRR
IT'S FINE!
THE STONE GUY SPOKE THE SAME WEIRD LANGUAGE AS THE ONES WE SAW IN THE GLOBE!
WHICH MEANS SOMEONE MUST HAVE CORRUPTED HIM TOO...
BUT WHO?

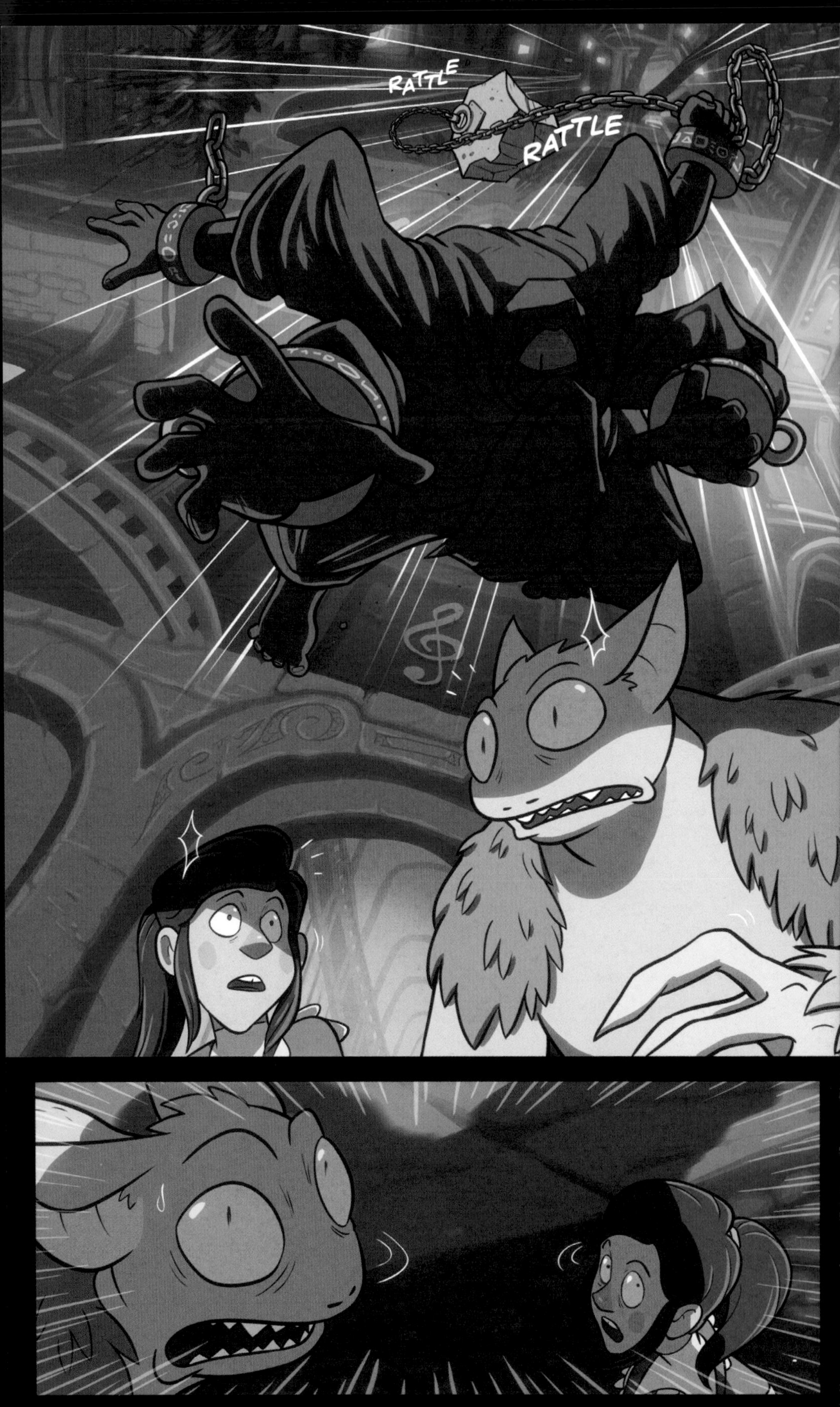
RATTLE
RATTLE

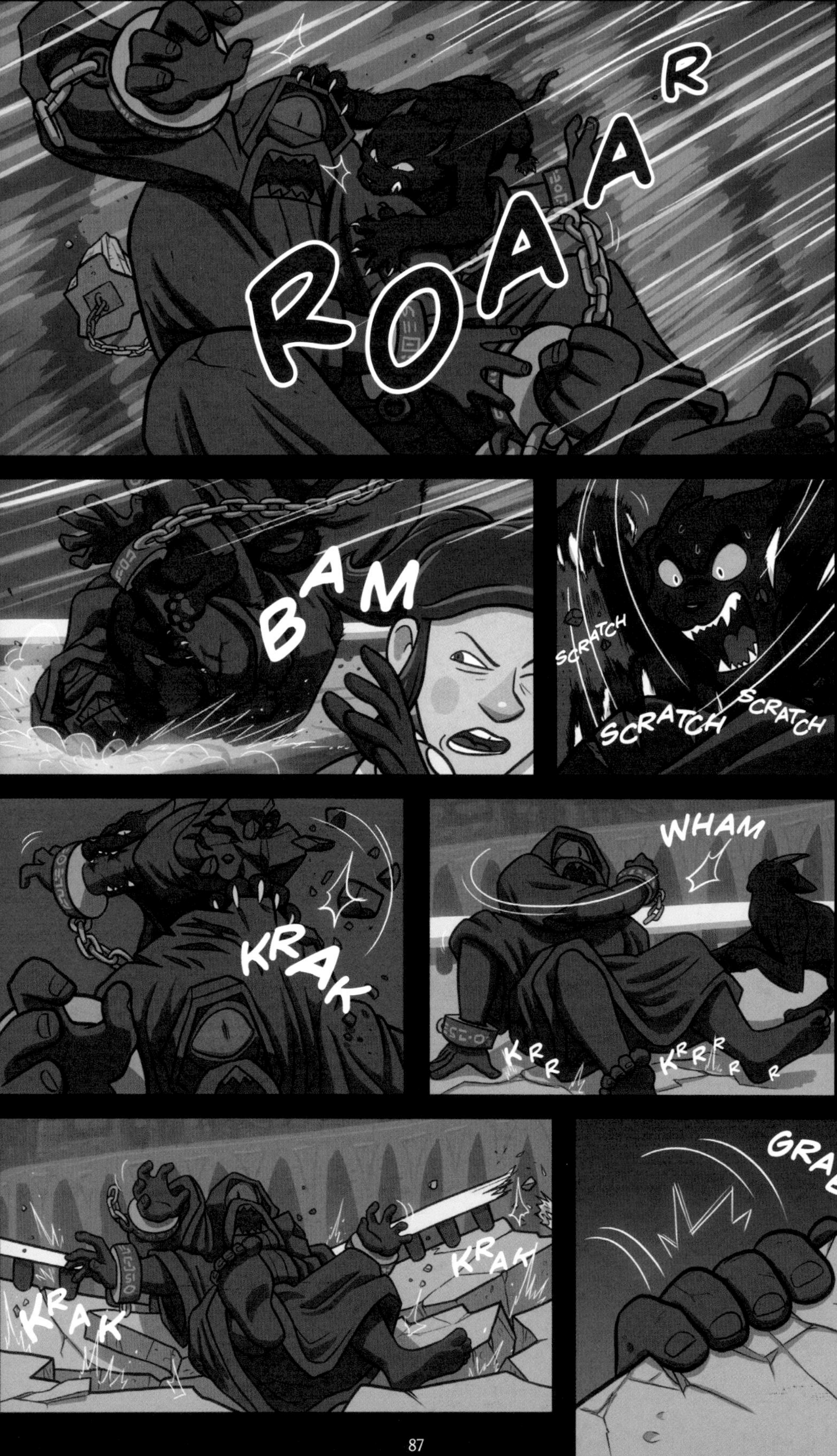
ROAAAR
BAM
SCRATCH
SCRATCH
SCRATCH
KRAK
WHAM
KRR
KRRRRR
KRAK
KRAK
GRAB

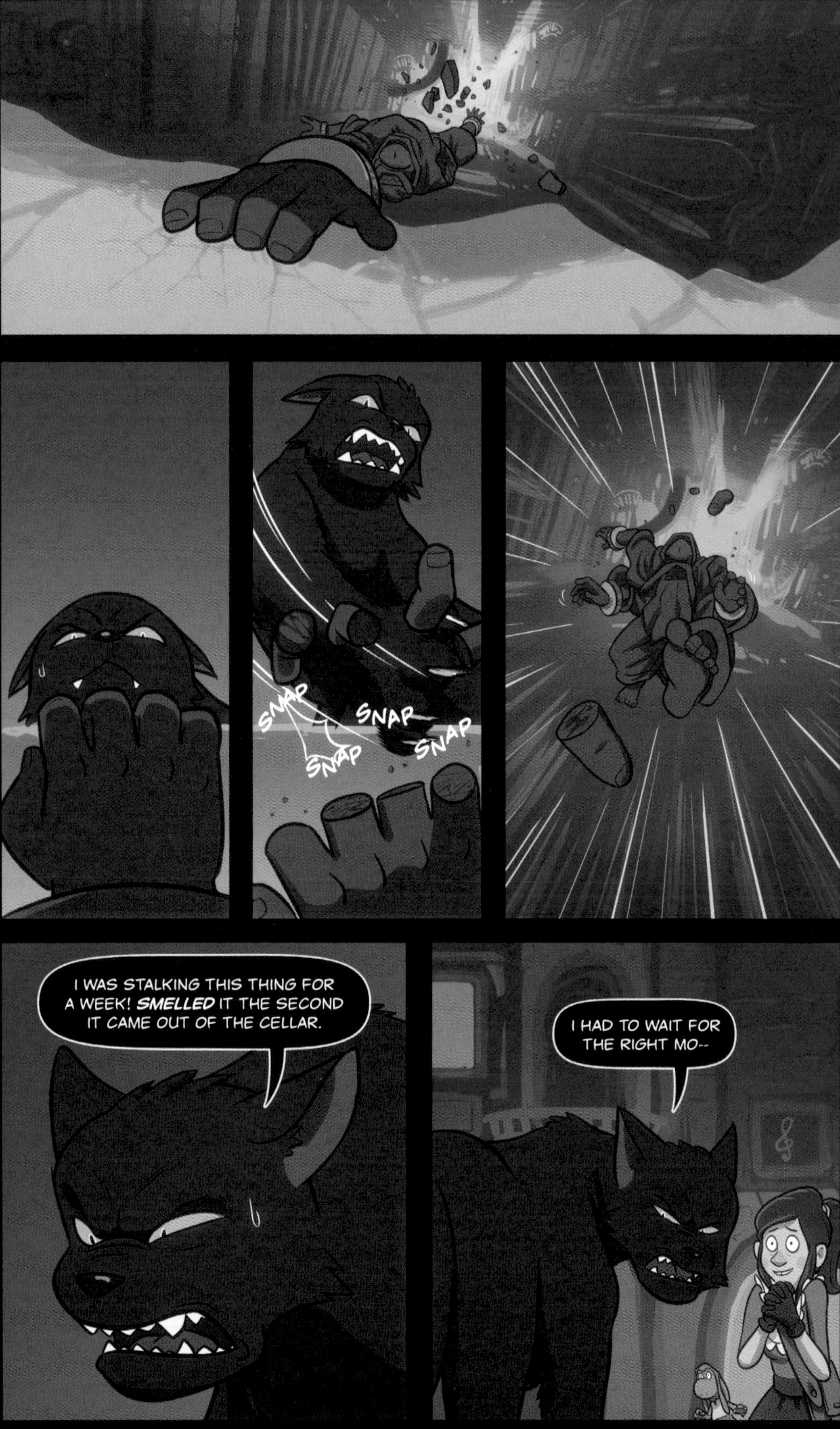
SNAP
SNAP
SNAP
SNAP
I WAS STALKING THIS THING FOR A WEEK! SMELLED IT THE SECOND IT CAME OUT OF THE CELLAR.
I HAD TO WAIT FOR THE RIGHT MO--

I KNEW YOU'D COME BACK!

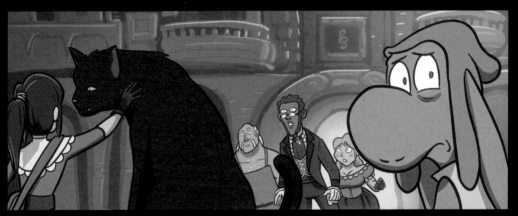

HOPE IT WASN'T TOO *LATE* TO MAKE A DIFFERENCE...

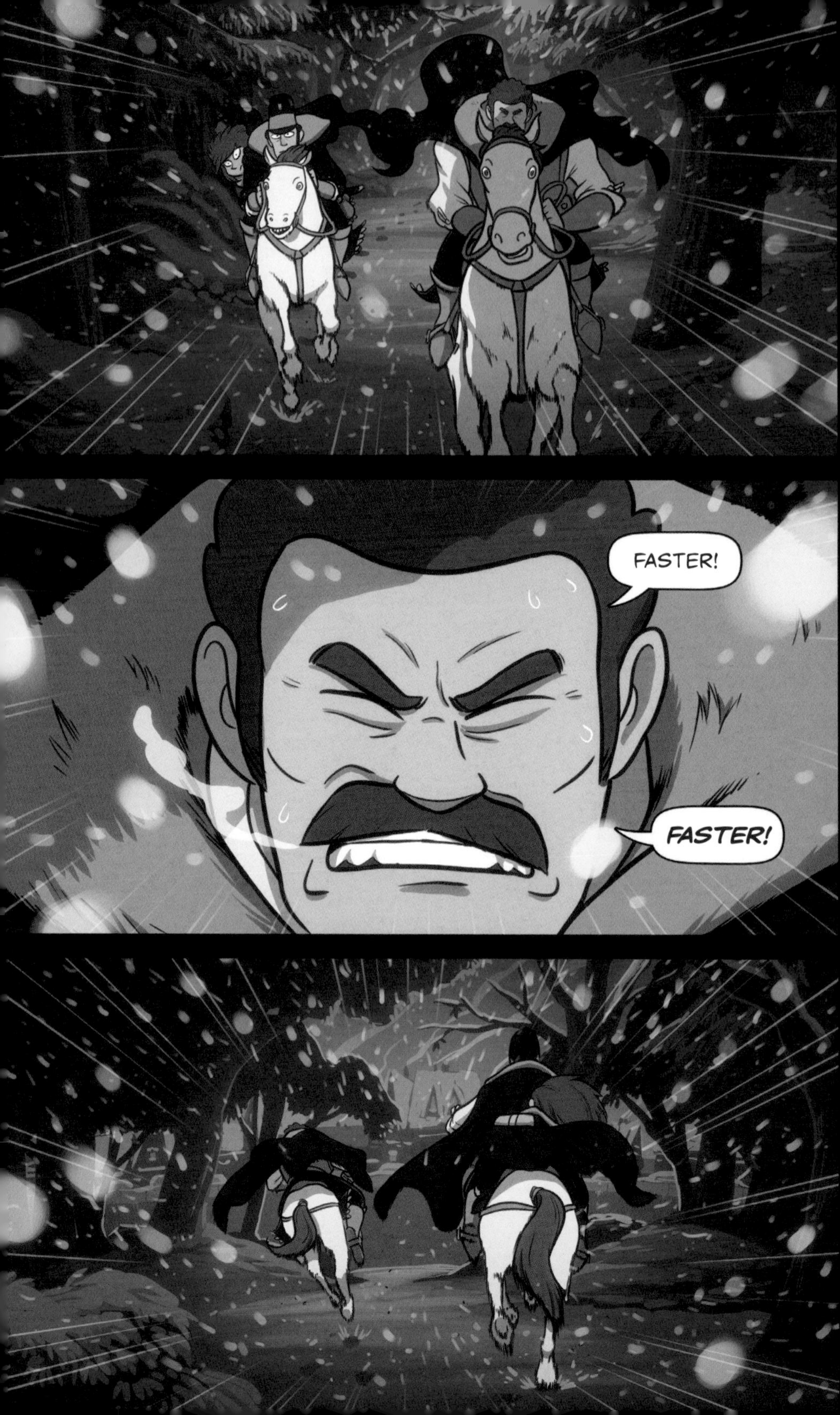
FASTER!
FASTER!

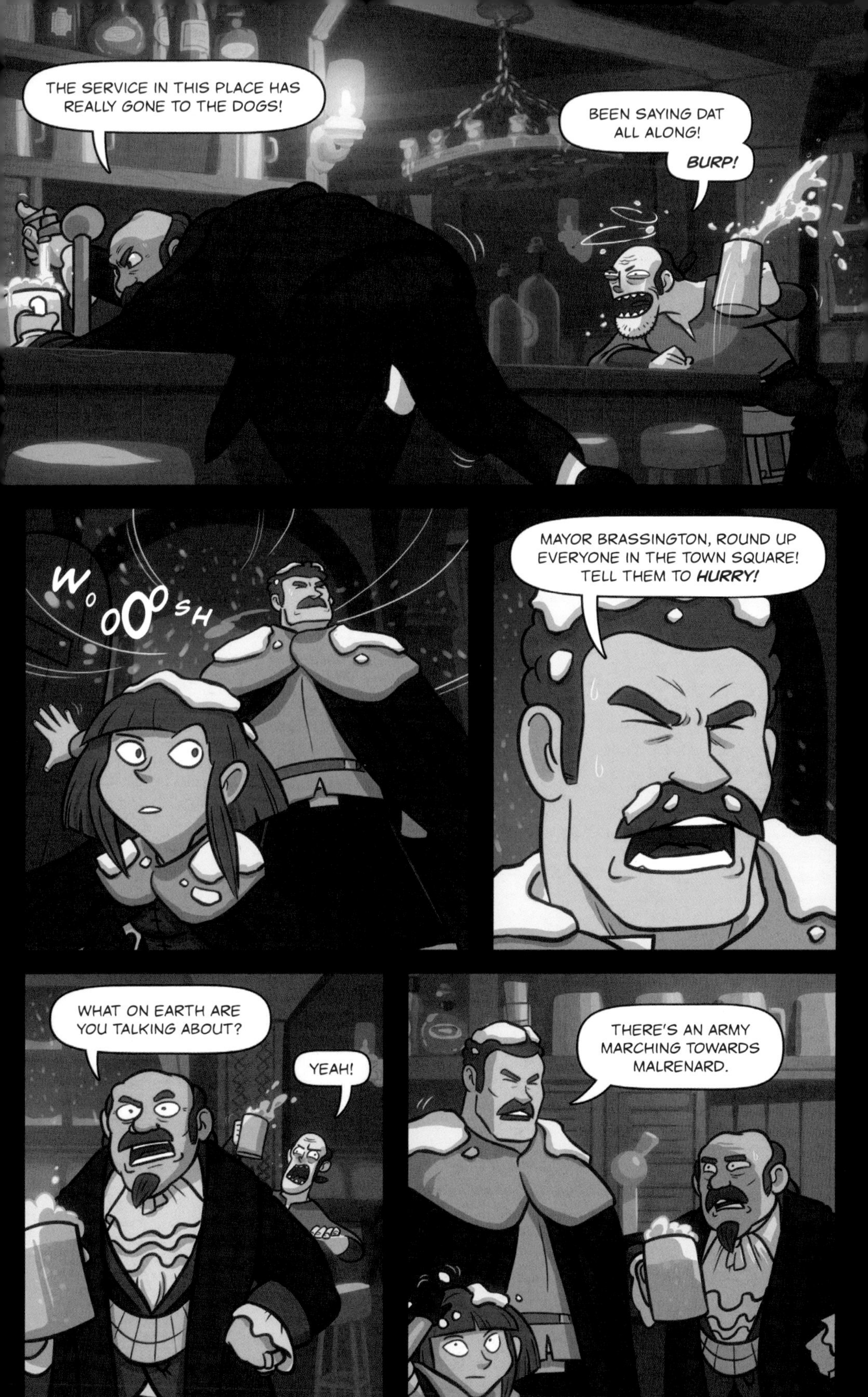
THE SERVICE IN THIS PLACE HAS REALLY GONE TO THE DOGS!
BEEN SAYING DAT ALL ALONG!
BURP!
WOOOOSH
MAYOR BRASSINGTON, ROUND UP EVERYONE IN THE TOWN SQUARE! TELL THEM TO HURRY!
WHAT ON EARTH ARE YOU TALKING ABOUT?
YEAH!
THERE'S AN ARMY MARCHING TOWARDS MALRENARD.

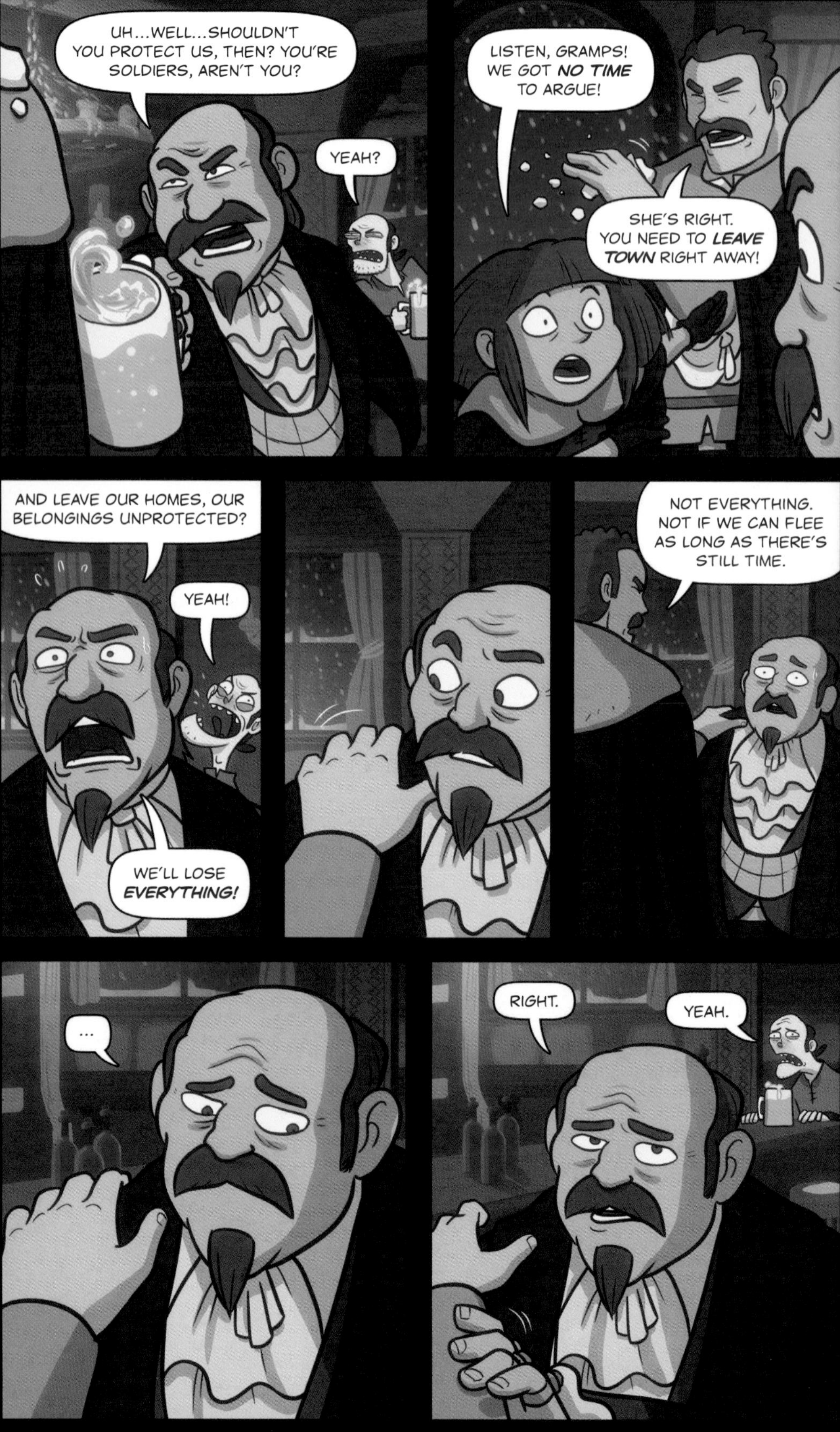
UH...WELL...SHOULDN'T YOU PROTECT US, THEN? YOU'RE SOLDIERS, AREN'T YOU?
YEAH?
LISTEN, GRAMPS! WE GOT **NO TIME** TO ARGUE!
SHE'S RIGHT. YOU NEED TO **LEAVE TOWN** RIGHT AWAY!
AND LEAVE OUR HOMES, OUR BELONGINGS UNPROTECTED?
YEAH!
WE'LL LOSE **EVERYTHING!**
NOT EVERYTHING. NOT IF WE CAN FLEE AS LONG AS THERE'S STILL TIME.
...
RIGHT.
YEAH.

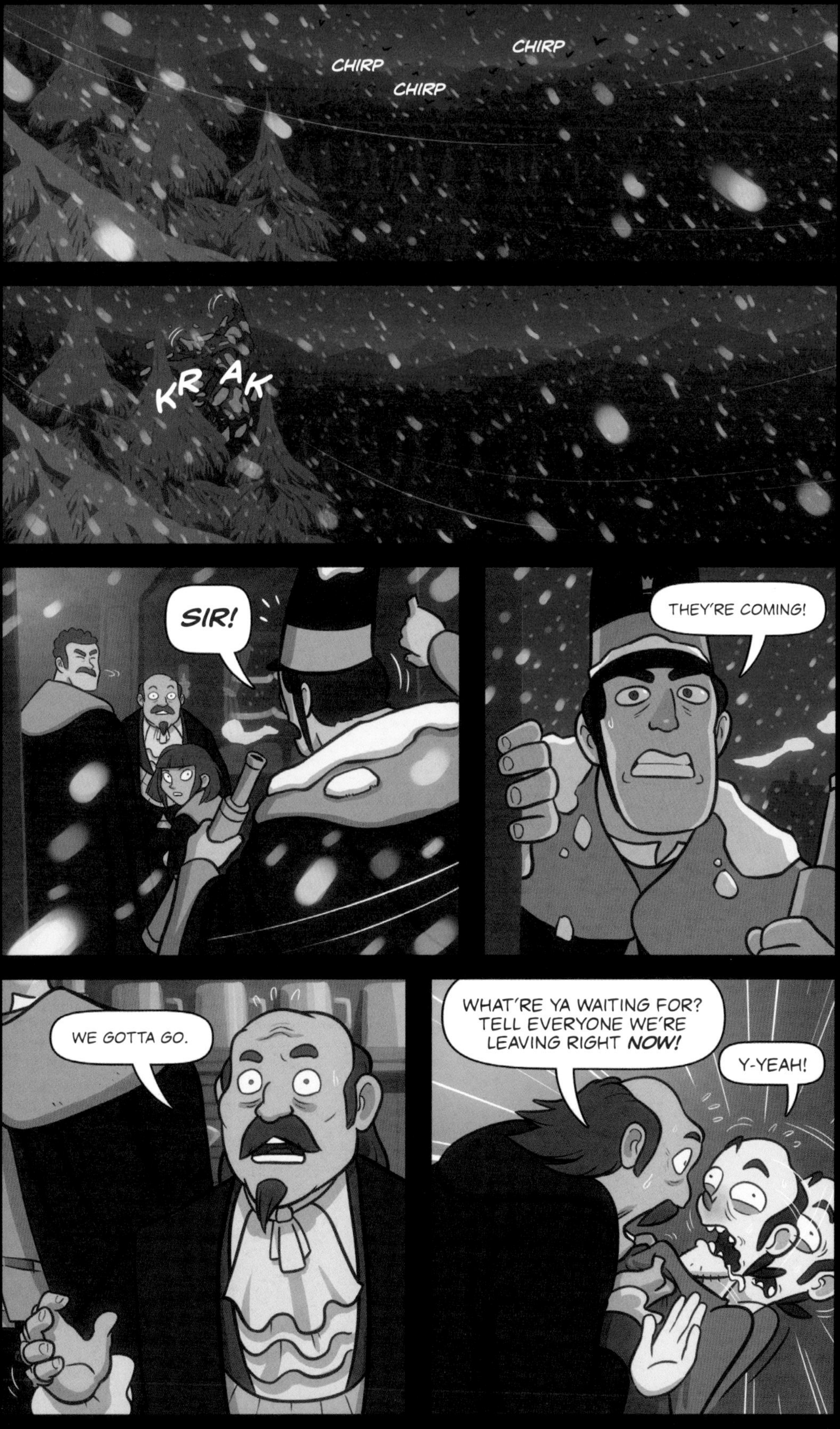
CHIRP
CHIRP
CHIRP
KRAK
SIR!
THEY'RE COMING!
WE GOTTA GO.
WHAT'RE YA WAITING FOR? TELL EVERYONE WE'RE LEAVING RIGHT **NOW!**
Y-YEAH!

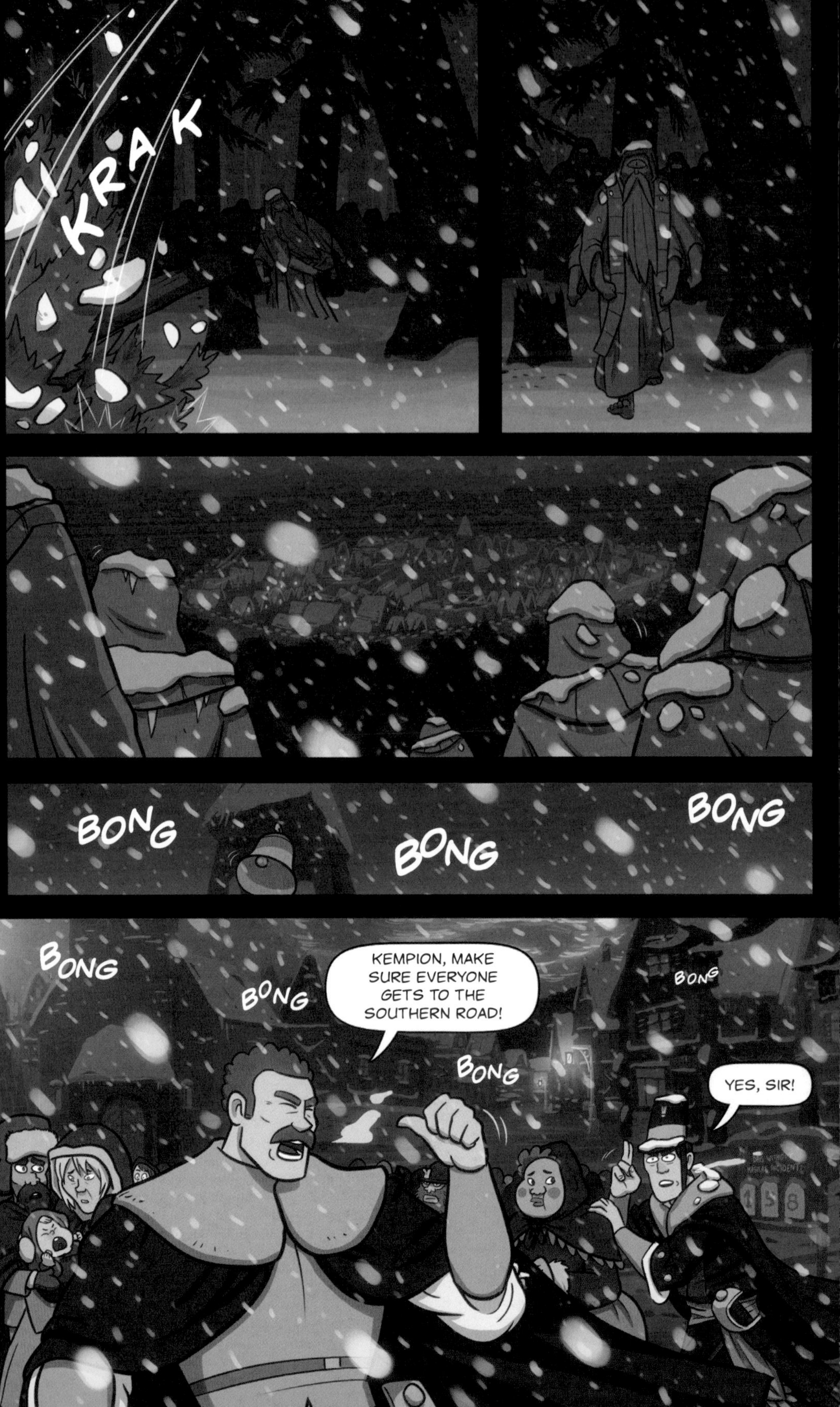
KRAK
BONG
BONG
BONG
BONG
BONG
KEMPION, MAKE SURE EVERYONE GETS TO THE SOUTHERN ROAD!
BONG
BONG
YES, SIR!

WAIT!
WE CAN'T TAKE THE SOUTHERN ROAD!
WHAT?
WE'RE TRAPPED!
IF THIS ARMY W-WON'T K-KILL US, THE WEATHER SURELY W-WILL!

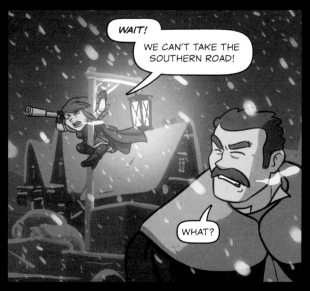

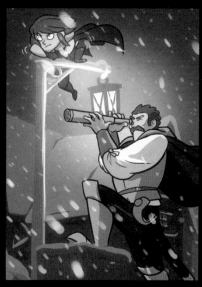

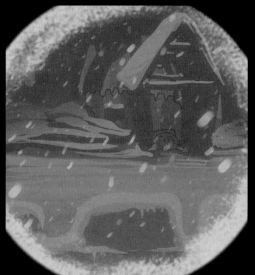

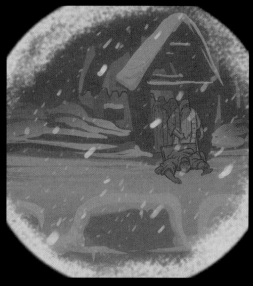

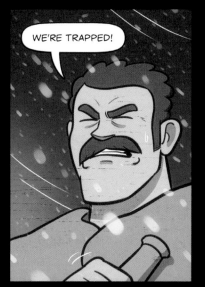

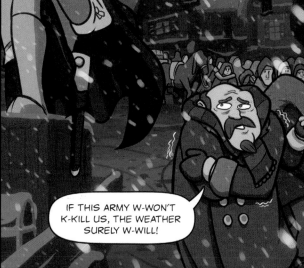

...

WE HAVE NO CHOICE.

EVERYBODY, LISTEN UP!

WE MUST GO TO HENRIETTA'S *HOUSE!*

HE CAN'T BE SERIOUS...

THIS IS CRAZY!

WHAT?

THAT PLACE GIVES ME THE CREEPS!

IT'S THE *ONLY* SAFE PLACE LEFT!

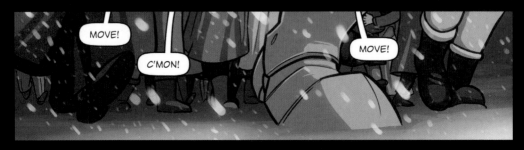
MOVE!

C'MON!

MOVE!

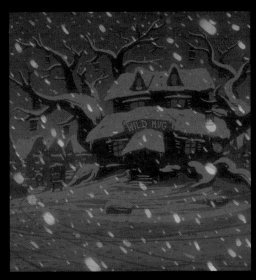

DAYS WITHOUT
MAGICAL INCIDENT:

1 5 8

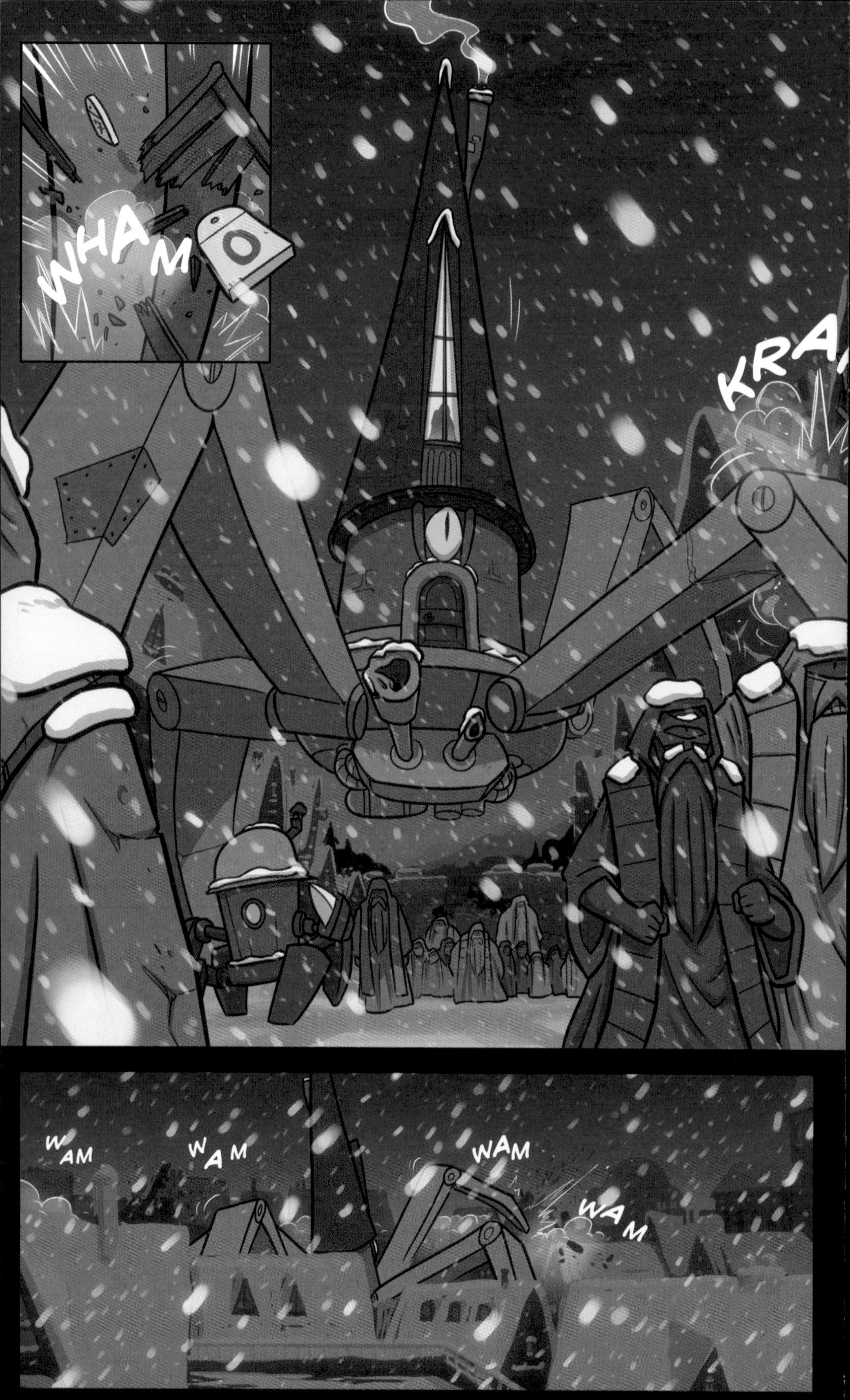
WHAM
KRA
WAM
WAM
WAM
WAM

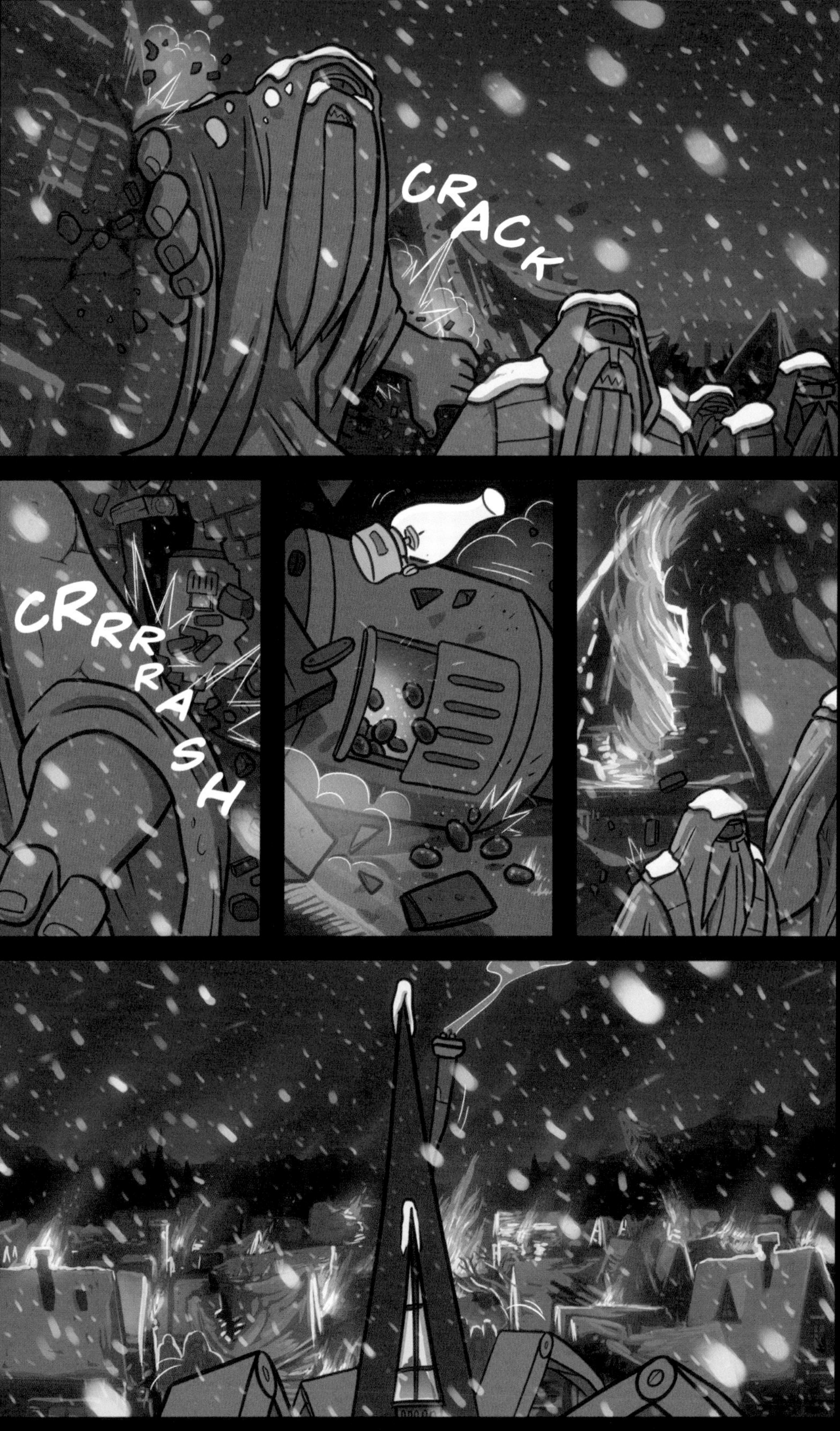
CRACK
CRRRRASH

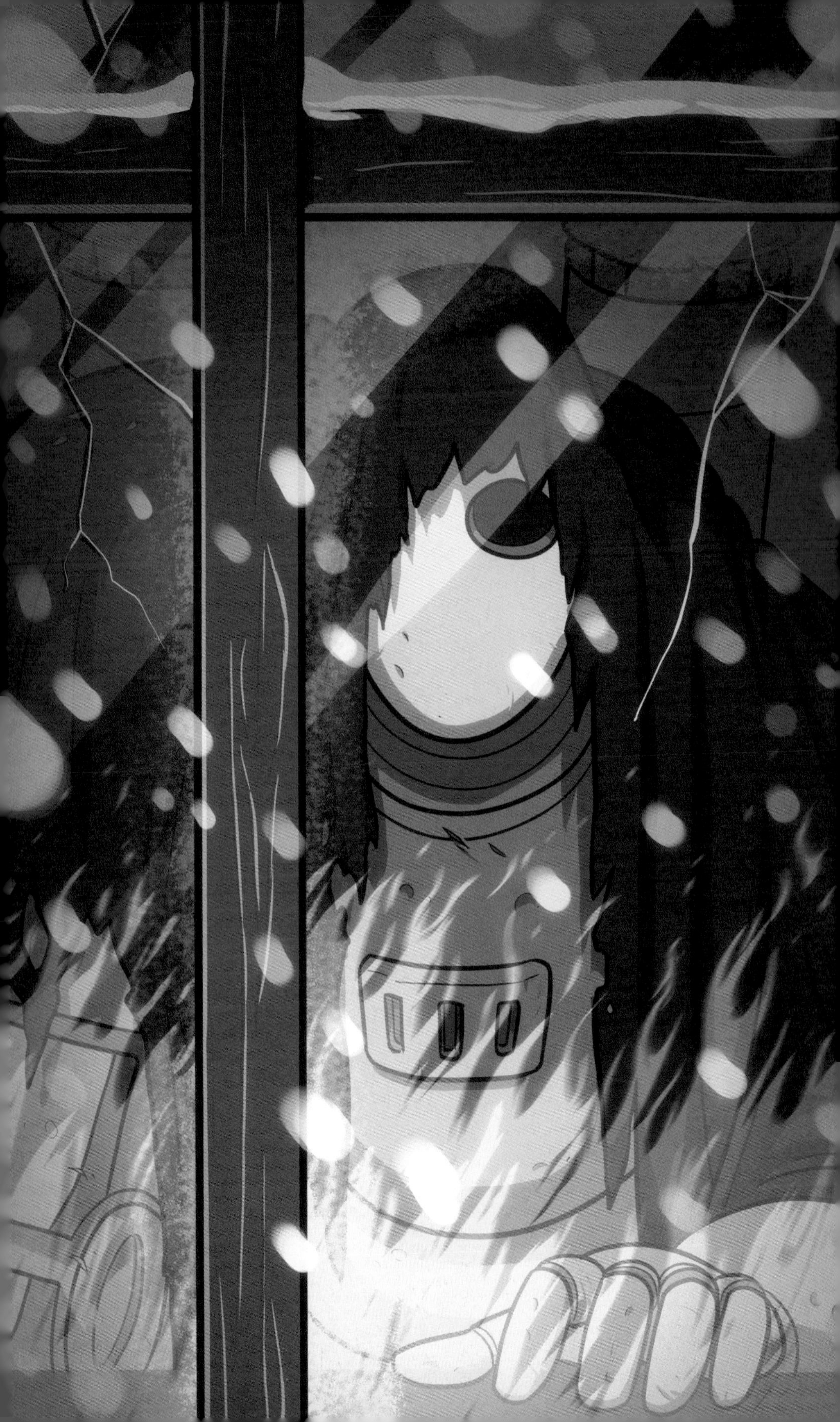

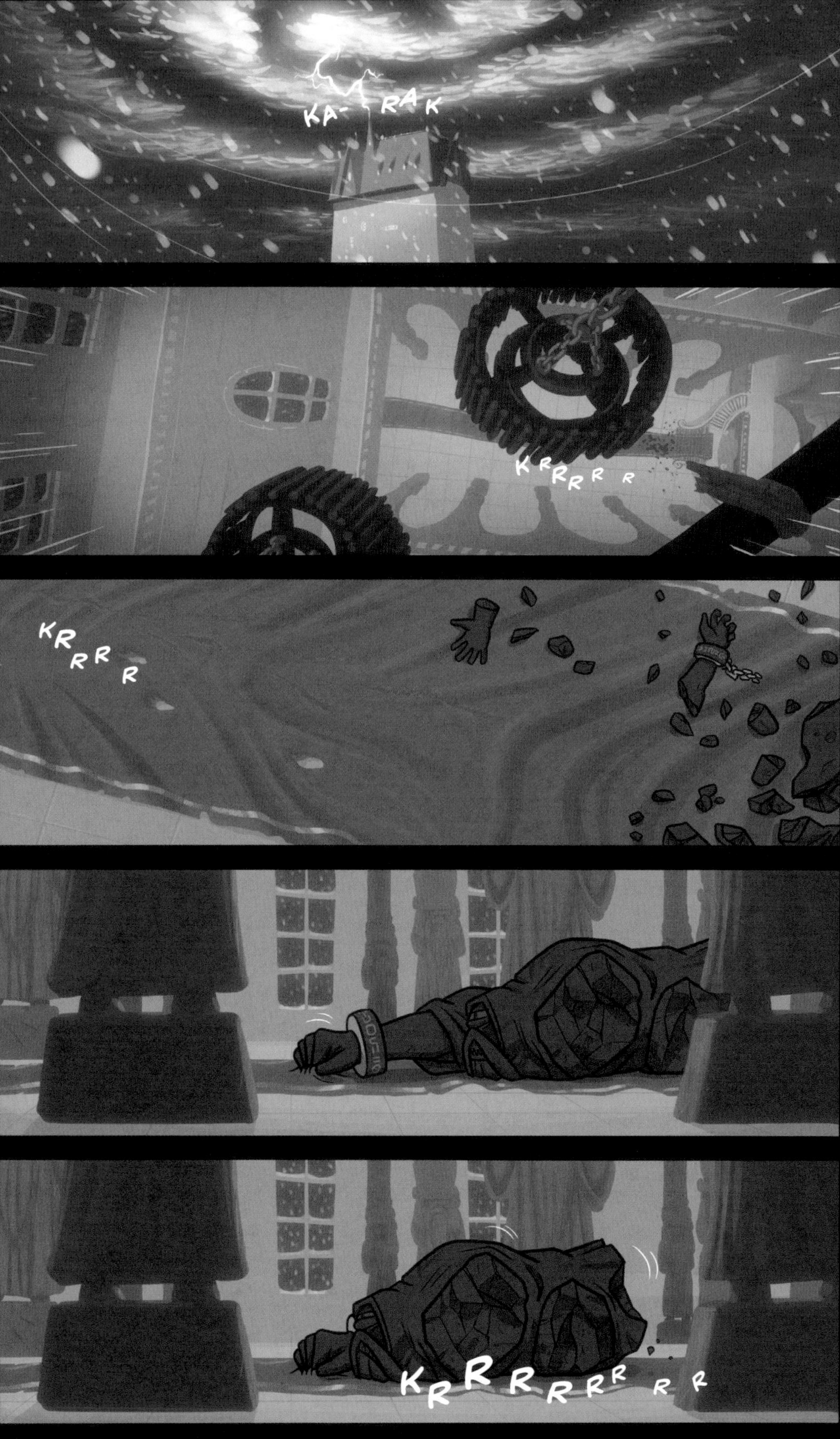
KA-RAK
KRRRRR R
KRRRR
KRRRRRRR R R

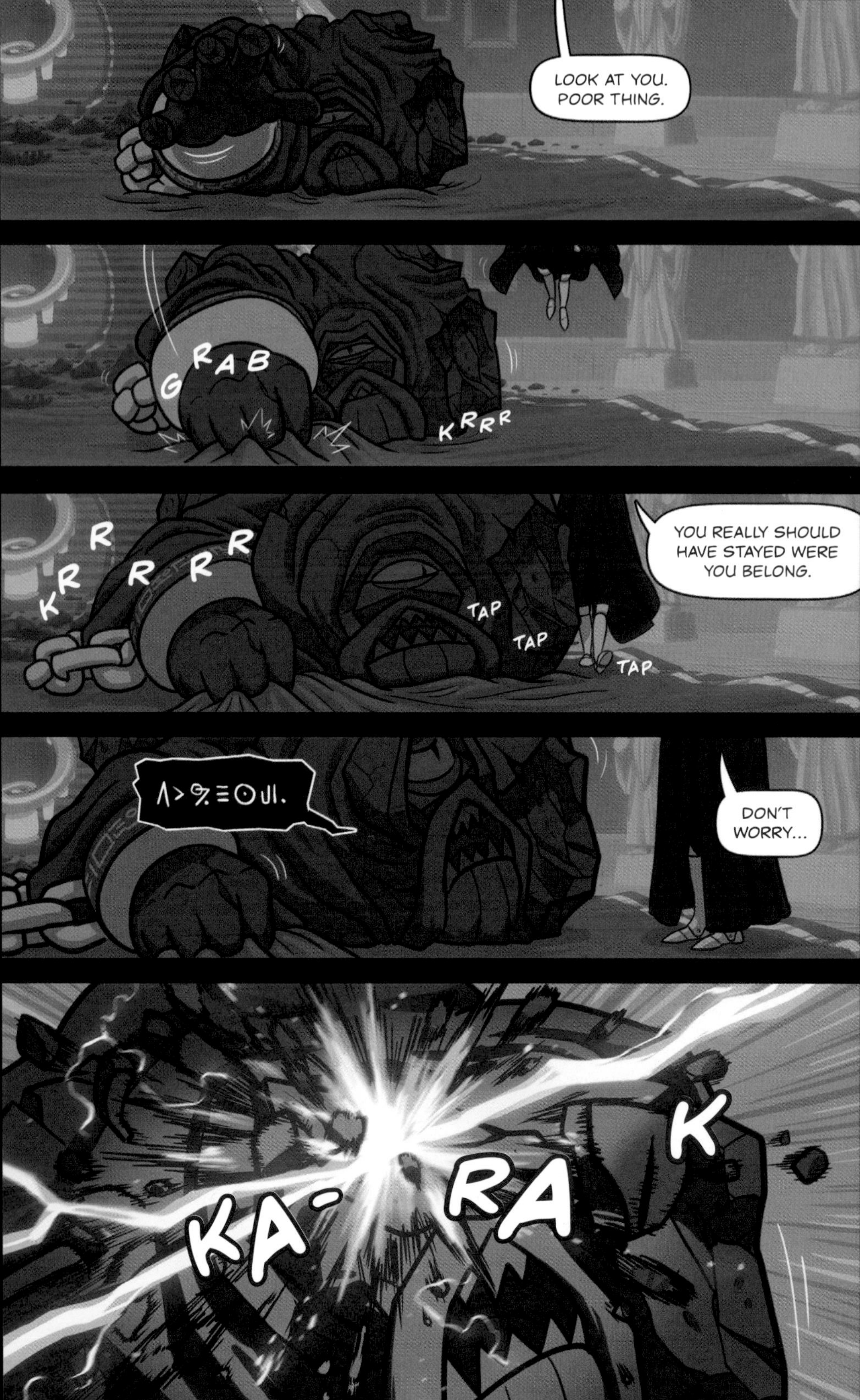
LOOK AT YOU. POOR THING.
GRAB
KRRR
KRRRRR
YOU REALLY SHOULD HAVE STAYED WERE YOU BELONG.
TAP
TAP
TAP
DON'T WORRY...
KA-RAK

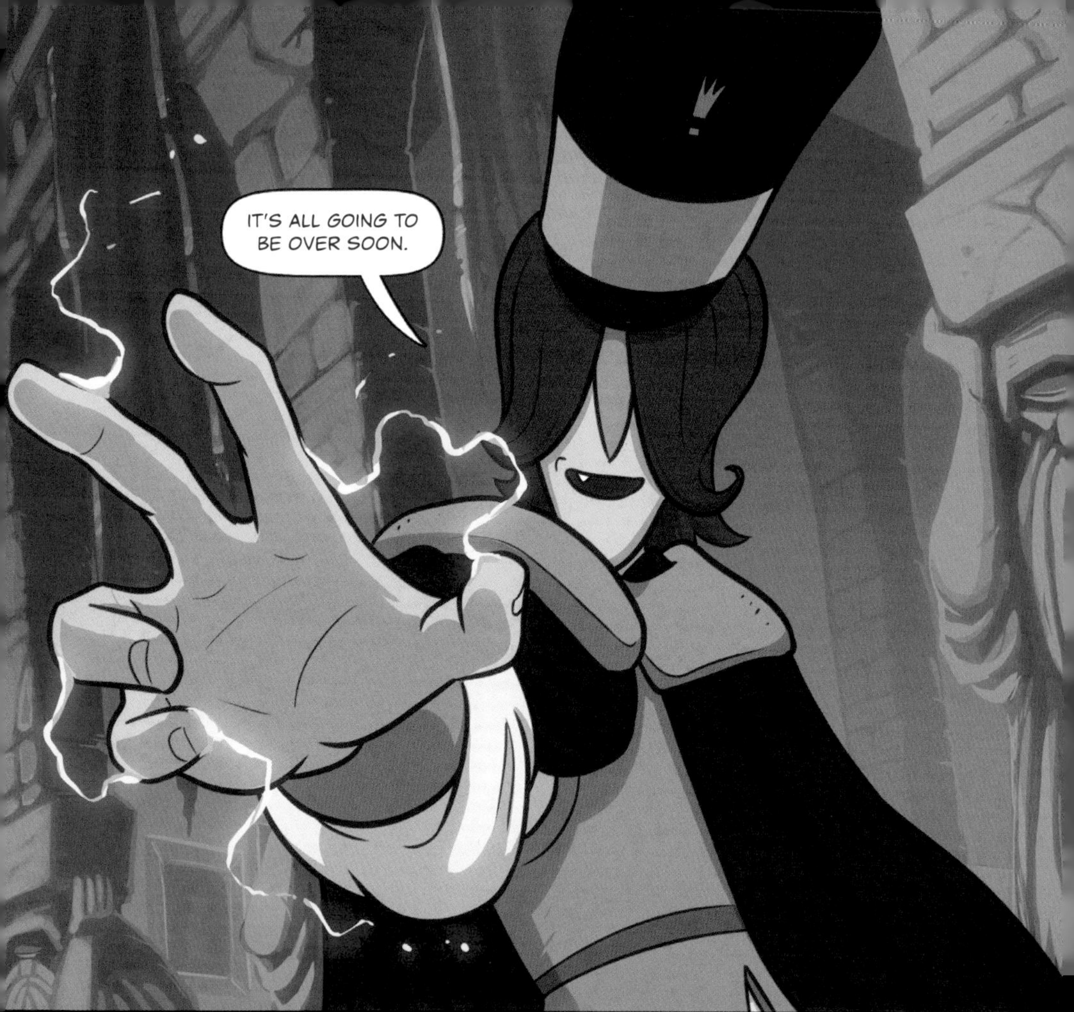
IT'S ALL GOING TO BE OVER SOON.

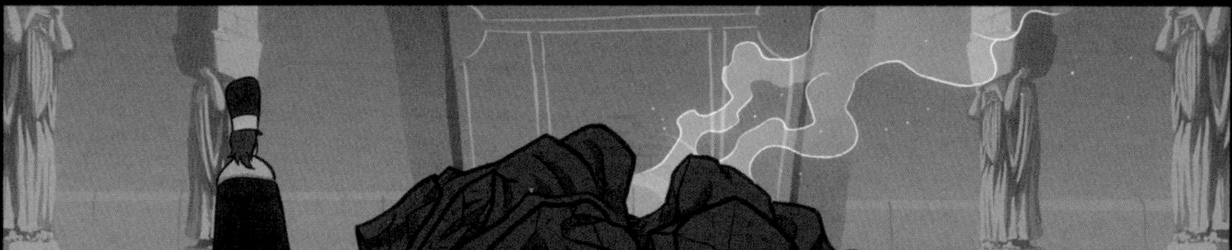

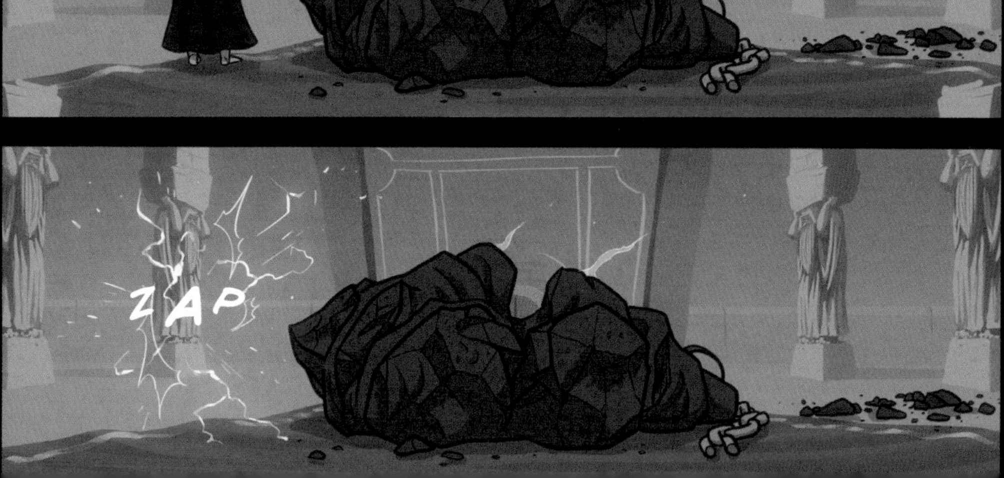
ZAP

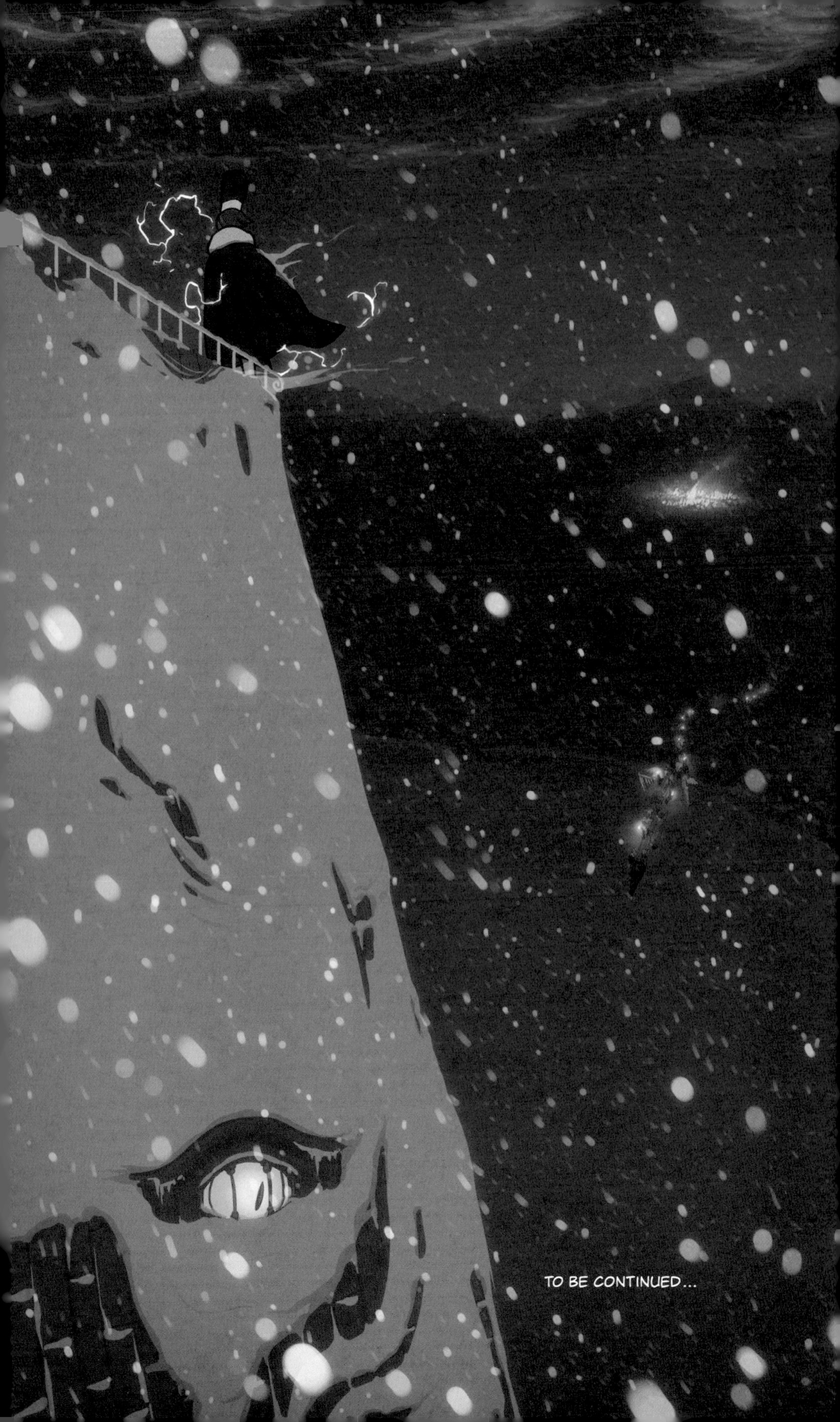
TO BE CONTINUED...

Henrietta's Farewell Cake

Cake Base

2 ½ cups (350 grams) flour
1/3 cup (50 g) cornstarch
1 ¾ cups (200 g) sugar
1/2 cup (60 g) cocoa powder
1 tablespoon baking soda
1 ¾ cups (400 milliliters) water
1/2 cup (100 ml) vegetable oil
2 tablespoons (20 ml) vinegar

Filling

24-ounce jar of sour cherries
1/4 cup (35 g) cornstarch
1/3 cup (60 g) sugar

Toppings

2 cups (400 ml) heavy cream
1 cup powdered sugar
1 teaspoon vanilla extract
1 cup grated chocolate shavings

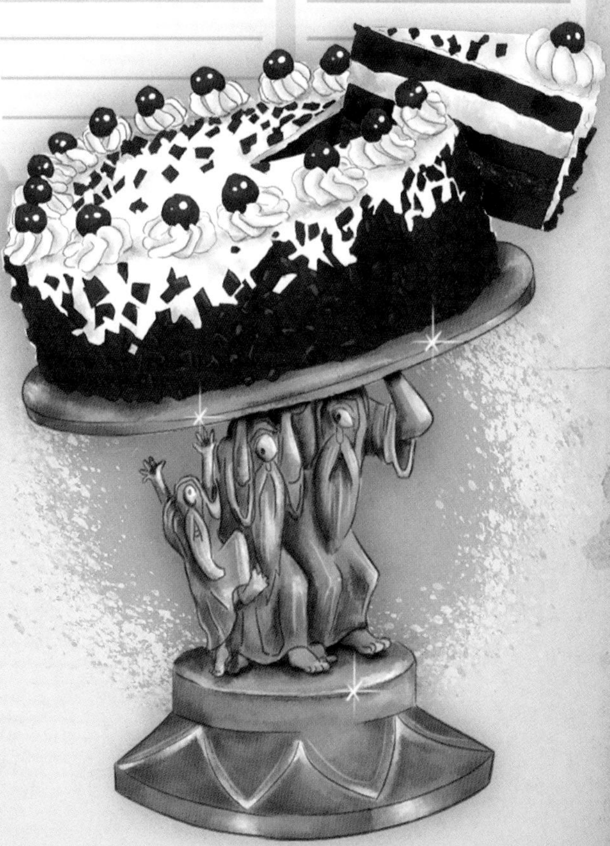

Preparation

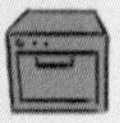

Preheat oven to 350° F. Grease a 9-inch cake pan.

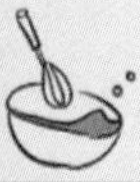

Mix all ingredients for the cake base. Pour mixture into cake pan. Bake in oven for 35 minutes.

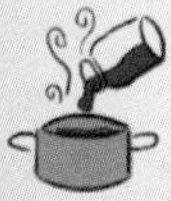

While the cake base is baking, begin to cook the filling. Drain cherries and mix the juice from the cherry jar with enough water to equal two cups. Boil the liquid with sugar and cornstarch. Reserve 12 cherries for decoration and mix the rest with the filling. Allow filling to cool.

Next...

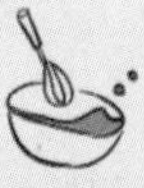

Whip cream until frothy. Add powdered sugar and vanilla. Continue whipping until stiff.

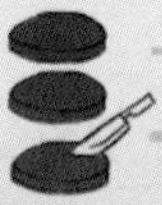

Once cake base is cool, cut into three equal layers.

Spread cooled cherry filling over bottom layer. Spread the whipped cream over the middle and top layers. Decorate with cherries and grated chocolate.

Enjoy!

THE ART OF

A HOUSE DIVIDED

ANOTHER LOOK INSIDE
THE ATTIC

CORNELIUS

Now that Cornelius has lost his trademark pot/crown, we had to think about what he might look like under the helmet. We wanted to distinguish him from the other kobolds, so we gave him a slightly different snout, humanlike teeth, and big eyes that let his intelligence (and irritable personality) shine through.

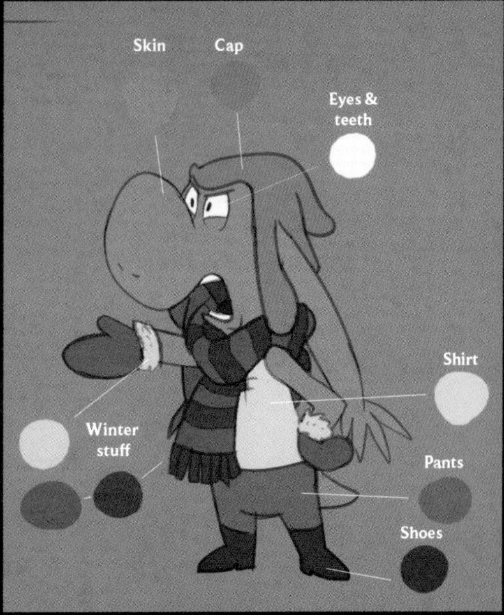

Skin
Cap
Eyes & teeth
Shirt
Winter stuff
Pants
Shoes

RUFFUS

Ruffus, the cursed little cupboard, actually predates almost all of our characters! Marius drew a cute table right next to the very first character design for Henrietta, years earlier. While Henri changed quite a bit in later iterations, Ruffus's original look stuck. It just took a while to find the right spot for him in the story.

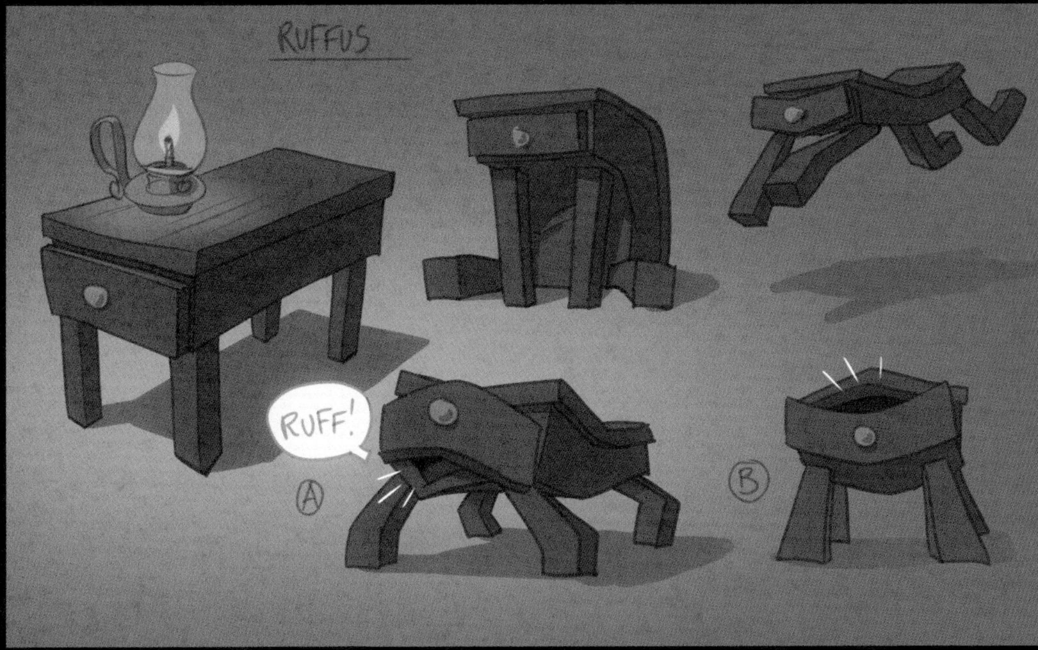

RUFFUS
RUFF!
A
B

THE HOUSE TRAIN

Although this is the first time we visit one of the train stations inside the house, eagle-eyed readers may have already spotted the train in the background of a panel in book two! For its big close-up in book three, the train was slightly redesigned. We wanted to give it a more distinctive, magical look, so we based it on an anglerfish and the fish's characteristic antenna.

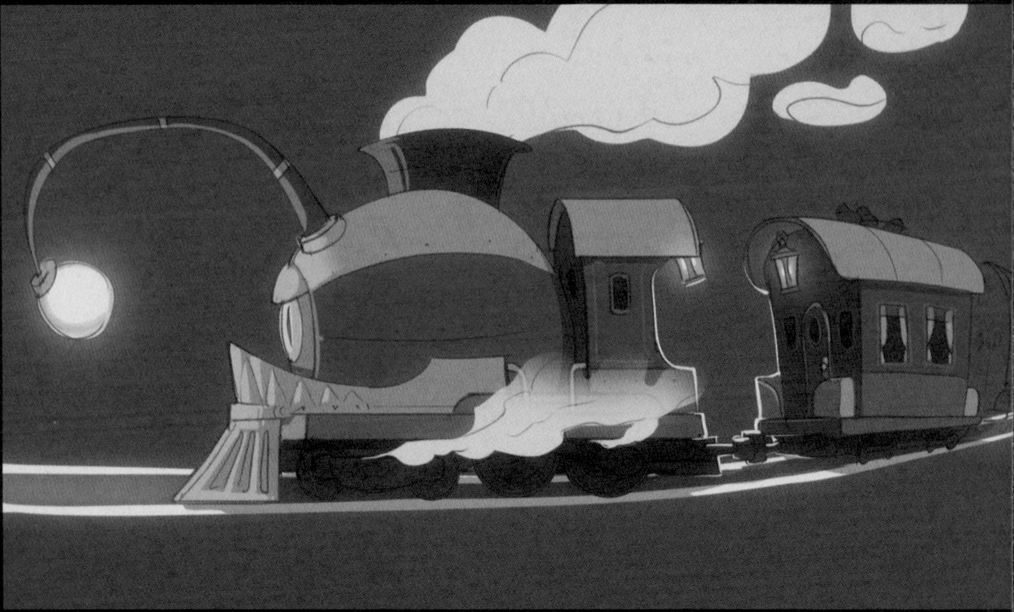

WINTER OUTFITS

With the story's change of season, our characters needed to change attires as well. Booner's men have their standard-issue winter cloaks, while our rogues simply didn't pack for such a long stay. At the start of the cover illustration, we knew Henrietta would need a cloak too. The color, a light-bluish gray, was chosen to harmonize with the cold background colors.

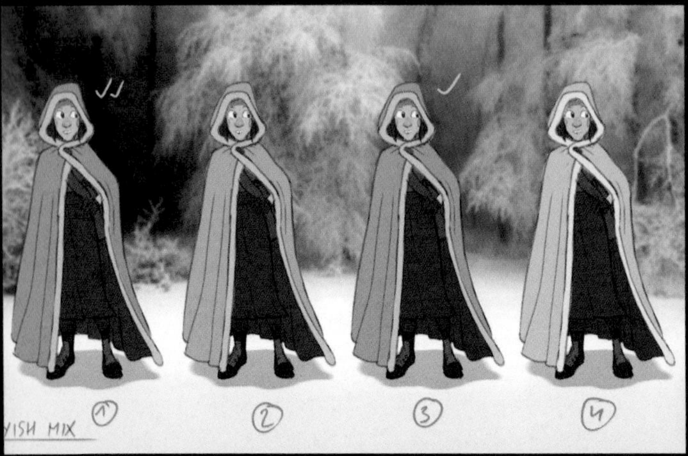
1
2
3
4

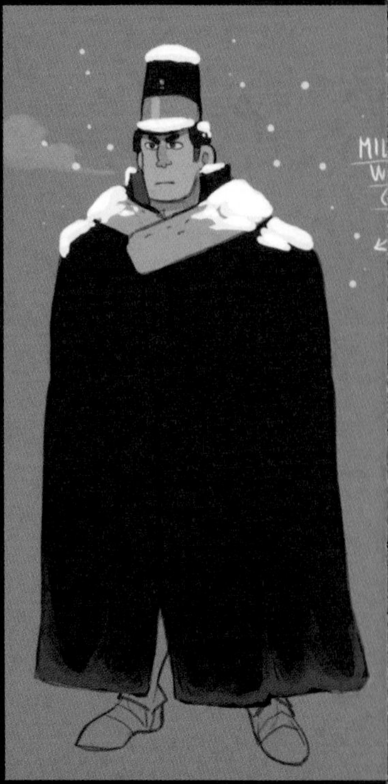

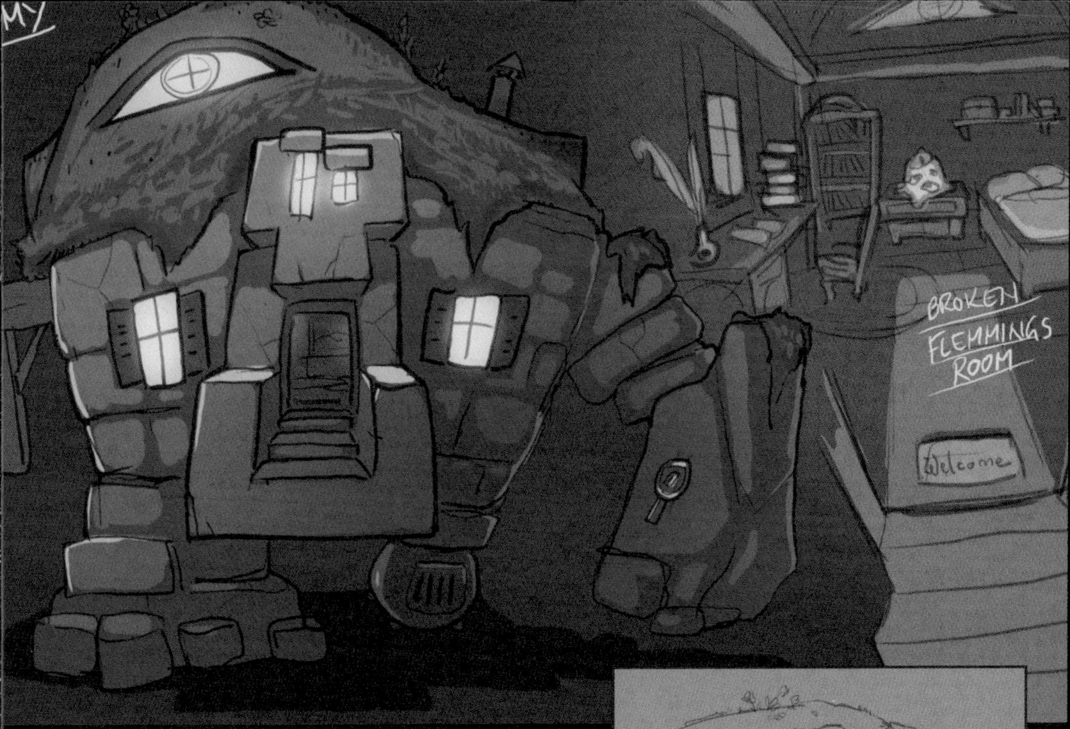
BROKEN FLEMMINGS ROOM
Welcome

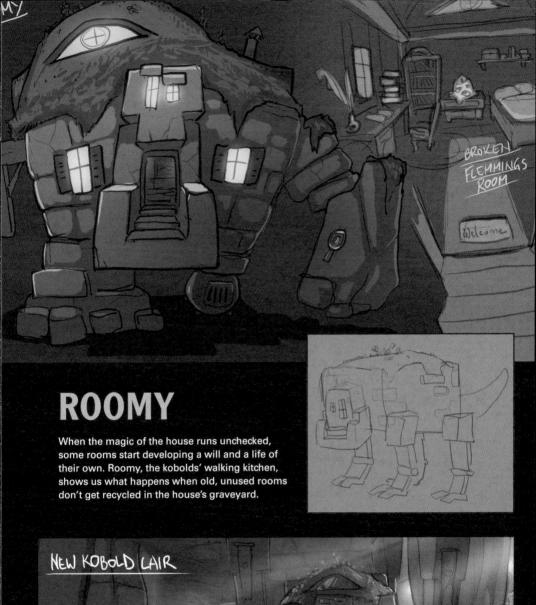

ROOMY

When the magic of the house runs unchecked, some rooms start developing a will and a life of their own. Roomy, the kobolds' walking kitchen, shows us what happens when old, unused rooms don't get recycled in the house's graveyard.

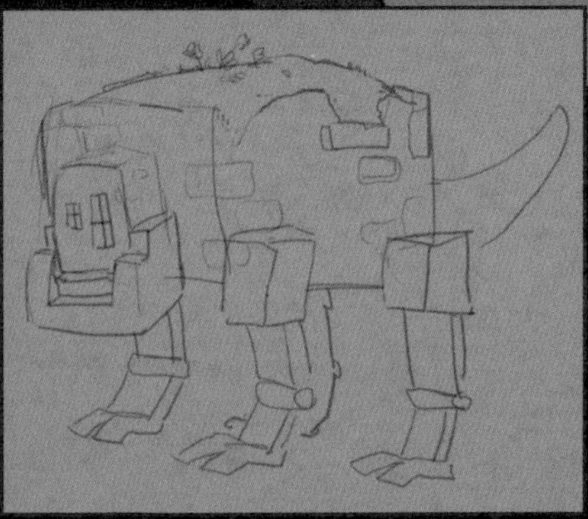

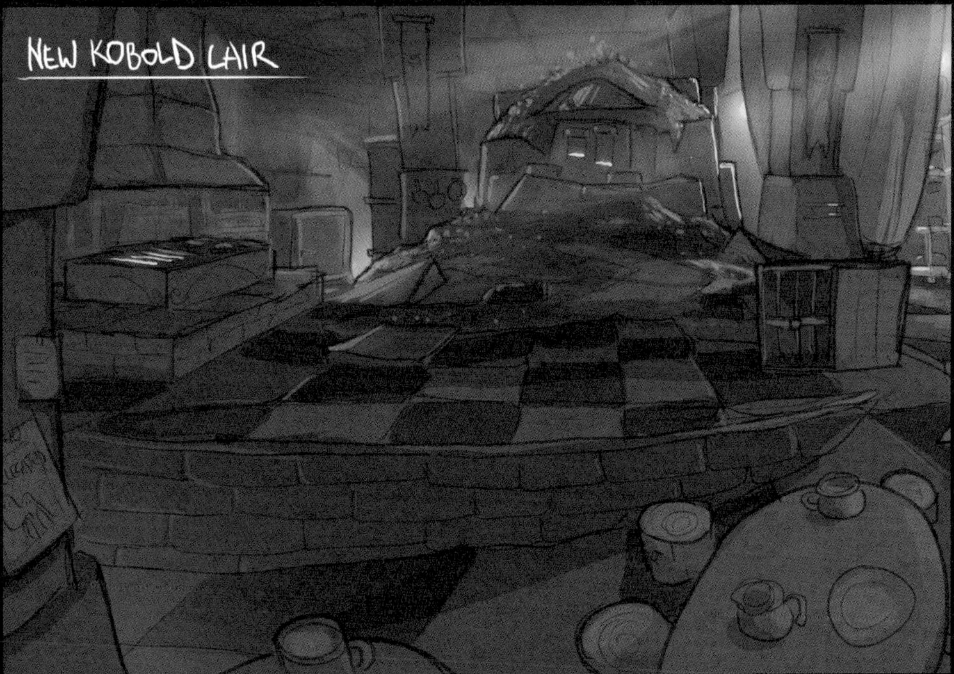
NEW KOBOLD LAIR

ABOUT THE AUTHOR

Haiko Hörnig spent his childhood in his parents' comic book store, where he developed a love for sequential art at an early age. In middle school, he quickly became friends with Marius Pawlitza. The two of them first enjoyed role-playing games together and later started to make comics. Since 2013, Haiko has worked as a screenwriter for animated shows and feature films. A House Divided is his first published book series. He is based in Frankfurt, Germany. He's also active on Twitter (@DerGrafX) and Instagram (@ahousedividedcomic).

ABOUT THE ILLUSTRATOR

Marius Pawlitza was born in Poland in 1984 and grew up in Ludwigshafen, Germany. Years later, he studied communication design in the German city of Mainz. It was a good excuse to spend as much time as possible playing video games and making comics with Haiko Hörnig. Since 2011, he has worked as an art director for different agencies and companies in Frankfurt, in addition to creating sequential art. On Twitter and Instagram, he's @pengboom.